T0130096

Borrowing
THE TRUTH

NICKY HINDMARSH

iUniverse LLC
Bloomington

BORROWING THE TRUTH

iUniverse books may be ordered through booksellers or by contacting:

iUniverse
1663 Liberty Drive
Bloomington, IN 47403
www.iuniverse.com
1-800-Authors (1-800-288-4677)

ISBN: 978-1-4759-9163-5 (sc)
ISBN: 978-1-4759-9165-9 (hc)
ISBN: 978-1-4759-9164-2 (e)

Printed in the United States of America.

iUniverse rev. date: 5/14/2013

"All truths are easy to understand once they are discovered; the point is to discover them."
- Galileo

For Josh, Adam, and Michael

CHAPTER 1

From the time Hannah and Martha had been little, it had been the custom each weekend for the sisters to travel to the family's cottage. It was a rare event to miss out on the two hour trip north, but on this particular weekend, Martha had been suffering from the flu and was not feeling up for the trip. Nineteen year old Hannah offered to stay behind with her younger sister and insisted that their mother and father go ahead.

"You and Dad are ready so there's no reason not to go." Hannah persuaded.

"Oh, I don't know. I don't feel right leaving you two here, especially when Martha's not well." Mrs. Hutton said with concern.

"It's just the flu. She'll be okay and as soon as she's better, we'll come up in my car. We'll be fine, so don't worry." Hannah said convincingly.

"Come on Jean. They're not babies anymore. We'll see them tomorrow morning." Their father said while putting his arm affectionately around his wife's shoulders.

"Oh, alright. Martha crawl back into bed and I'll look forward to seeing you both tomorrow. We'll call you once we get there." Mrs. Hutton said quietly to Hannah.

"Good plan Mum. Call as soon as you arrive and I'll give you an update on our patient." Hannah promised.

Martha and Hannah's parents were soon on their way, but not first without Mrs. Hutton warning Hannah and Martha to drive carefully since a heavy snowfall had been predicted.

"We promise Mum and you do the same!" Hannah said hugging

her parents and kissing them goodbye. Martha, while looking pale and very tired, came downstairs to say goodbye. "I'll just blow you kisses so you don't catch my germs."

"Are you crazy? How can we go without kissing those lovely washed out cheeks of yours?" Martha's dad scolded as he leaned over her and placed a kiss on each cheek.

Martha managed a smile. "Oh Dad, you say the sweetest things."

John Hutton hugged his youngest daughter. "Take care of yourself and get some colour back in those cheeks. We'll look forward to seeing you soon."

Hannah and Martha stood waving to their parents, little realizing that in less than six hours their lives would be turned upside down.

Later that evening, Martha was beginning to feel better after a long afternoon nap. She and Hannah had just finished their dinner of beef stew and hot buttered crescent rolls when a knock at their front door interrupted their conversation.

"I'll get it." Hannah said sternly, "I don't want you catching a cold now on top of the flu!"

Martha sipped on her tea while Hannah ran to the door. After about half a minute, Martha was startled by the sound of her sister's anguished cries.

"Oh my God! Oh no! Martha." Screamed Hannah as she ran into the room, her face white and distorted with anguish. Martha jumped to her feet and ran towards the sound of her sister's wretched cries.

"What's the matter? What's wrong Hannah?" Martha demanded as Hannah fell into her sister's arms. Hannah's response was indecipherable as Martha tried aimlessly to understand her sister through her sobs.

"Hannah, please you're scaring me. What is it?" Martha demanded. Hannah completely collapsed to the floor and as Martha bent down to her, she felt a gentle hand on her shoulder and a soft voice spoke to her.

"Miss Hutton." A strange voice interrupted.

"Yes?" Martha answered automatically while raising her head to the voice. She felt her heart rise to her mouth as she looked to see that the voice belonged to a uniformed police officer. Another police officer stood behind the one that spoke. Martha's mind tried to make sense of the imposition of these two men who looked as though they wished they were anywhere but standing in the Hutton's home. As the officer spoke again, the other officer knelt down to try to comfort Hannah.

"Are you Martha Hutton?" The officer asked.

"Yes, yes." She screamed. "What is going on?"

"Please let's sit." The officer instructed and continued. "I'm afraid its your parents, Miss Hutton. I regret to inform you that they have been killed in a car crash."

Hannah extended her arms to Martha to hold her. The officers sat quietly as Hannah and Martha sobbed their disbelief and shock at the incredibility of what they had just heard. After a few minutes, Martha was able to ask what had happened.

"Your parents were travelling on a portion of Highway 49 near Stolpe when, according to two witnesses, their car was run off the road by an oncoming car that forced them over an embankment. They died instantly - they didn't suffer."

The girls listened though their tears went uncontrolled. Constable Barker hated this part of his job. He knew there was no other way than just to continue without dragging it out.

"Unfortunately, at this point, we only have two witnesses – a Mr. and Mrs. Philpot who were traveling on the same roadway, and they're not too clear on what they in fact saw. But you may rest assured that we are investigating. Sometimes there is a delayed reaction by the witnesses and they come up with something they didn't think to mention in the first round of questioning."

"What do you mean run off the road?" Hannah asked suddenly realizing what Constable Barker had said.

"Mr. Philpot seems to think it may have been deliberate. So we have to pursue that likelihood."

"Deliberate?" Hannah said with disbelief. "You mean someone did this on purpose and then left them there to die?"

"We can only go on what the witnesses have told us, and we can't say that conclusively, but it would appear to be the case. We will investigate further and Detective Burgess here from Special Investigations will be in charge of your parents' car accident."

Finally, as if on cue, the other officer spoke.

"I'm sorry to have to meet you under these circumstances. This is a terrible shock for both of you, and I do want to assure you that I will investigate your parents' accident more thoroughly."

"I don't understand." Martha cried. "Why would someone do this deliberately? How can this Mr. Philpot be so sure that it was deliberate? I just don't believe that anyone would do this on purpose. It just doesn't make any sense to me."

"According to Mr. Philpot", Detective Burgess continued, "it seemed that the other car came out of nowhere and as it approached from the other direction, it suddenly swerved into the path of your parents' car and forced it off the road."

Hannah tried to force the image out of her mind but found it hard to keep her composure.

"So why…" Hannah faltered, "So why do you think it was deliberate? Why could it not have been someone losing control of their car? Maybe they were going too fast?"

Hannah tried desperately to find a reason that this terrible tragedy was an accident rather than such a cruel and senseless end to her parents' lives.

"Miss Hutton, we cannot say for sure, but based on what the witness has said, it seems that it was. Mr. Philpot was behind your parents' car and he could see the other car approaching in the other direction. It then swerved abruptly in the path of your parents' car, hit them, and then kept going. We are hoping that more witnesses step forward to at least verify or disqualify what Mr. Philpot said."

"Did he say anything else?" Martha asked abruptly and clearly not happy with the explanation thus far.

"Mr. Philpot explained that the road conditions at the time were quite good and were free of ice or snow. In other words, the road conditions were perfect. It caught them off guard when the car started to swerve towards your parent's car. The only explanation that may seem feasible, although not comforting, would be that the driver was under the influence of drugs or alcohol. It may also have been someone out for a good time and when they saw what they did to your parents, got scared and bolted."

Hannah and Martha both shook their heads in disbelief and gripped each other's hands in support while fresh tears spilled from their eyes. "So you don't know who did this?" Martha asked.

Detective Burgess wished he could do more for them, but he had nothing to go on.

"No, not yet, but it is very likely that the driver will be found. We have the approximate time and the direction the car was travelling in. Hopefully, someone else further down the road may have remembered the car for some reason or another. Perhaps they stopped at a destination close to the accident such as a gas station or a local diner. Someone may have noticed the driver or even overhear a conversation that may have taken place that would connect the car to the accident. I know it will be little comfort to you, but I want you both to know we are committed to investigating this thoroughly."

Hannah quietly whispered thank you, but his sudden kindness made her cry again.

"Miss Hutton," he went on, "I really think it would be best for you and your sister if you called someone. Do you have a relative or someone who might be able to stay with you? You shouldn't be alone."

But as the days turned into months, Hannah and Martha were in fact alone, having only each other.

CHAPTER 2

Ten years slipped by and during the initial years after their parents' deaths Hannah's and Martha's lives had become preoccupied with the police investigation. As it turned out, no other witnesses had stepped forward to identify the offending driver. The fact it was a deliberate accident haunted Hannah, but the police investigation had come to an end when no concrete evidence helped further the case. Sadly, Mr. Philpot had died later that same year of a heart attack. Mrs. Philpot, the police said, was heartbroken and had little time for anyone else's problems. If she knew anything more about the accident, she wasn't saying.

Luckily, Mr. Hutton had provided well for his daughters, but Hannah realized that she could no longer afford to stay in university to continue with her law degree as planned. She also found that the recent tragedy of her parent's deaths was making it difficult for her to concentrate on her studies. She also felt it important that she and Martha stick together and by doing this, Hannah would have to get a job since she could not give up the house her parents had worked so hard for. It was to some extent a welcomed change for Hannah to get out in the working world.

Hannah began her first job working for a large accounting company, but found the position to be a bit challenging as she did not have a knack for numbers and the demand for overtime became more than she was prepared to dedicate herself to. It happened to be her lucky day when about six months after her parents' death, Mr. Peterson, a very old friend of her father's and a partner in the law firm of Peterson, Peterson and Reynolds, came to the house to see how she and Martha were making out.

"Uncle Paul!." Hannah exclaimed.

"I just came by to see how my girls were doing."

"Come in and have a drink with me."

Settling in with their drinks, Mr. Peterson looked at Hannah with concern. "How are you doing, really?"

"Really?" Hannah looked away. Dear Uncle Paul was almost like a father to her which only accentuated the fact that she missed her own father so much.

"It's hard – and there are times when I feel how unfair it is not to have my parents here. I miss them so much." She couldn't help her tears now as they flowed like little streams down her face.

Mr. Peterson sat beside her and held her hand until she had calmed down.

"I'm sorry." Hannah said.

"Don't be sorry, that's really what I came to see." Mr. Peterson explained.

"What?" Hannah said amazed.

"I'll bet that's the first time you've really cried since your parents' deaths, isn't it?" He said looking at her with kindness.

Hannah leaned against his shoulder. She could smell his pipe tobacco that was so much a familiar part of him.

"How come you're so smart?" Hannah laughed enjoying the comfort of this dear old friend.

"I've been around awhile and I've learned a thing or two." He replied. "What I've learned is its better to cry than hold it all in."

"I shouldn't put this on you though." Hannah confessed.

"You're not putting anything on me. Your parents are worth those tears, not to mention that it's not healthy to keep all that sadness bottled up inside you. You don't have to be strong through this you know – it's not expected." Mr. Peterson said tenderly.

"I suppose I expect myself to be strong. I have to think of Martha." Hannah said dabbing at her tears.

"Martha's okay, believe me. And so are you. All I'm saying is let yourself be sad. It's only natural. One day the empty sadness will be replaced by quieter memories of your Mum and Dad."

"Uncle Paul, you make everything better. Thank you." Hannah said innocently.

"Well, I do have another reason for coming over. How would you like to come and work for me?" He said hopefully.

"Work for you?" Hannah replied with astonishment.

"Oh." Mr. Peterson faltered. "That's not fair. I'm assuming that you would prefer to work with me rather than where you are working now. I guess the impression that I had from you the last time we spoke was that you weren't too thrilled working with the company you are with now, and I thought perhaps I could offer you a change."

"Well, no! It's just that I didn't expect this. You caught me off guard." Hannah explained.

"Does that mean you might?" Mr. Peterson laughed.

"Yes, I would love to, but what would I do? I'm not very good with a keyboard!" Hannah confessed.

"I know it must have been hard for you to give up your dream of going to law school…" Mr. Peterson held up his hand as Hannah began to protest. "I know why you gave it up, and I would have done the same thing. One of our law clerks gave their notice two days ago, and I thought of you. I know I could hire someone with lots of experience, but I really think you would be ideal for the job. I'll give you all the help you need and so will the others that will work with you. Hannah, I know you'll do a great job, otherwise I wouldn't offer this position to you."

Hannah looked at Mr. Peterson intently, feeling there was more to this kindness.

"Alright, okay I admit I want to help too. What's so wrong with that?" Mr. Peterson confessed. "But at the same time, this is partly my firm and I need to protect that too. In the beginning, your responsibilities wouldn't initially be extensive, naturally, but eventually and most certainly as your knowledge grows, so will your responsibilities. I'm confident that you are someone who will work well with others, and particularly with my clients. I hope someday that you might be more of an assistant to me and my associates, but of course…" Mr. Peterson stopped and looked at Hannah who was now waving her hands in front of his face.

"I've only said yes four times but you haven't heard me. I really would love to work with you, but and I mean this, if it doesn't work out for you, I will accept that and leave, no questions asked." Hannah said honestly.

"It's a deal." Mr. Peterson laughed, extending his hand to shake hers.

CHAPTER 3

Hannah did not let her uncle down. She dedicated herself to her job, and although she made mistakes she learned from them and, as her uncle had promised, her responsibilities had grown. In time, she had two junior clerks reporting to her and Sally, Paul's assistant, who had been hired the year before, became pivotal to her progress. Although the same age as Hannah, Sally had taken on a protective and caring role with Hannah and the two soon became close friends. They spent a lot of time outside the office socializing together and enjoying the many friends they shared. With every outing, Sally hoped that Hannah would meet someone since she was convinced that a male influence would benefit her. Although Hannah dated often, she never felt anything more than friendship for most of the men she dated.

"Hannah." Sally would say, interrupting Hannah's work. "I have to get you hooked up with someone nice."

"I take it you don't feel like working today?" Hannah muttered without looking up at Sally.

"Don't change the subject, and yes I feel like working. However, I am just taking my coffee break."

Hannah now looked up and laughed. "My dear friend, we don't have coffee breaks here, and furthermore, I can't get married because I'm busy right now."

"Oh you know what I mean." Sally leaned forward feeling that at least Hannah may be interested. "Why don't you come out with us this weekend? It will be fun."

"Who is us?" Hannah resumed her work, although feeling a little curious.

"Well, there's going to be a group of us and we thought we would just have a night out on the town. There's a great jazz group playing at Hero's and I know you'll love it." Sally said with excitement.

"Who is us?" Hannah repeated while she resumed working.

"Hannah, we went there about four months ago and the same group was playing. I could have stayed all night because they were so good. Please come." Sally pleaded.

"Who. Is. Us?" Hannah insisted and looked fixedly at Sally.

Sally sank back in her chair defeated. "Okay, Grayson has a nice friend and we thought maybe you might like him."

Hannah started to say something, but Sally interrupted. "Wait Hannah, I know what you're going to say. You think I'm childish and interfering, but Daniel is a nice man and he doesn't know anything about you or that we are even inviting you. And there are about five others who will be joining us."

Hannah was now resting her chin in her hand watching Sally as she continued. "Hannah I admit I worry about you. I'm doing this too because I like your company and so does Grayson."

Hannah smiled, although she was a bit surprised that Sally suggested that Grayson enjoyed her company. She had the distinct feeling that Grayson didn't really like sharing Sally with anyone and those times when they were all out together, Hannah often felt like an intruder. Despite her feelings, she didn't want to indicate any hesitation in case Sally picked up on it.

"Sally, I don't think you're interfering and I don't think you're childish. You are incredibly sweet to me and I appreciate how thoughtful you are. You have become a wonderful support to me in so many ways, and one of the bonuses that I got coming to work here was meeting you and finding a true friend. It's sometimes hard to go out when I feel a bit like a third wheel, but I just have to get over that don't I? I know that everyone would like to see me settled down and I understand that, but I think if I am meant to meet someone it will happen when it happens."

"So will you come with us?" Sally asked delicately.

"I will. It sounds like a lot of fun."

In the end, Hannah had a great time and Daniel turned out to be as Sally described – a nice man. For Hannah there had been something missing and although they had dated a few times, they both agreed that it wouldn't work being anything more than just good friends.

Martha's laughter brought Hannah back to the present. Adam was teasing her. Hannah felt a sense of relief that Martha was so happy.

"What is it?" Martha said to Hannah, pulling herself away from Adam.

"You two make me feel like I'm missing something or at least I may have something worth waiting for." Hannah explained.

"Hah, sure." Adam scoffed jokingly. "You have so many men lapping at your heels that you don't know what to do with them! 'Oops, no.' Adam mocked Hannah using a high voice. 'Looks like he has a hair out of place. I will not go out with him.'

"Very funny. I don't think I'm too good for them. I just haven't met anyone lately who makes a difference. I like them better as friends." Hannah explained as she leaned back in her chair and yawned. "Well, you two have fun. I'm going up to bed."

"That's a nice way to end the conversation, feigning tiredness." Adam teased.

Hannah kissed Adam and Martha good night and said, "Never mind Adam as long as you two are happy together, that's enough for me."

"Well, it shouldn't be." Adam said seriously.

Hannah shot Adam a friendly warning glance. "For now it is Adam so please doing worry. Night-night you two." She said as she climbed the stairs to her bedroom.

Now in her bedroom with the door closed, the streetlight illuminated the room in a soft golden light. She thought about the concern her family and friends had for her future. Maybe Adam was right. Did she somehow think that she was too good for her dates? 'That's crazy.' She whispered and sat down at her night table to turn on her lamp. She studied her face in the mirror to closely assess herself. She pulled the tie from her hair to let it fall and settle softly around her shoulders. She studied her grey eyes in the mirror imagining they were someone else's eyes looking back at her. 'What do they see?' She thought. Although she wouldn't say she was beautiful, her looks were sensual and mysterious. Her hands slid over the contours of her body that was sheathed in a transparent nightgown. Slowly she let the straps of her nightgown fall away. Her eyes closed while she let her thoughts drift seductively to imagine the face of a man she scarcely knew.

Hannah slowly opened her eyes and softly stared back into the mirror. I am not beyond loving someone she realized. She turned off the lamp and stood to walk to her bed. She slipped under the covers and stared through the window into the still night, wondering about the possibilities. Her heart and head both told her not to feel any urgency. There is a reason that it hasn't come before now and I am willing to wait she thought. She adjusted the covers over her body and settled into a contented sleep.

CHAPTER 4

The following work day proved to be unimaginably long, with one demand after another, all of which resulted in Hannah not getting anything productive done. She silently admitted to herself that most days were rewarding, but not today. She was happy to get home where she retreated to her living room to relax after dinner, but the sense of contentment that she expected escaped her. The fire that she had lit presented a backdrop to her restlessness, its flames brandishing long arms as though to encourage her to dig deeper into her thoughts. In the weeks to come, a great deal more would encourage her discontent, due to the truth that she would painfully discover. She would then question her instincts and wonder how she had not pieced together events that, had she been paying closer attention, would have allowed less upsetting results.

While Hannah wrestled with her uneasiness, her thoughts were abruptly cut short as she witnessed the silhouette of a person passing outside her front window. She waited expectantly for a knock at her door but none came. Hannah decided it must have been only her imagination. As she drew her interest from the window, she was suddenly drawn back to it again as there, very clearly, was the reappearance of the shadow that destroyed her acceptance of simple imagination. This shadow moved slowly and surreptitiously, halting briefly. Despite the sheer window blind that offered a delicate barrier between the two, Hannah watched as its head turned to look inward, its prying eyes discovering that she was alone. A lump of fear rose to her throat and, despite the warmth in the room, a shiver shuddered through her and she went instantly cold. She gradually drew herself forward on the chesterfield, her hands gripping onto it as if to encourage support. Her eyes welled with tears momentarily blurring her vision.

Her heart was banging in her chest as if to call attention to her vulnerability. She could not move despite wanting desperately to investigate with the hopes that she would distinguish a friendly face, putting an end to her alarm. Her instincts prevailed however, telling her that this visitor was not well intended. How could it be when a simple knock at the door would allow an unwelcomed guest to become a welcomed one? The shadowed figure turned away from the window and slowly crept away. Hannah wanted to leap up and rush to the window and to discover its identity, but she couldn't move, wouldn't move as she silently wished for it not to return. Endless minutes passed as she sat motionless, her hands still clutching onto where she sat, waiting for time to pass until her heart slowed its hammering signaling that there was nothing, no more shadow, and no more fear.

Several minutes passed when, from the kitchen, the telephone's brittle high pitched ring momentarily confused her and Hannah found herself faltering in her seat. Quickly, she collected herself and darted to the phone.

"Hello?" Hannah whispered but paid no attention to the caller's response as she whirled around so that she could keep her eye on the kitchen window to make sure the shadow had not relocated. Nothing seemed to be there.

In fact maybe something was there. Hannah crouched down on the floor, hiding behind the kitchen table. A shadow danced menacingly against the window. Hannah had turned off most of the lights inside the house earlier so that the only illumination was reflected by the fire. She now found it very difficult to focus on the window. It was too dark – it threatened again to expose her vulnerability.

"Oh God what's going on?"

"Hannah, Hannah, what's the matter? What are you doing?"

The voice surprised her, but realized that it was coming from the telephone.

"Kate?" Hannah whispered.

"What's the matter? Who are you talking to? Am I interrupting something?" Kate fired her questions in quick order.

"I think someone is outside my window!" Hannah confessed.

"What do you mean someone is outside your window? Who is it?" Kate demanded.

"I don't know!"

"So you didn't see who it was?"

"No, it was too dark. I had all the lights off because I had lit a fire, and I looked up and I saw someone pass outside my front window, twice." Hannah qualified.

"Are you sure you didn't see who it was?" Kate asked.

"I'm sure."

"Alright, do you want me to come over, or maybe I should call the police."

"No, don't call the police, I feel ridiculous. Maybe it was just my imagination." She knew in her heart she had seen someone. Why was she second guessing now? Where was Martha?

"Your imagination? Great! So someone is playing peek-a-boo with you, you're scared half out of your mind, and you don't want me to call the police. Where's your sister?"

"Well," Hannah said quietly, "I was wondering about Martha too. I don't know where she is, probably with Adam somewhere. I wish she would come home."

"I can come over."

"No, I'll be okay. Martha will be home soon and Adam will be with her. I'll have him take a look around outside the house."

"Oh, so you need a man to help you. Maybe you should ask Joe to come over to investigate."

"What? Where did that come from? I scarcely know him and I wouldn't think of asking him to look around my house. He'd think I was out of my mind." Hannah replied while becoming a bit annoyed. Her friend meant well, but her tone indicated a bit of insincerity that seemed out of place. She decided that rather than go any further with the conversation, she thanked Kate for calling, but was tired and needed to go to bed.

CHAPTER 5

After Hannah hung up the phone, she felt her fear dissipate as she thought back to the day when she met Joe almost three months before. It was a warm autumn day when she decided to go for a run, when, without warning heavy clouds formed and it started to pour down with rain. Hardly able to see for its force, she ran making a bee-line for the local public school's entrance for shelter. As she was busily shaking the raindrops from her hair, a deep voice sliced into the hum of the sleeting rain.

"So you got caught too!"

Startled, Hannah spun around and came face to face with a man a few years older than she, likely in his early thirties.

"Oh, I didn't see you. I'm sorry to invade your space!" Hannah exclaimed.

"No need to apologize. I'm grateful for the company. I was beginning to get a bit lonely and I am more than happy to share." Her new companion smiled, his cheeks presenting beautiful dimples as though for her benefit.

She was momentarily speechless, not only by his mere presence, but because he was exceptionally handsome. His eyes were a remarkable grey-green shielded by a thick meshing of black eyelashes. His rain-soaked deep brown hair lay softly against his head, as little wet curls struggled to spring back to life. Hannah couldn't help but smile as she was quietly mesmerized by their attempts to resume order. Rain drops jumped from his curls and tumbled down his sculpted face. He extinguished their existence using the bottom of his soaking T shirt exposing a muscled stomach equally as tanned as his face. Her smile broadened innocently at the beautiful man that was presented before her.

"Do you find me amusing?"

"Oh no, I'm sorry. Well, you are soaking wet." Hannah qualified.

"I am?" He laughed as she stated the obvious, and then leaned in as if to disclose a secret. "So are you!"

"I hope you didn't think I was laughing at you. It's not what I meant." Hannah confessed.

"I can take it. Don't worry your rain-soaked lovely head about it. Hopefully one day, you will see me not drenched to the core and you won't feel the need to laugh. I'm pretty cute bone dry." He said teasingly.

His banter left her surprisingly tongue tied and she felt lost for a way to respond. Hannah looked quickly away so that he wouldn't see how he had left her lost for words.

"It looks like it might be clearing finally." Hannah feeling a weather report could change the subject.

"Oh, I hope not so soon! I'm enjoying this." He laughed.

Hannah turned to the handsome face once again. "I don't think I've seen you around here. Have you just moved into the area?"

"No, actually I'm just in town on business. Joe Hastings." He offered as he extended his hand to her and she responded by offering him her hand.

"Hi Joe, I'm Hannah Hutton. What type of work do you do?" Hannah asked hoping she was not being too personal.

"I'm with the Special Investigations Unit for the Provincial Police. Heavy stuff." Joe said laughing.

"Interesting stuff more like." Hannah responded.

"Yes, it can be Hannah. But like any job, it can also be frustrating. Mine comes with long hours and sometimes with the result of lots of unsolved cases that become cold cases. But they're always worth keeping on top of. What about you, Hannah Hutton? What do you do?"

"I work with a law firm as a legal assistant. I really enjoy it. Heavy stuff." Hannah laughed, repeating Joe's comment.

"What law firm are you with?"

"Paul Peterson and Associates. Its downtown." Hannah offered simply.

"Oh yes, I think I've heard of them. They deal with mainly civil and criminal litigation, am I right?"

"You are right."

"That can be really interesting work, better than most other areas of law I think."

"I can't disagree with that." Hannah said smiling.

Well, Hannah I'd better be off. Normally I hate it when the rain stops me from my runs, but I can say today that with all honesty I'm so glad it did rain."

"It was really nice to meet you."

Joe smiled and looked warmly into her eyes. "I hope one day to run into you again."

"I would like that too." Hannah admitted simply.

"You're not married or significantly attached?" Joe dared with an impish smirk.

"No to both."

"I'm glad because I couldn't take my day being ruined after such a beautiful encounter!"

They looked into each other's eyes wordlessly confirming an unspoken attraction. Joe then looked away and seemed distracted by something that seemed to catch his attention on the road nearby. Hannah followed his gaze but could see nothing that seemed out of the ordinary.

"Well, this is our spot." Joe said returning his attention to Hannah. "Don't share it with anyone else but me."

"I won't." Hannah laughed. "I promise."

"Bye Hannah Hutton. Thank you for a wonderful morning."

Hannah crossed her arms and leaned against the wall as she watched Joe sail out of the school yard and slowly out of sight. She looked up to the sky where the sun now began to push brilliantly through translucent clouds. Despite the sudden warmth of the sun, she was uncomfortably wet through she set off on her course. Her thoughts replayed the images of Joe and the impact of their brief encounter that had surprisingly left her weak in the knees.

CHAPTER 6

Hannah thought often of Joe, the next was a few weeks after her first encounter, and again, by accident. One day while shopping, Hannah waited outside a store while Kate ran into the drug store to buy some shampoo. She seemed to be taking an unusually long time and as Hannah went into the store to look for her, she found Kate talking with a man whose back was to Hannah. 'So that explains the delay', Hannah thought with amusement. As she approached them, the expression on Kate's face stopped her and forced her to turn around and retreat. She walked no further than four steps when she heard a male voice call her name. She reeled around to find the male voice coming from Kate's direction.

"Joe! I was wondering what was keeping Kate so long." Hannah said smiling while caught off guard that Joe knew Kate. "It's nice to see you again!"

"Been caught in any rain storms lately?" Joe teased.

"No, not lately." Hannah said lightly looking to Kate expecting a pleased reaction because they all knew each other, only to find a scowl cross her face.

Something is clearly wrong, Hannah thought. I think I must really be intruding after all.

"You two know each other?" Kate asked or rather demanded incredulously.

"Only by chance because we ran into each other while out running!" Hannah laughed.

But Kate wasn't laughing and Joe simply looked uncomfortable, and so to shift from the awkwardness of the situation, Hannah exclaimed excitedly. "But what a coincidence that you two know each other!"

Neither Kate nor Joe offered an explanation. Both stared at her blankly, although Joe offered a slight smile as if to acknowledge how uncomfortable this must seem to her.

"Well," Hannah decided since she was the only one talking. "I think I'll just finish a little shopping, and Kate, I'll meet you outside when you're through."

"Speaking of running, I really have to go, but it was nice to see you again." Joe offered to Hannah.

Kate opened her mouth to say something, but Joe said a hurried goodbye to Kate and quickly left the store.

Kate started routing around in her purse for something and finally looked to Hannah and said, "I forgot my cell phone and I have to make a phone call using the pay phones. I'll meet you in ten minutes outside Jenkins Deli."

"Sure, I don't mind waiting." 'Again', Hannah thought silently.

Hannah had never seen Kate seem so rattled. Obviously Joe has had this effect on her, but why? Her thoughts were broken by a salesgirl asking if she could help her with anything.

"Oh, no thanks, I'm just leaving."

In order to put the ten minutes to good use, and realizing that she would soon need a new coat for winter, Hannah decided to go to her favourite store, Richards' Clothier, that was tucked away at the west end of the shopping mall. After walking the distance, to her disappointment, there was a sign on the door that read: 'To our valued customers. We have relocated to new premises. Please visit us on line for our new location opening soon.'

'Well, that's disappointing.' Hannah murmured to herself.

Hannah checked her watch and since she had wasted all of four minutes, she decided to make her way back to the meeting spot and deposited herself outside Jenkins Deli to wait for Kate. After waiting for more than twenty minutes, Hannah began to become a little impatient, not to mention a little annoyed. She went over to the phone booths where she saw no sign of Kate.

'This is ridiculous', she thought, 'I'm going to take the bus home.'

As Hannah made her way outside through the parking lot, she suddenly stopped dead. There again was Kate appearing to be in a heated debate with Joe. Kate wasn't making a call after all; she only meant to chase after Joe.

'Dodging these two is beginning to lose its charm.' Hannah mumbled to herself.

Her annoyance lifted as she realized Kate was crying, and Hannah found herself feeling very concerned for Kate. She wondered why Joe was making her cry. Joe appeared unbothered by her tears based on the stern look on his face. It bothered Hannah to think that Joe could make her friend so unhappy.

'And he seemed so nice. I guess you really can't tell a book by its cover.' Hannah said to herself as she continued to watch the interaction between them.

Now Joe was holding onto Kate's shoulders appearing to console her, but all the while looking slightly annoyed. Hannah decided she wasn't going to interrupt them again and with this, she turned and went back into the shopping mall and used the east exit to go home by taxi rather than her earlier decision to take the bus. That evening, Hannah had decided she would save any embarrassment or awkwardness for Kate and picked up the telephone to call her.

"Kate, I'm sorry about this afternoon. I waited for about twenty minutes, and since I didn't see you, I thought I would just take a cab home. I hope you weren't angry." Hannah offered hoping she sounded convincing.

"Oh no Hannah, I'm not angry at all. I know I was a bit later than we had agreed, but there was a sale at Richards' Clothier that I couldn't resist. Anyway, I got to Jenkins and since you weren't there, I assumed that you couldn't wait. It was my fault completely." Kate explained.

Hannah felt hurt and then angry. Not only is she lying, Hannah thought, but she is so smooth at it. Hannah did not want to continue the conversation any longer because Kate's deceit was so unexpected.

"Look Kate, I have to run, otherwise my bath's going to overflow. I just wanted to apologize."

"Well, just don't do it again." Kate said with a laugh.

"I'll try not to." Hannah replied hoping to keep the sarcasm from her tone.

Hannah hung up the phone in utter amazement. 'Don't do it again.' She mimicked. 'She must be kidding!'

CHAPTER 7

Days went by before Hannah heard anything from Kate. She began to feel uncomfortable with the silence and during that time Hannah had satisfied herself with thinking that there must be a good reason for Kate's need to lie to her. She decided she would let it go, and not hang on to one negative incident considering all the time they had been friends. The days and weeks that followed settled into their usual comfort of friendship without any mention of Joe, until now.

"Speaking of Joe, I wanted to ask you a question Hannah. I hope you won't mind."

"I don't mind. Shoot." Hannah invited the question despite feeling she was being lured into a conversation that she would regret.

"Remember the day we were shopping and we ran into Joe? Well, I have been meaning to ask you how you know him. I remember you mentioned you had met him running." Kate prompted.

"Yes, we met running, and so actually I don't really know him at all. It was coincidence that we got caught in the rain and we got to chatting until the rain lifted. That was it really." Hannah explained, although feeling a bit resentful that she had to defend how she knew him. Her instincts, although not knowing why, was to make light of the situation and not give the actual location of their meeting and the obvious attraction they felt towards one another. Hannah felt that Kate would not be happy with that information.

"Oh, I got the impression you two knew each other well." Kate prompted.

"Really?" Hannah asked, genuinely confused. "I wonder why you would get that impression. We barely spoke."

"Well, it wasn't what was being said, it was what was in the eyes. There was just a look that said you knew each other well." Kate explained.

"Oh, really? Well, Miss Look in the Eyes, I hate to disappoint, but you're way off." Hannah laughed. "But I like the theory. However, I will say that the look you might have been getting was me walking into a private conversation, and I was concerned because you seemed upset."

"Oh, don't be silly, I wasn't upset. You shouldn't have been concerned. I think your imagination was getting the better of you again Hannah." Kate stated.

"My imagination is getting the better of me again? I don't understand." Hannah remarked.

"Just now when I called you thought there was someone creeping around outside your house?" Kate reminded her.

"True, and thankfully, your call distracted me and I feel much better. But you're right, I must have a vivid imagination." Hannah offered being happier talking about her wayward imagination rather than discussing Joe.

"I'm teasing you, but I could tell you were upset. Will you be alright now Hannah?" Kate asked sincerely.

"Yes, I will. Thank you for calling. I think its best if I climb into bed since I'm feeling really tired all of a sudden."

"Okay, good night Hannah. I'll call you later in the week. Maybe we can take in a movie?"

"Sounds great. I'd really like that Kate. Good night."

Hannah had considered asking Kate how she knew Joe, but something told her that she wouldn't get a straight answer. She felt that Kate displayed an unspoken possessiveness of Joe that translated into a 'don't ask' message. Despite that, Hannah felt much calmer and almost silly about the shadows that had passed her windows earlier. Her eyes had now adjusted to the darkness around her and she realized that the old weeping willow outside her kitchen window had turned out to be the culprit. But a shiver ran through her nonetheless as she thought of the shadows that passed her living room window. That had definitely not been a willow tree.

Hannah had no sooner hung up the phone when she heard Martha's key in the lock. She turned on the kitchen light to check the time. It was almost midnight. Hannah groaned. She had wanted to get to bed early tonight so that she would be fresh for work in the morning.

It suddenly dawned on Hannah that Kate must have called her at about 11:15. 'That's strange', she thought, 'I wonder why she called. Since we were sidetracked by those shadows, Kate must have forgotten why she phoned me.'

Hannah's thoughts were broken as Martha opened the front door and walked down the hall and then poked her head in the kitchen.

"Hi." She whispered.

"Hi Martha. Why are you whispering?"

"I don't know. I suppose because it's late." Martha smirked.

Another head poked through the door over Martha's.

"Hi Sis!" Adam, Martha's boyfriend of one year, said as he bent to kiss Hannah on the cheek.

"How dare you keep my baby sister out so late!" Hannah scolded affectionately.

CHAPTER 8

The next morning, Hannah woke a little earlier than usual although she was thankful as her night was consumed with unsettled dreams. As she prepared a light breakfast and put the kettle on for tea, a nice start to her day she decided, she was momentarily startled by Martha's appearance in the kitchen.

"Boy, are you jumpy. Good morning." Martha laughed.

"You did startle me. I had a restless sleep and I must be a bit edgy." Hannah leaned in to kiss her sister's cheek. "Good morning."

"I think you need a vacation. Better yet, why don't you come to a Halloween party with us this weekend?" Martha said brightly.

"You think a party is better than a vacation?" Hannah laughed as she poured some tea for Martha.

"Well, when you're with your loving sister and wonderful brother-in-law to be, yes I think its better." Martha laughed back as Hannah busied herself with pouring her own tea.

"Oh really? Well, if you really think you're so wonderful, I suppose…" Hannah stopped mid-sentence and turned to look at her younger sister. Martha's face was full of expectancy and reflected a cautious smile.

Hannah walked over to the kitchen table where Martha was seated and handed her a steaming cup of tea.

"What do you mean future brother-in-law?" Hannah said quietly.

"Well," Martha said quietly and then slipped her left hand from under the table to expose an exquisite ring featuring one solitary yellow diamond encircled by a halo of mother of pearl.

"Oh Martha it's gorgeous and so unusual. I'm so happy for you.

Congratulations." She opened her arms to hug her sister. "And you're right, Adam is wonderful and you're so lucky. Oh this is wonderful news! Tell when did this happen? Were you surprised? Did you pick the ring? Or did he pick the ring?"

"Hannah, Hannah, one question at a time." Martha laughed. "It happened last night actually just after you went to bed. Adam and I made a drink and went into the living room and it was nice because you had left the fire going..."

"Oops, I forgot about that, but lucky that I did..." Hannah conceded.

"Yes, it was lucky that you did because it was the perfect setting for what was about to happen. Adam had been acting strangely all night, so distant and lost in thought. I didn't realize that he was actually looking for the right moment. I wondered why he kept behaving so peculiarly, and then when he drove me home and he wanted to come in, I began to think the worst!"

"Why the worst?" Hannah questioned.

"Well, you know Adam always full of jokes and fun. But last night, it was none of that; at least he was not his usual self. Then when he wanted to come into the house on a weeknight when he usually drops me and goes straight home, oh, I don't know, my imagination started to get the better of me. I just thought that maybe he was working up the courage to tell me we should cool off because we were seeing too much of each other." Martha confessed.

"Sometimes I think you're really crazy. You know he loves you." Hannah said comfortingly.

"Well I do now." Martha laughed, holding up her new ring that she had only admired at least three hundred times. "I honestly had no idea that he was about to propose."

"So, tell me. How did he propose?"

"Well..." Martha began.

"I got down on my knees, and I told her how much I loved her..."

Hannah looked up, momentarily startled to hear a male voice. Adam peaked his head around the corner, sporting a lively case of bed head and an unshaven face.

"And what are you doing here?" Hannah asked with mocked dismay.

"Celebrating!" Adam admitted grinning proudly.

"You really are a brat, Adam. But I love you and thank you for proposing to my sister. I know she will be well looked after and I'm proud and thrilled to death to have you as my brother-in-law." Hannah confessed as she kissed Adam on his bristled face. "And furthermore, you're supposed to 'celebrate' on the night you get married, not the night you get engaged."

"What could I do Hannah, Martha absolutely begged me." Adam said mischievously.

"Hey!" Hannah and Martha screamed in mock disgust and threw their toast at him.

"Thanks girls! Now I don't need to make my own breakfast." Adam laughed.

"Oh God, maybe I should reconsider." Martha laughed shaking her head.

"Yes, maybe you should." Hannah responded with delight.

"So, Hannah," Martha began while getting up to make some fresh toast. "We were thinking that we would like to get married in July of next year if that's okay with you."

"Of course it's alright with me. You shouldn't have to ask my permission when to get married." Hannah offered.

"Well," Adam interrupted, "that's actually another reason I'm here Hannah. Of course Martha and I would be getting a place of our own, but we just don't want to leave you high and dry. We want you to be emotionally ready for this marriage and July may be a little soon for you to be totally on your own without Martha. It will be quite an adjustment. Martha and I respect your wishes too, and we both agree that you should have some say in this."

Hannah shook her head in disbelief. "Thank you for thinking of me, but there's really no need to worry. If you decided to get married tomorrow I'd be in full support of that – more so than if you decided to wait five years. If I thought you were setting aside plans and hushing things up just to make me happy, or what you thought would make me happy, then that would hurt me more than you could know. Just put yourselves in my position. Do you really see me as being so lonely and dependent on you both?"

"No, no." They said in unison.

"Sometimes though Hannah, you seem so pensive, so deep in thought and you're very hard to read. I don't like always pestering you with 'what's wrong' or 'what are you thinking about', so I can only assume that you're lonely and maybe a little unhappy. And we think that we just may be able to interrupt some of that loneliness or unhappiness by being here with you." Martha explained.

Adam placed his arm lovingly around Hannah and nodded in silent agreement.

Hannah felt her eyes threaten the release of tears but smiled at both Adam and Martha, despite the threat. "And so this is all because I don't have a 'fella'? She said, hoping to lighten the conversation.

"No, not because you don't have a 'fella', as you put it." Martha said defensively.

"But, I think that's part of it." Hannah continued for her.

"Yes, of course it is. So, we've put an ad in the paper for you, advertising for one." Adam said standing up and announcing in a falsetto as though to imitate Hannah's voice 'I am a beautiful young woman with no visible warts and I would love to meet a man who will take long walks on the beach with me and share my toast in the morning.'

"No visible warts! Oh no! Are you sure you know what you're doing Martha? You know you can say no if you like. Remember, you have to put up with this so called sense of humour for the rest of your life!" Hannah pleaded while laughing.

"Yah, I love his humour. I can take it." Martha laughed while kissing her fiancé.

"Hey, I'm not kidding, I'm serious. The phone will start ringing any minute now." Adam pressed.

"Alright you two. Before the phone rings and I'm too busy fighting off all the offers, let me explain a few things for you. Yes, I would love to have someone in my life, just as you have each other. But, for now it hasn't happened and I really believe that it's affecting everyone else more than it's affecting me. I appreciate your concern, I really do, but I don't want it to become the objective of my friends and family to help 'Hannah find a man'. While well intended, it becomes a little embarrassing, believe me. I'm neither lonely nor unhappy. I admit I am a little preoccupied with things lately, but it has nothing to do with my love life, and God forbid it should now affect yours. So please, do me the greatest favour and do not worry about me because I want you to go ahead with your plans without guilt or weighed down with worry about me. This is a wonderful time in your lives and I want you to approach it unchained and without emotional burden. I am your greatest supporter, and I give you my blessing. Without any doubt in my mind, if Mum and Dad were standing here Martha, they would say the same to you and would be thrilled to know that you were making such a wonderful choice in Adam."

"I am quite a catch." Adam agreed, trying to look humble, while Martha giggled.

"You're such a goof Adam." Hannah said shaking her head.

"Yes, Adam you are. We have to be serious now." Martha suggested.

"I was being serious." Adam implied. "Look at me; I'm gorgeous, witty, incredibly sexy…"

Hannah and Martha just stared expressionlessly at Adam with mock disinterest.

"Did I mention how sexy I am?" Adam repeated.

"Uh huh." Martha and Hannah agreed without interest.

"It's become a bit of a problem. Women following me, throwing panties…"

"Poor you. I feel really badly for you." Hannah laughed.

"I'll be okay." Adam assured.

"Well now that we have made sure Adam's okay, maybe we can get back to focusing on Hannah." Martha hinted lightly.

Adam slipped his arm over Hannah's shoulder and nuzzled his nose into her cheek. "Talk to us Hannah."

"The only thing that needs to be talked about are your wedding plans." Hannah suggested.

"We'll talk about the wedding plans after we talk about you. What are you preoccupied with?" Adam probed.

"Nothing important." Hannah said lightly.

"Look, Hannah, couldn't you share this with us?" Martha pleaded.

CHAPTER 9

Hannah realized there was no reason to drag out an explanation as she looked from Martha and then to Adam. It wouldn't hurt to share her feelings with the two people who are the closest to her.

"Alright, but I'm probably just over thinking things. What I mean by that is it may be my imagination, but something is not sitting right and I can't put my finger on it." Hannah paused briefly and checked to make sure she had their full attention and continued.

"Kate's been behaving strangely. She's not quite herself and I know she has deliberately lied to me about things that would not need lying about. I feel uncomfortable and a bit annoyed when she does that, but I can't bring myself to say anything. So, I have to pretend that things seem normal when they aren't. I was talking to her just before you came home last night."

"What did she call about?" Martha questioned simply.

"Well, actually, we never got to why she was calling because I was completely distracted by someone sneaking around outside." Hannah confessed. She then disclosed to Martha and Adam what had transpired just prior to Kate's call when the phantom paid a visit, assuring them that the whole event was likely nothing.

"I hardly think someone creeping outside the house late at night is nothing. Do you think you know who it was?" Adam inquired.

"No, I couldn't see. By the time I had assured myself that whomever it was had gone, Kate called. I wasn't brave enough to go to the door and look outside before that." Hannah admitted.

Adam got up from the kitchen table. "I'm just going to go out and investigate. There may be an explanation to all this."

"As for Kate," Martha continued as Adam left the kitchen, "maybe something is bothering her and she can't bring herself to tell you. So it probably has nothing to do with anything you've done. You might just want to take the bull by the horns and come right out and ask her if something is up. You never know, maybe she called last night in an attempt to explain herself."

"Yes, maybe, but I have approached her a couple of times, although I admit I was subtle about it, but she always skirts the issue or makes light of it. I'm just concerned about her and I want her to be alright, but I have to admit it's affecting me. I feel that our friendship is a bit shaky, which may happen, but I don't like feeling as though it may be something I have done. It shouldn't be important, I know, but we've become good friends and I would hate for it to be destroyed over something unspoken."

Before Martha could comment, Adam bounced back into the kitchen. "Nothing looks out of the ordinary. It may just have been someone who may have had a wrong address." Adam proposed.

"Yes, of course," Hannah said with some relief. "It was probably a wrong address."

"Well, wrong address or not, I think it may be wise just to notify the police so that they can at least have a patrol car come by the area from time to time." Martha decided.

"Oh I don't want to trouble the police about this Martha. Let's just let it lie." Hannah decided hoping to dismiss the whole issue.

"Okay, you're the boss. But, promise me if it happens again you will at least call the police." Martha asked.

"I promise." Hannah said reluctantly.

"So, what about going to the party this weekend?" Martha said brightly.

"Yes, the Halloween party. Hannah you have to come because it's also doubling as an engagement party for Martha and me. We thought it would be more fun to have a theme and the timing is perfect for Halloween." Adam added.

"It sounds like fun, but do we have to be dressed up? I can't imagine what kind of costume I can come up with in such short time." Hannah said.

"Yes, you have to wear a costume, but it doesn't have to be elaborate. We are also asking that everyone be masked. That's an absolute must — you can't get in unless you have a mask on." Martha warned.

"Sounds interesting and I think I can come up with a mask. Where is the party going to be held?" Hannah asked.

"Adam's brother, Joshua is going to have the party. Adam had told Josh that he was going to propose to me this week, so he took it upon himself to turn his party into a Halloween engagement party so we could announce it at the party." Martha said lovingly.

"I guess Joshua didn't think you'd turn Adam down." Hannah deduced with a smile.

"Well, actually, I don't think he wanted me to change my mind. I can hardly back out now with a party in the works." Adam grinned.

Hannah and Martha both groaned at this. "I think you really should reconsider." Hannah concluded laughing with Martha.

"Yes, I agree. I'm calling it off." Martha teased Adam, as she cuddled into his arms.

"I think we had better talk about this later on because I am going to be late for work. I really have to go." Hannah said ruffling Adam's hair.

CHAPTER 10

The week that followed went smoothly and was rather ordinary. There were no more incidents of shadows passing by the windows, although Adam took it upon himself to keep watch for a few evenings, setting himself up in a corner of the living room with all the lights out, much to the amusement of Hannah and Martha.

After speaking with Adam, Joshua had extended an invitation to the party to Kate as well as Sally and Grayson. Hannah had realized that she wasn't able to make a costume on such notice and so decided to rent an outfit from a local costume supplier. She decided to go as the Pink Panther and found a sequined pink cat suit with a complimenting bejeweled mask shaped as a cat's face. Kate's selection was a playboy bunny costume featuring an oversized white bunny tail. After selecting the costumes, Hannah got caught up in the excitement of the engagement party, and was looking forward to making the most of the evening.

"You will be a hit in that playboy suit". Hannah suggested to Kate.

"You never know, Hugh Hefner might show up, which would mean a whole new career move for me." Kate decided.

"You never know." Hannah laughed.

The night of the party, the Hutton household was in a flurry. Martha and Adam, in keeping with the theme of the night decided to go as Romeo and Juliet. They were dressed and ready to go long before Hannah. Adam insisted on encouraging her to get a move on by continually going to the bottom of the stairs and calling to her.

"Oh, I don't know about this outfit. I feel really under-dressed." Hannah admitted from the top of the stairs.

"All the more reason to get down here." Adam said enthusiastically.

"Trust you." Martha said shaking her head and then placing a light kiss on his cheek.

"Just give me a minute and I'll be down." Hannah pleaded.

Hannah had been ready to go for about half an hour, but she felt the pink panther outfit may be just a little too revealing. She had tried the costume before renting it, and compared to Kate's outfit, it seemed mild by comparison. 'It fits just a little too well – just like a second skin.' Hannah thought examining herself for about the hundredth time in the mirror.

"Hannah, come on!" Martha sounded exasperated.

"I'm not sure about this really. I think I'd better let you two go on without me while I find something else to wear." Hannah shouted from the bedroom.

"Don't be silly. Come down and let us have a look." Martha encouraged.

"Okay, but please don't laugh." Hannah said. As she descended the stairs, Adam let out a slow whistle.

"Well hello Hannah." Adam drawled imitating W.C. Fields' voice. "I don't think we have to worry about your big sister enticing the men, do you Martha?"

"Knock it off Adam. I feel self conscious enough as it is. I don't think this is going to work for me. I feel like a bubblegum prostitute in this thing." Hannah complained.

"Hannah, you are being ridiculous. You are absolutely gorgeous. What are you worried about?" Martha asked gently.

"It's too tight for one and I feel like I'm going to spill out of the top if I make one false move." Hannah confessed.

"Okay, make a false move and let's see. We might as well test it now." Adam teased hopefully.

"Don't listen to him Hannah. You look amazing so why don't we just go and have a good time. There will be all sorts of people there in various outfits and you'll soon feel comfortable. And don't forget, you'll have a mask on." I wouldn't let you go out of the house if I thought you looked awful, and believe me, you look amazing. It's seductively tasteful."

Hannah felt better with Martha's encouragement and decided to do as she said. Once they had arrived at the party and upon seeing some of the costumes, Hannah became more at ease. Martha was right, many of the costumes were equally as daring or more so, and Hannah felt a sense of security once veiled behind the mask. Their first stop, mercifully, was at the bar where they ordered a drink that helped to ease Hannah's sense of discomfort.

Hannah then worked her way through the room seeking out some of Martha's friends whom she 'recognized' despite the masks, and chatted casually and happily. They all greeted her warmly and complimented her on how beautiful she looked. From time to time, despite the masks, Hannah couldn't help but notice the favorable glances from many of the men who had arrived at the party. She found herself unpredictably enjoying their interest and smiled confidently to acknowledge their attention.

After about half an hour, Hannah checked her watch and was surprised to find that, despite agreeing to meet Kate at the party, she was nowhere to be seen.

"I wonder what happened to her." Hannah said to no one in particular.

"Were you talking to me?" A male guest masquerading as a Zorro asked.

"Oh no I was talking to myself. I'm expecting a friend who hasn't shown up yet." Hannah explained.

"Well maybe she's here and you just haven't recognized her yet." Zorro leaned in closer to Hannah. She caught her breath as she sensed something familiar in the sound of his voice but she couldn't place it. His black mask obscured most of his face erasing every facial detail with the exception of his mouth and piercing eyes. Hannah also caught a faint scent of cologne that appealed to her senses.

"No, I know what she's wearing." Hannah said mechanically.

The stranger simply smiled at this letting his eyes take in all of her. Hannah became a little uncomfortable as an awkward silence settled between them.

"You seem very familiar, but I can't place you. Have we met?" Hannah asked.

"I'm not sure we're supposed to reveal our names. I thought that was the reason for the masks."

"Oh, yes, you're right. I shouldn't ruin the theme for the night. I understand all masks off at midnight, so I guess I'll have to wait until then." Hannah laughed, as, looking over Zorro's shoulder, she caught sight of Kate arriving. "Oh, there's my friend now."

Zorro followed Hannah's look as though to verify the arrival of Kate, who was dressed seductively in the playboy outfit, the mask and all else scarcely disguising anything at all. Halting to look only briefly, Zorro took hold of Hannah's hand. "Well, I'll leave you to your bunny friend, but with any luck, I'll see you later." He confessed.

"Yes, but you don't have to leave." Hannah implored wanting to discover the identity of this charismatic man. She momentarily left his gaze and turned away from him to wave at Kate.

"Kate, I'm over here." Kate responded by waving back and made her way through the crowd that had now tripled in size since Hannah arrived. Hannah turned to Zorro to introduce him to Kate, but to her surprise, he was no longer by her side. She turned each way to try and find out where he had gone but he had quite literally vanished.

"Wow what a mob." Kate laughed.

"It is a mob." Hannah agreed. "Kate you look great! You should wear that outfit more often."

"I certainly would be a big hit at the office wouldn't I? And what about you? You just may give me a run for my money. I don't know if I can stand the competition." Kate confessed. "That cat suit leaves nothing to the imagination."

Hannah was silenced by her remark, feeling suddenly uncomfortably aware of the appropriateness of her outfit. It was little comfort to her that Kate's outfit was far more revealing and with far less material covering her than the pink cat suit. Gratefully, her thoughts were interrupted by Joshua standing on a chair while holding up his hand to quiet everyone.

"Thank you everyone for your attention. I just have a couple of things to say and then you may all get back to having a great time with great friends." Joshua paused and smiled while murmurs of agreement rippled through the room. "First," he continued, "Thanks for coming out tonight. I hope you're all enjoying yourselves. You all look incredible in your costumes and remember midnight is the witching hour when everyone removes their masks and your identities will be disclosed. And no one is allowed to leave before then, so don't even think about it!" Joshua paused once again to more rumblings and laughter until the voices settled into silence again. "Second, this party began as a Halloween costume party but then it became an even better occasion to offer me the pleasure of formally announcing the engagement of my baby brother Adam to Martha Hutton." Cheers of congratulations and surprise went through the room.

"I will make an exception now to reveal the identities only of Adam and Martha – perhaps some of you have already guessed who they are given their costumes – but would Romeo and Juliet come and join me?" Martha and Adam squeezed through the crowd to hugs and pats on their backs. Joshua leaned forward to grasp Martha's hand and gave her a brotherly hug, and then hugged his brother.

"Would everyone raise their glasses in a toast to the newly engaged couple? Glasses lifted high in the air while Joshua beamed proudly and toasted: 'To Adam and Martha, may you have a long, loving and happy life together."

Murmurs of 'to Adam and Martha' chorused followed by cries of congratulations midst cheers of happiness. Hannah stood proudly by as Adam and Martha thanked everyone and laughed amongst their friends as Martha proudly showed off her ring. Hannah's attention was momentarily distracted as she looked to her right to find Zorro leaning casually against the bar. As his gaze caught hers, he smiled slightly and tipped his glass to her. She followed his lead, smiled and tipped her glass to him. Kate, who was standing slightly to her right, caught the exchange and her attention was diverted to the beneficiary of Hannah's attention.

"Who is that?" Kate inquired.

"I have no idea. I was just returning a toast that he offered." Hannah explained not wishing to draw importance to her actions. When she looked away from Kate and back to her mysterious friend, he had vanished. 'Another disappearing act', Hannah thought silently.

"Well, that's exciting. Maybe he is completely gorgeous under that mask." Kate suggested.

"I guess I'll find out at midnight if he's still here." Hannah said lightly.

"True. In the meantime, let's see if these outfits might do some work for us. Let's get a drink to give us a little more courage for conversation" Kate said grabbing Hannah's hand and leading her back to the bar.

"Okay," Hannah said laughing but thinking she didn't really need liquor to help her make conversation.

"What wonderful news for Martha and Adam. I had no idea they were even thinking of marriage, but they make such a wonderful couple don't they?" Kate offered as they arrived at the bar. Despite Kate's earlier declaration for the need of a drink, she ordered a soft drink instead.

"Yes, they are perfect together. I am really excited for them." Hannah said sincerely.

"Will they be getting a place of their own, or will they stay with you?" Kate questioned.

"Oh, certainly they will be getting their own home, and I can't blame them. They need to start off their marriage properly − just the two of them, the way it should be." Hannah philosophized.

"Right." Kate said simply and looked intently at Hannah. "Okay, well, why don't we work the crowd? Let's have some fun."

CHAPTER 11

Hannah followed Kate as they squeezed through the partygoers. They stopped at a recognizable group and as they chatted superficially about one thing and another, Hannah's attentiveness was fractured as she searched the room for the mystery man. She felt disappointed as her search went unrewarded.

'Another vanishing act.' Hannah confirmed to herself.

"What did you say?" Kate asked.

"Nothing, I was just thinking out loud." Hannah laughed, feeling a bit embarrassed that she had been caught talking to herself.

Hannah and Kate made their way to the back of the house where Joshua's sunroom had been cleared of most furniture so it could be converted to a dance room. Installed in the corner was a DJ disguised as a ghoul. The only light that illuminated the room was hosted by candle lit pumpkins and orange pin lights that had been strung in a crisscrossed pattern from the ceiling. The effect was extraordinary as shadows and light radiated a haunting yet romantic backdrop.

"This is spectacular." Hannah marveled. "I didn't realize Joshua had such talent."

Just then the DJ announced that the dancing would begin and apropos to the theme of the evening, he started out with the Monster Mash, to everyone's delight.

Hannah got caught up in the enjoyment as her partners changed from one to another. She soon found herself needing a breath of fresh air and excused herself from her present dance partner to retreat to the outside patio just off the sunroom. Despite the time of year with the expectation of a cool night, it was a warm evening. Except for a soft gentle wind, the night was still. Hannah was thankful for the solitude and wandered from the patio area and onto the extensively treed lawn. Nearly all of the trees were still heavy with autumn painted leaves. Contented with the solitude the backyard offered, music could be heard in the distance. Hannah sought the sanctuary of a large willow tree, its limbs so long that they swept the ground. As the branches danced gracefully with the soft zephyr, Hannah raised them so that she could break through their protective shield. Light from the backyard patio lanterns filtered streams of delicate radiance through the willow's branches. Obscured now from the rest of the world, Hannah leaned her back gently against the willow's substantial trunk and closed her eyes to enjoy the drifts of music that floated down the yard. After a few brief moments, her solitude was broken.

"May I have this dance?" A soft voice spoke. Hannah turned, momentarily startled and surprised that she was not on her own. Her surprise turned to quiet pleasure to find Zorro, still masked, extending his hand to her.

Hannah smiled and extended her hand to his. "Yes, thank you." She said simply.

He pulled her to him, not letting go of her one hand. He then slid his other hand around to her back and cradled her against him as she responded by placing her arm around his neck. Despite this stranger, she felt safe and happy to be near him sensing still that he wasn't a stranger at all. The music played in the distance as they danced slowly in silence, quietly content in each other's company. The music quieted and they slowly pulled back from one another. Zorro softly pulled the mask from Hannah's face.

"I'm not sure that's allowed." Hannah said half seriously with a smile.

"I won't tell, if you don't." Zorro smiled. "You are more beautiful than I remembered. Hannah felt her knees weaken at the nearness of him. She thought if he were to let her go now she would surely fall. Then she realized what he had just said to her.

"What do you mean 'than you remembered'? I do know you, don't I?" Hannah pressed. She pulled back and gently touched his mask. "Who are you?" She began to take off his mask, but then stopped. What if it were better not to know? Perhaps he wouldn't be all that she imagined and then what?

"It's okay. You can take my mask off. I can't be here at midnight, so I think we can break the rules." He offered.

Hannah halted only briefly and then decided she had to know who this man was. She gently pulled the mask from his face. "Joe." She said with a familiarity that implied a closeness that they had not yet experienced.

"I hope you're not disappointed." He said sincerely.

"I'm not disappointed. I'm…" Her words caught and she couldn't decide how far to confess her feelings of pure delight. She realized now that there would be no one else who she would prefer to have standing before her than Joe.

His hands came up to cup her face and held her gaze, then he slowly bent to kiss her on her mouth, so gently. She felt weak from his touch and his closeness as he continued to kiss her. Hannah's eyes closed at his seduction and he then guided her gently back against the willow tree pressing into her while his kisses lingered against her mouth. Slowly, he stopped, pull back away from her, and lovingly pushed back a lock of her hair that had fallen down her face.

"Thank you." She smiled.

"You're welcome." And he laughed. "I'm so glad you were here tonight. You really do look beautiful."

"Thank you." She said again.

"You're welcome." He repeated. And then they both laughed.

"I guess I'm lost for words." Hannah confessed. "But I'm happy I saw you again too."

He ran his thumb gently and lovingly down the curve of her face and said, "I can't stay Hannah. I should have left awhile ago, but I was waiting to see if I could have the chance to meet with you again privately. I was watching you from a distance and when you went for your walk, I discreetly followed. It's a perfectly beautiful setting."

"Thank you." She said for the third time. He looked at her with mock surprise and then they laughed again.

"How about I do the talking?" Joe teased, while she nodded still laughing.

"I have to go. I want to see you again but I can't promise anything right now. I'm working on a case that is consuming most of my time, and my social life currently has to take a back seat. Since our first meeting, I haven't been able to get you out of my mind, and you being here gave me an opportunity to let you know how unforgettable you are." He bent down and kissed her again, and pulled away. "I thought I'd stop you before you said thank you again."

Hannah smiled, but this time was without words. She felt so conflicted with the joy of seeing him and the disappointment that it would likely be awhile before she would see him again.

"Do you know Martha and Adam?" Hannah asked realizing this fact had not been disclosed.

"No, actually, I don't know them at all." Joe said simply, but didn't offer why he was attending the same party that she was attending.

"It's so strange that I would run into you again." Hannah suggested.

"Do you want me to walk you back to the house?" Joe offered, again not being tempted to explain his presence.

"No, I think I'll just stay here. I don't think I'm ready for sharing myself with anyone else right now." Hannah confessed. "I'd like to be alone for a bit, and then I'll go back to the party."

"I understand. I'm going to leave around the side of the house so I don't interrupt the party. I'm not sure I would be able to find Josh anyway." He hesitated and then continued. "Hannah, I wonder if I might ask that you keep our encounter to yourself for now. I know it's a strange request, but I promise you, it's for good reason."

Hannah felt reluctant to respond immediately. "Oh, I suppose…well, I wouldn't necessarily…" Hannah found herself floundering for the right thing to say, wishing she could make some sense of his request. Please tell me he isn't married, she silently pleaded. If this was the case, she wouldn't want to admit her meeting with Joe to anyone. She suddenly felt foolish for not having suspected this.

"Hannah, will you promise? It's very important." He urged.

"Yes, of course. I won't say anything, I promise." Hannah said wishing very much now to be alone.

"Don't worry. I'm not married. Goodnight Hannah" He said as if reading her mind, and she simply nodded feeling so grateful for those words. Joe bent down to kiss her lightly again on the mouth and Hannah responded willingly.

CHAPTER 12

Hannah lingered hidden behind the willow's branches for some time before returning to the party. She rested delicately against the trunk and closed her eyes to a million thoughts that ran through her mind and his request that she keep her silence. She decided not to worry just now about the 'what ifs' and believe that his intentions were good and felt it was time to leave the seclusion of the willow tree's screen and return to the party. As she pulled back the heavy branches the light from the house illuminated an object on the dewy lawn. She stooped down to discover it was Joe's mask. Hannah decided to keep it as a souvenir and closed it gently in her hand as though it were a precious gift.

As Hannah walked back to the party, she was oblivious to the fact that Joe had not been the only one interested in her movements that night. In fact, she had been followed by someone else, their eyes waiting and watching as an eyewitness to her encounter with Joe.

Hannah arrived at the patio door to be greeted by Martha, who looked a little concerned.

"Hannah, where have you been?"

"I was just out for a stroll in the yard. Don't look so concerned, I'm fine." Hannah assured her.

"I thought you had been abducted."

"Abducted by a masked man?" Hannah teased.

"You've been gone for quite awhile." Martha said impatiently as she was greeted with the casual response from Hannah.

"I had? It didn't seem that long to me. I just wanted to get some fresh air"

"Yes, you were gone for a long time. Are you feeling okay?" Martha now feeling a bit worried.

"No, I'm fine." Hannah was almost wishing she could pull Martha aside and confess her encounter with Joe. But keeping to her promise, she stayed silent. "I guess I feel a little sentimental because of my sister's good news."

"Oh Hannah please don't be sentimental. Nothing is going to change between us." She assured her sister and giving her a warm hug.

Hannah felt somewhat guilty that she had used Martha and Adam's engagement as a reason not to admit her meeting with Joe. She did concede to herself however that one of the reasons she went for a walk was to think back over the days when it was just she and Martha as a family, each looking out for the other. The evening for many reasons was bitter sweet. While her happiness for Martha was genuine, she knew that their relationship would take a different path and it was only natural that it should.

"I'm really happy for you Martha. I wasn't being selfish with my thinking; I know everything will be the same with us. Let's forget it and have a good time." Hannah said and took Martha by the arm and led her to the bar. "Let me buy you a drink." She joked.

"Sounds good to me." Martha laughed as she followed behind her sister. "Hey what's this?" She asked pulling a willow's long narrow leaf from her hair. "Must have been quite a walk! Were you lying down gazing up at the stars?"

"Not quite." Hannah laughed.

"Oh, and you found someone's mask?" Martha suggested as she touched the mask that Hannah had rescued.

"Yes, I found it on the ground." Hannah confessed accurately. They were then interrupted by Adam who appeared to have had a few too many. This distraction offered Hannah an opportunity to place the mask into her purse. She felt a little childish but somehow possessing it offered her confirmation and a simplistic reminder of her encounter.

"There you are!" Adam cried as he noticed Hannah and Martha on their way to the bar. "Where the heck have you been Pinky?"

"Had a few have you?" Hannah observed with a laugh.

"Just a couple, but I'm fine. I've been waiting to have a dance with you. Will you dance with me?" Adam asked looking a bit like a lost puppy.

"Of course I'll dance with my future brother-in-law."

During her dances with Adam, Hannah recognized Sally dressed as a cheerleader, giggling and having a wonderful time dancing with Joshua. She looked over at Hannah briefly and waved, and despite being masked had recognized her costume. After about three dances, Hannah and Adam agreed that they could use refreshment and left the dance floor. They collected Martha who was waiting in the wings, and all linking arms, headed towards the bar.

"Who was Josh dancing with?" Adam said with a slight slur.

"That's my friend Sally who I work with. I think you've met once before at our place when we threw a Christmas party last year." Hannah explained. "Josh came with you."

"Oh, that's right. Josh thought she was pretty special, but she has a boyfriend, am I right?" Adam asked.

"You are right Adam. They are actually living together now."

Their conversation was diverted by a scene that was playing itself out next to the bar leaving them all speechless. Kate was standing unsteadily on a bar stool and looking quite drunk. She had drawn a small crowd, all of whom seemed quite amused by her antics.

"How long have I been gone?" Hannah asked Martha incredulously.

"Over an hour at least. But you're not responsible for..." Martha started to say before Hannah cut her off.

"I know Martha, but this is quite unlike Kate, or at least I think it is." Hannah replied. "I'm going to try and lead her away from here, but I might need some help. Will you help me Adam?"

"Sure, do you think I should just throw her over my shoulder?" Adam asked seriously as though this wouldn't be a problem.

"No, I don't think we had better do that. It may not have a pretty ending, especially if she doesn't want to come down off that bar stool." Hannah surmised. "Why don't we just ask her to come down, and see if that works?"

"Okay, you do the talking and I'll be your backup." Adam agreed as if he were on a very serious mission. Despite the concern Hannah had for Kate, she managed a quick glance in Martha's direction to exchange a smile acknowledging Adam's slightly inebriated determination.

Hannah moved closer to the bar stool that unsteadily displayed her friend and smiled up at Kate in an effort to act as though she saw her doing this every day.

"Hey there." She called up to Kate.

"Hanniepoo! Where have you been?" Kate shrieked with a quizzical look and slurring her words.

Hannah felt a little embarrassed as all eyes fell on her. "I've been to the moon and back." Hannah explained as she approached Kate and held out her arms to her in an effort to keep her from falling off the bar stool.

"Oh, to the moon. Why didn't you take me? Did you go all by yourself?" Kate looked childlike as though she had truly missed a trip to the moon.

"Yes, I went by myself." Hannah continued the conversation while holding her hands up to Kate to signal her to come down from the stool. Kate responded automatically and with the help of Adam, allowed herself to be led away from the crowd.

Hannah decided it best to take Kate outside and maneuvered her onto the patio and after a bit of coaxing settled her into a lawn chair. To Hannah's relief, the patio seemed quite deserted. A few minutes later Martha and Adam appeared with coffee and a few sandwiches.

"Here, this may help." Martha said handing the coffee to Hannah.

"Thanks."

"How is she doing?" Adam whispered as though on a covert mission.

"Oh, she's okay. I think if we try and sober her up a bit she'll be fine. Being outside is going to help too." Hannah replied as she settled beside Kate in an effort to have her sip at the coffee and take a few bites of the sandwich.

"Oh, moon food. I just love moon food, don't you Hannie?" Kate cried enthusiastically. Hannah burst out laughing as Martha and Adam joined in.

"I think we'll be okay. Why don't you two go and enjoy your party." Hannah smiled. "Thanks for the food and coffee."

"If you need anything, just yell." Adam replied taking Martha's hand. "We'll come out and check on you from time to time." He assured and walked away, albeit a little wobbly.

"Moon food!" Kate declared happily as she waved goodbye with her sandwich.

"Moon food." Hannah verified with a smile. "You my dear Kate are a crazy woman."

Kate's attention moved from her sandwich to Hannah. "Really?" she questioned obviously taking Hannah seriously.

'I have to watch what I say.' Hannah thought. "No, I didn't mean it seriously. I think you're funny, that's all.' Hannah explained hoping that Kate's cheerful disposition would return.

Kate let the remainder of her sandwich drop to her knee and let her hands cradle her forehead. "God I am crazy. I'm crazy and drunk, aren't I?"

Hannah felt the best response was a light one. "It's nothing that we all haven't done by getting drunk. Don't worry; everyone here has had something to drink. You are just enjoying yourself."

"That's the problem though. I'm not enjoying myself. I'm making a fool out of myself by drinking too much." Kate was attempting to speak without sounding inebriated, but Hannah could still detect that her words were slightly slurred.

"You didn't do anything to feel foolish about Kate. You're being hard on yourself."

"I'm drunk and there is nothing worse than a drunken woman. So for that reason, I'm a fool." Kate concluded.

Hannah felt there was nothing she could say so she remained silent, never taking her eyes from Kate's face. Kate's hand dropped from her forehead and looked back at Hannah. A slight smile crossed her face as she declared quietly. "You know why I did this, Hannie? You know why I wanted to get drunk?"

Hannah said nothing except to shake her head. 'Maybe if she keeps talking, she'll sober up a little.' Hannah thought.

"I'll tell you why. Because I'm very, very sad and it never seems to go away, no matter how hard I try to be happy. I'm just very, very sad, never, never happy." Kate said in a gloomy repetitive monotone. It was apparent that she was still affected by the alcohol she had consumed, but it seemed to be putting her in a calmer and more worn-out state. Perhaps just being outside and away from the party atmosphere had settled her down.

"Why are you so sad?" Hannah asked quietly. Kate's head dropped to her chest for what seemed like endless minutes. Hannah began to think that she may have fallen asleep.

"Kate?" Hannah whispered, lifting her hair from her face.

Kate looked up abruptly, her face streaming with tears.

"Kate, what's the matter?" Hannah said, startled by the turn around in Kate.

"My husband is the matter." Kate said plainly. "He doesn't love me anymore and its killing me inside."

"What do you mean your husband? You're married?" Hannah exclaimed wondering if this was fact or fiction. The whole idea was ridiculous since Hannah had known Kate long enough and there was never any evidence of her being associated with any man, let alone a husband. Surely Kate's imagination was being confused with reality due to her present state of mind.

"I know you didn't know. That's because I never told anyone when I moved here. I wanted to start a new life and forget a very unhappy experience. But, try as I might, it has stayed inside me and it has been dying a long and slow death. And it's my fault that it is that way, because I can't get used to not having him in my life. I still love him."

"But Kate, you're not serious are you?" Hannah realized, feeling a little guilty that Kate may not have been confessing all if she had not had so much to drink.

"I know I have had too much to drink, but I am serious. I've kept it from you for too long."

Hannah felt completely at odds. Admittedly, she felt a bit resentful that Martha's engagement party would be the time Kate would come clean with such a huge confession. "Kate, I'm not sure we should keep talking about this. Maybe we should call it a night. Once you have had a good night's sleep, you can decide in the morning whether you want to tell me the rest."

"I want to tell you now Hannah. I have never felt good about the fact that I've kept this from you, and considering my behavior tonight, you deserve to know the truth since you've been such a good friend to me."

Hannah nodded, still unsure that hearing her out would be the best plan, but conceded. "Okay, tell me what you think I need to know." Hannah said simply.

"I feel since my marriage broke up my life has been a waiting game for something I believe will never take place and that's the reinstatement of my marriage or, more to the point, to have my husband love me again." Kate confessed as a tear slipped down her face.

"But maybe there's hope Kate. Surely if your husband knew how you felt..." Hannah seemed lost for words. Obviously this would have been something Kate would have already confessed to her husband, but clearly there had to be a lot more to her marriage breaking up than simple miscommunication.

"My husband knows how I feel. He knows only too well and he won't consider getting together again. I love him so much and I don't think I will ever be able to let go. I can't seem to accept that he will never love me again."

CHAPTER 13

Hannah felt helpless as well as stunned. She was now looking at Kate in a completely different light, as if through new eyes. How could she never have realized that Kate's other life had existed when she thought she knew her so well. Kate's dark moods through the few years Hannah knew her were now explained. Hannah felt badly that she was never more sensitive when those moods hit.

"Kate, I wish you would have told me long ago so that I may have been more supportive. You've obviously been dealing with this alone and it may have helped to have someone to talk to."

"But that would have defeated the whole purpose of leaving that life behind. The point is that I wanted to forget and if I had a life that didn't remind me of what I no longer had with friends that didn't know it would be easier for me to forget and to get on with my life." Kate explained sensibly. Slowly Kate seemed to sober as the confessions to her past fell from her lips.

"But was it so bad that you had to leave so you could forget?" Hannah asked quietly.

"The disintegration of my marriage was, I admit, foreseeable in view of the events leading up to the breakup. So, in answer to your question, yes, it was bad." Kate spoke resolutely. "I wanted so much to please him, to make him see that I loved him and would do anything for him, but, I suppose when I look back, I may have overdone it. Hannah I think because I became so determined and so focused on being a better and more loving wife, the more it drove him crazy. So, at first, he just used to walk away from me and ignore me. Then, when that no longer worked, he started to become impatient and threatened to never see me again if I didn't leave him alone. It was so confusing for me, because all I thought I was doing was showing him how devoted I was to him. He saw it so differently. Unfortunately, the more he pulled away, the more I clung on. I was so afraid of losing him yet all the while I was causing him to leave. It was a vicious cycle and I was too fearful to let go and I realize now that I needed confidence to not be reassured every single day. But then, that fear led me to thinking that he must be seeing someone else. He seemed so distant, so disinterested in me. My fear turned to panic and I'm ashamed to say I began following him.

My whole life was dictated by where he went without me. I hated that he preferred to be alone or with other people and not with me. I was so consumed by it; I don't know how I managed to get anything else done. I became such a different person. If I knew he was going out, I would pretend that I had plans too, and I would sit in my car and wait for him to leave the house and then I would follow him."

Kate paused for a bit and stared at her hands as though they were the most fascinating things she had ever seen. Finally, in an almost trancelike state she continued.

"Then one night he had plans to go out and as usual, he was leaving me behind. I acted as though it didn't bother me, but of course it was like little knives going through my heart. Before he went out, I made an excuse that I was going out with friends when in fact I simply got in my car, drove down the street, and waited for him to leave."

Kate looked up at Hannah as though suddenly realizing she was there and said, "Is this okay that I'm telling you this? Here we are at your sister's engagement party, and I'm selfishly taking your time by pouring out all my troubles. This really isn't fair to you."

"No, I want to listen and I think you really need a friend right now. I'm just sorry I didn't know about this before." Hannah offered sincerely.

"Hannah, I really made a mess of things." Kate said appearing to be satisfied that she wasn't taking up Hannah's time. "I followed him to this little bar on the edge of town. This made it worse for my insecurity because I thought he was going out of town so that he wouldn't be seen by anyone he knew. He went into the bar while I sat in the parking lot and waited."

"What were you waiting for?" Hannah couldn't understand why she would go to all that trouble just to sit outside in a parking lot.

"I didn't have the courage to go into the bar. It just seemed easier to wait in the parking lot to see if he would come out with someone and then I would know once and for all. The trouble was every female that went into the bar I imagined was going in to meet Joseph."

Hannah, who had been leaning towards Kate with her chin propped in her hand and listening intently, straightened slightly. This was the first time she had mentioned her husband's name. She had seemed to be deliberately avoiding mentioning it, but Kate appeared not to have noticed the slip-up, if in fact it was one. Regardless, she continued without missing a beat.

"I wish now that I had just come to my senses and left to go home. I now know that it would have been better to live silently with my imaginings rather than my reality. As they say, hindsight is twenty-twenty, but I was drawn to the inside of that bar like a bee to honey. Then it started to snow, and my vision was becoming obscured by the heaviness of the snow accumulating on the windshield. I was frustrated because I couldn't see who was coming and going clearly so I decided I would just go in and settle in a corner of the bar and watch from a distance. I was convinced that enough people were inside that I would not be noticed at all. So, I pulled the hood of my coat over my head and went into the bar. It was so dimly lit that I was content that I had not been seen." Kate sat quietly for a moment and shook her head as if to drive the visions of that night out of her head.

"Kate, you don't have to tell me this. I can see that it's hard for you." Hannah suggested.

"No, as embarrassed as I am to tell you, I feel as though a weight is lifting from me. I think I've been playing it over and over again in my head for so long, and I just need to say it out loud, like a confession." Kate said honestly.

"Okay, as long as you're sure. Tell me what happened." Hannah had to admit that she was captivated and was anxious to hear the rest.

"I ordered a tea because I was shivering so much. I wasn't sure if it was from nerves or from the cold and I sat and waited. Finally, I caught sight of him. He was leaning against the bar chatting with a man, and I felt relieved that he was just there with a buddy. I decided to finish up my drink and slip back out of the bar and go home. I kept an eye on him to make sure he wouldn't see me as I put my coat on. Then, out of nowhere, this girl came up to him and put her hands on his shoulders and planted a kiss on his mouth. I felt like someone had punched me in the stomach, and I sank back into my seat because my knees had gone to rubber. I watched as they joked and laughed together as though there was no one else in the room."

"How horrible for you." Hannah offered genuinely.

Kate continued seeming not to notice Hannah's sympathy.

"My hurt began to turn to fury. I felt foolish and I felt betrayed. I couldn't believe that he would do that to me since he knew how much I loved him. I suddenly felt the strength to meet him head on and I wanted to let him know what I thought of him and I would give this other woman a piece of my mind too. So, full of fury and feeling completely justified, I ran over to where they stood and confronted both of them." Kate faltered.

"What did you say to them?" Hannah asked incredulously.

"I started on my rampage. I called her every name in the book and I even took her by the arm and pulled her away from him. I then turned and started to strike Joseph on the chest. I couldn't stop. By this time, I was crying bitterly and shouting at him. In the meantime, the woman, who I had completely embarrassed, had run to the washroom to escape me. I remember the 'sound' of the silence that fell over the bar. It was like slow motion. All eyes had now focused to watch this jealous, insane woman make a complete fool of herself. There was no pity in the faces that watched, just disgust. It took a bouncer to finally pull me away and escort me outside. It was humiliating. Joseph followed us only to make sure that I would not return. In fact, he put me in my car and said he was sick and tired of my behavior and asked that I stay out of his life once and for all. He told me that if I were ever to come around him again and interfere in his life, he would get a restraining order against me. He ended the conversation by telling me to go home and he slammed my car door shut as if to finalize our relationship, and then ran over to the car where the girl and his buddy were now waiting and they sped off. He must have thought that if he went back into the bar, I would have been stupid enough to follow him."

"I'm so sorry Kate. I don't know what to say." Hannah said feebly.

Kate fell silent for a few moments. "You know," she continued, "I don't think I've ever been so obsessed with anything or anyone in my whole life. You would think after all that, I would crawl into obscurity and not wish to be seen again. I presume, on some level, I did do that. Moving here to Evanston offered me a sanctuary and I could live a completely new life by starting over. I didn't see my husband for a long, long time. It was as though we had both vanished by fading from each others' sight."

"But it must have helped you to be here and away from the temptation to be near him. I never guessed there was anything that bothered you. You always seemed to be relatively content." Hannah offered.

"For the most part I was. I had to be. But then I wanted to apologize for my dreadful behaviour that night. I thought at the very least we could be friends. After that night at the bar, I thought long and hard about everything. I literally felt sick at the thought of losing my husband, but I knew it was over. Strangely enough, when I did see him again, it was here in Evanston. I couldn't believe it. There he was as plain as the nose on my face. So what did I think? Stupidly, I thought he had come looking for me, but I was wrong. It was just a strange coincidence; a lucky coincidence for me, and an unfortunate one for him. He made it clear that he was here on business, and was actually surprised that I was living here. I felt the rejection all over again."

All Hannah could do was to take Kate's hand and grip it tightly in support. Clearly, she was lost for words, not completely understanding that level of commitment where you could get so lost and misdirected by loving someone who clearly did not feel the same way about you. To Hannah, it was nothing short of self inflicted torture.

Their conversation was interrupted by screams of laughter as the clock chimed midnight prompting the go-ahead for everyone to take off their masks. Silently Hannah was grateful for the distraction as she felt speechless by the subtle assault of information that had besieged her. As the voices inside died down and the laughter subsided, Hannah wordlessly took hold of Kate's hand as a show of unspoken support.

Kate finally looked up at Hannah, sighed and leaned back in her chair. "God, I've talked myself into an early hangover. My head is killing me." She said rubbing her temples.

"Look, why don't I run in and tell Martha that we'll grab a cab home since I came with them." Hannah suggested.

"Normally, I would say no to your offer, but I think that would be a good idea, so I'll say yes. Thanks." Kate conceded.

"Okay, I'll meet you round the front of the house."

CHAPTER 14

Hannah ran inside the house to find Martha and Adam and told them of her plans. They insisted they come with her, but Hannah wanted them to stay and enjoy their party. It was late enough and people were starting to leave and they agreed that it would be better to stay behind and see everyone off.

"Have you seen Sally? I want to say goodnight to her." Hannah asked.

"No, the last time I saw her was on the dance floor with Josh. She may have already left." Martha guessed."

"Okay, but if you see her, tell her that I had to get Kate home."

On the way home, Hannah spoke supportively but lightly of Kate's situation while she simply listened. She presented optimistic expectations suggesting that, in time, Kate's husband may give her a chance to redeem herself and perhaps a reconciliation may come from it. Hannah silently thought that this would likely never happen given the circumstances, but she hoped that she might be able to lift Kate's spirits. At one point, Hannah turned to Kate for a response, and found that she was fast asleep leaning against the cab door. 'Oh good I don't have to carry on this cheery pretense any longer.' Hannah thought.

Finally arriving at the house, Hannah jiggled Kate's arm to wake her. "We're here." She said softly.

"Oh, I'm sorry, I must have fallen asleep." Kate said as she fumbled for her keys while Hannah dug in her purse to come up with money to pay for the cab fare. "I'll go open my door. Can you come in for a minute? I forgot to leave my lights on, and I get a bit spooked going in late at night."

Hannah would have preferred to just run across the street to her own home so that she could digest the whole evening, but felt it would have been impolite to decline her request. "Sure I can." She said willingly as she settled up with the cab driver and quickly jumped out of the car and ran up the driveway to the front door of Kate's home.

"You don't have to stay, but I'd love to have a tea if you would like one too." Kate invited.

"That sounds nice. Why don't I make the tea while you get changed and ready for bed. Then when I leave, all you have to do is tuck yourself in." Hannah offered kindly.

"Oh that's so nice. Thank you. I'll be right down." Kate called as she ran up the stairs.

Hannah put the kettle on to boil, made the tea and decided to put out some biscuits that they could enjoy, realizing that she had had very little to eat that night. She placed everything on a tray and went to the living room to wait for Kate. As she sipped her tea almost ten minutes went by and Kate had still not come down the stairs to join her. Since Kate's tea would be getting cold, Hannah decided to carry it upstairs for her to drink in bed as Hannah felt there was really no reason to prolong the evening. As she walked up the stairs she called out to Kate but there was no reply. Once she had arrived at her bedroom door, she found her changed from her costume into her nightgown but fast asleep on her bed.

'Poor thing.' Hannah thought, and decided to place the tea beside her bed to signal to Kate that once she woke, Hannah had left her to sleep. Hannah wandered quietly towards Kate's night table on the other side of her bed to turn out the light. She quietly admired her room that was filled with photographs and banners likely from her high school and university days. 'Wow, I never liked high school that much to keep banners on my wall.' Hannah thought to herself. She hesitated by a group of photos that were clustered on a shelf near her bed stand, some of which were recent and some that were taken years ago. Hannah smiled at the fashions from about ten years ago. 'How could we have worn those clothes?' She said half out loud. She picked up one fading photo where a group of smiling friends were clustered together. She recognized Kate as she gazed lovingly up at a young man whose arm was draped casually around her shoulder. Her attention was then drawn to the young man who was capturing Kate's undivided attention. Despite the lack of light in the room, Hannah thought she recognized the young man's features. Her heart seemed to stop and then revive itself as it hammered crazily in her chest. It was without a doubt a photograph of a more youthful Joe. She was frozen with disbelief and overwhelming disappointment. Despite there being no wedding photographs within the grouping, Hannah was sure that Joseph, Kate's awful husband, was the same Joe with whom hours ago she had shared an intimate conversation.

Hannah replaced the photograph carelessly, hearing it clatter as it fell forward on its face as she ran from the room. She couldn't risk going back to right it, she simply had to leave. She ran swiftly down the stairs and out the front door and didn't stop until she got to her own front door, only to find it was locked. Foolishly, she had left her purse in Kate's living room. She turned and leaned heavily against her front door as her heart continued to hammer over and over again in her chest. She couldn't go back to Kate's house again to retrieve her keys from her purse. She felt bewildered and needed to collect her thoughts. She slid down the length of the door to sit on the stoop to wait until Martha and Adam came home. Perched under the outside light, she couldn't settle on which emotion to focus on as her thoughts ricocheted from embarrassment to annoyance to fury. How could they both intentionally keep the fact that they were married to each other from Hannah? Ironically, tonight, they both had the perfect opportunity to tell her. What were they playing at? They must have decided that she would find out, so what was the point of their deception?

It was too much of a ridiculous coincidence, but all the pieces were now beginning to fit in place. Hannah recalled the day in the shopping centre when Kate had run into Joe. She was so upset that day because he must have told her that he had come to Evanston on business and not there to see her. Joe even pursued Hannah with little regard for how it would compromise her friendship with Kate. No wonder he had asked her not to say anything to anyone. They had been married! Now she was annoyed. It was all too much. She had been dragged into their mess and they clearly were unconcerned for how it all might affect her. Now she was furious. If Kate had suspected that Joe might be paying attention to her, why wouldn't she just tell Hannah that she had been married to him? Instead, she was convinced Joe was trying to get her out of his life, so why would he be in the very town that Kate had moved to? The more she thought about it, the more confused and hurt she felt. Tiredness washed over her and she now wished Martha and Adam would come home so she could go up to her bed. She needed to sleep.

CHAPTER 15

"Hannah. Hannah, wake up." Hannah felt her shoulders being gently shaken as she slowly woke from her sleep.

"Come on Pinky, you can't sleep out here." Adam said holding out his hand to her.

Hannah felt herself dip in and out of consciousness briefly before she was fully aware of her surroundings. She looked up sleepily to see Martha and Adam crouched next to her.

"Oh my God, did I fall asleep out here?" She asked as Adam helped her to her feet.

"You certainly did Pinky." Adam teased. "What in the world were you doing sleeping on the front step?"

Hannah looked behind Adam to see Martha looking very concerned. Hannah explained that she had left her purse at Kate's and didn't feel right going back into the house again to retrieve it.

"But you felt better about falling asleep on the front step in a cat suit?" Martha asked incredulously.

"I wasn't planning on falling asleep out here honestly." Hannah assured her. "Can we go inside now?"

"Sorry Hannah, but you were very vulnerable out here. It's really late." Martha explained as they went inside and locked the door.

"I know, I know." She assured her sister as she kissed her on the cheek. "Good night, I have to go to bed."

Adam leaned in to kiss her good night as well. "Nighty-night Pinky." He said with a smirk.

"Good night Adam. By the way, are you going to stop calling me Pinky soon?"

"That depends on what outfit you wear tomorrow." He offered.

"I'll take that as a no then. I'll see you two in the morning. Good night."

Hannah climbed the stairs to her bedroom and was grateful to be able to change out of her cat suit. She pulled back her duvet and slipped under its cool shell and stared out the window into the clear dark night where the moon had diminished to its minimum phase. Hannah attempted to make sense of the disorder of the night and now wished she had listened more intently to the finer details of the conversation with Kate. When all said and done, it was clear that Joe was off limits, and despite her earlier humiliation and irritation that he and Kate had duped her, she felt a bitter disappointment. This was a complete contradiction to Hannah's personality as she was quite confident in her ability to sift out associations that were not a benefit to her. She was never one to suffer fools or to be pulled into deceptive relationships. Conversely, she was not a person who was distrustful by nature and entirely gave people the benefit of the doubt if what they presented to her was, in fact, the truth. Drifting off to sleep, she conceded that she would pull back from both associations and allow their deceit not to affect her or become foremost in her mind. Easier said than done.

The next morning Hannah wandered down to the kitchen to find Martha enjoying her breakfast. She'd only had a few hours sleep and looked forward to preparing a hot breakfast with lots of coffee.

"Did you have a good sleep?" Martha asked.

"I actually did thanks." Hannah confessed.

"Did you have a nice time last night, or was your whole night ruined because of Kate?"

"No, I did have a nice time actually, in spots." Hannah said.

"In spots?" Martha laughed.

"Well, I had a few dances, nice conversations, and a beautiful walk in the garden..." Hannah reported as she poured herself a coffee.

"I guess you weren't counting on having your night orchestrated with having to look after Kate. That was unfortunate."

"No, I didn't expect to have to do that, but it was alright. We ended up having a long conversation about her past and I learned a lot about her that I didn't know before." Hannah offered. "Its funny, you know that expression 'you think you know somebody', and it is just so true. My only regret is that I wasn't able to say goodbye to everyone and I was outside for the mask unveiling."

"Oh, I know, but I think you wouldn't have been surprised by who was there." Martha assured her.

"I'm not so sure." Hannah admitted although Martha did not pick up on the intimation.

"You seem a bit preoccupied Hannah. Is there something that you are keeping from me?"

"Yes and no. Kate's past came up and I think she was telling me in confidence. I don't like keeping things from you, but given that she was a bit drunk last night, I would feel better about checking with her first to find out if I should keep things to myself." Hannah offered.

"That's alright. I just want to make sure it has nothing to do with you and you're not affected by what she said." Martha said resolutely.

Hannah sat considerately for a moment thinking how unwittingly perceptive Martha was. She keeps tapping into the reality of what is happening without actually witnessing it. Hannah thought she concealed her sentiments well, but possibly she was only fooling herself when she likely wore her emotions on her sleeve.

"It's a bit hard not to be affected when a friend has confided in you. Those kinds of confession can go either way. Kate will either rely on me to be her confidante or she will avoid me completely because she may be embarrassed by the confession. It's hard to say. And I must admit, I'm not sure which way will be worse." Hannah admitted.

CHAPTER 16

Hannah spent the rest of the weekend by herself, quietly strategizing about how she would deal with both Joe and Kate. She felt strongly that keeping her distance from both would be best and if Kate were to engage her in any further conversation, she would simply listen and reduce any emotional connection.

Luckily, when Hannah went to recover her purse from Kate's home on Sunday afternoon, Kate was unable to have a conversation with her since she was embroiled in a telephone conversation with an old friend from university. All this was quickly explained to Hannah after Kate greeted her persistent knocks at the front door. Kate covered the mouthpiece of the phone as she apologized for not having the time to talk.

"Its okay Kate, I don't want to come in, I just need my purse back that I left here last night."

Kate held up her index finger to indicate that she would just be a minute, and true to her finger's promise, she returned with the purse that she quickly handed to Hannah. Hannah mouthed her thanks, and Kate smiled and nodded, and quietly shut the door to her friend.

After returning from work the following Monday, Hannah was welcomed by a florist's delivery note that had been stuck on the front door. The note indicated that there was a delivery for their address, but since no one was home, the parcel was delivered to their neighbour directly beside them. 'Must be for Martha after the announcement of their engagement', Hannah thought to herself. She ran over to her next door neighbour's home as directed by the note and rang the front door bell.

"Hi Gary." Hannah greeted happily after he had opened his door to her. "I understand you have a parcel for us?"

"Hi Hannah, come in and I'll get it for you. Just a second." Her neighbour left her standing just inside the door as he retrieved the long box of flowers. "Here it is." Gary said, handing it to her.

"Thanks so much. Martha will appreciate these." Hannah granted.

"Our pleasure Hannah, but I think the parcel is addressed to you, not Martha." Gary corrected.

"Oh." Hannah said momentarily surprised. "I wonder who it's from."

"I don't know. You're welcome to open them here but I'm sure you would prefer the privacy of your own home." Gary said patiently.

"No, it must be a mistake. They have to be for Martha because she and Adam became engaged recently." Hannah explained to her neighbour. His response was a soft smile and he simply shrugged his shoulders and leaned against the door jamb expecting that Hannah's visit was going to take awhile.

"They can't be for me; I'm not even seeing anyone." Hannah insisted and looked to Gary as though he would make sense of the situation. He continued to stare back at Hannah again wordlessly offering her a slight smile. His silence made her realize that she was prattling on like an idiot and felt ridiculous when she realized that her confession was likely boring him.

"Maybe it's a secret admirer." Gary offered in an attempt to settle her confusion while appearing as though he would be happier if he could wrap up the conversation.

Hannah laughed and protested feebly while silently hoping that Gary wouldn't witness the blush that rose to her cheeks. She thanked him again for his kindness and left cradling the long carton to her chest as though it were precious cargo. She walked slowly across his lawn to hers, silently wondering who sent them. Now behind closed doors, she entered the kitchen and placed the box on the table and gently untied its ribbon. Inside rested a dozen long stemmed creamy centered white roses. Hannah was taken by their splendor and the uniqueness of their pure shade. Tucked inside their deep green thorny stems nestled a tiny envelope simply reading 'Hannah'. She pulled the note from it's sheathe and it read 'I look forward to a time when I can be free to enjoy your unmasked beauty. Z.'

'Zed for Zorro.' Hannah thought delightedly. She stared at the card feeling truly torn between her loyalty to Kate and her strong attraction to a man she could never have. She then felt conflicted with his attempt to be somewhat anonymous. 'Well, I just can't keep them.' Hannah said out loud as if determined to stick to her conviction.

"Can't keep what?"

Hannah jumped, startled at not having heard Martha come into the house. "Oh, just these…" Hannah said nonchalantly as she pointed to the roses.

"Hannah, they're beautiful. Why won't you keep them?" Martha asked incredulously.

"Because I don't know who they're from." Hannah kept her back to Martha so that she couldn't see her blushing. 'God, I'm lying to my own sister. What is the matter with me?' She reproached herself silently.

"Didn't they come with a card or a note?" Martha asked.

Hannah realized she was still clasping the card in her hand, but turned it over to Martha. "Yes, here's the card…" Hannah walked out of the kitchen to the living room so that Martha would not witness her discomfort.

"Oh, this is so romantic Hannah…your unmasked beauty. That should give you a clue. Did you meet someone at the party?" Martha asked as she followed Hannah into the living room.

"I don't know who it is." Hannah repeated abruptly.

"Oh." Martha simply said as she felt the sting of Hannah's denial.

"I'm sorry Martha. This isn't fair to take this out on you. I actually do know who sent the flowers, but the point is, he shouldn't be sending me flowers at all. He really hasn't any right to." Hannah admitted.

"Do I get the sense that you wish he did have the right to send you flowers?" Martha ventured.

"I would be lying if I said no." Hannah said sinking into a chair.

"Do I know him?" Martha asked still caught up in the romantic possibilities that may exist for her sister.

"No, or at least, I don't think you do." Hannah replied honestly.

"So, I'm guessing he must be married." Martha inferred.

"He is. Well, actually he isn't anymore, but he was."

"So, that's okay then. It only matters when they are married, and since he isn't, then he's fair game." Martha allowed.

"Its more complicated than that, and I'm not comfortable with allowing myself to be involved in a relationship that may come with a lot of baggage. So for now, I want to pretend like he doesn't exist, and if I don't talk about him, I might be lucky enough to convince myself of that."

"I understand, and I know you will do the right thing. I just hope that you won't sacrifice a wonderful opportunity when you don't need to." Martha suggested.

"Time will tell."

"Does his name start with Zed?" Martha asked with hoping still to discover the sender.

"No." Hannah smiled back.

"Well, Zed or no Zed, I hope it works out for you."

Hannah came over and kissed her sister on the cheek, and thanked her for understanding her reservation in discussing anything further about her secret admirer.

"How do you think Kate is doing?" Martha asked conceding and changing the subject.

"Why do you ask that?" Hannah enquired, a little surprised.

"I don't know, I thought after all that went on at the party, I would ask how she was." Martha laughed.

Hannah was unnerved that Martha's thinking linked Kate so closely to their conversation about Joe.

"Well, I'm really not sure. I haven't heard from her since then, although I'm sure she's fine." Hannah felt she was over-explaining but hoped she sounded unbothered.

"It was just a general question about Kate, Hannah; I wasn't looking for a deep hidden message." Martha was trying to be lighthearted, but looked at her sister adding... "Is everything okay? You seem bothered by something."

"Yes and no." Hannah began. "While I was as you say, babysitting Kate last night, I had a conversation with her where she confessed a lost love that she hasn't gotten over, and so your remark startled me. Of course, she had a lot to drink and you know when people drink they tend to confess all. I'm just wondering if she'll even remember the conversation. Although, as we talked, she seemed to sober up very quickly."

"Oh, I know. I remember that she got quite drunk so soon after she got to the party. I wondered if the drinks were too powerful for her. She was drawing quite a crowd on that bar stool. And then you came to her rescue. That was sweet of you to do that."

"Thanks, but I thought she would benefit from some fresh air. I thought the situation was going to go from bad to worse if she stayed inside. At least it looked like it was heading in that direction when we got to her. I guess on some level, I didn't want her taking the focus from your wonderful night." Hannah offered with an affectionate smile.

"And I did have a wonderful night. Nothing could have spoiled it. But, as always, thank you for looking out for me."

"As always, it's my pleasure." Hannah laughed.

"So are you able to tell me about your conversation with Kate and tell me who the lost love is that Kate spoke to you about, or is that private?"

Although Hannah silently wondered if she should mention any of the details, she was anxious to discuss it with Martha knowing that she would be discreet. "It was actually someone she was married to." Hannah offered and then waited for Martha's reaction.

"Wow – I didn't know she was ever married. Did you?" Martha looked genuinely surprised.

"No, I didn't either. That is what Kate fully intended though. She didn't want any of us to know so that she could live a new life without emotional ties. I will have to call her and see how she is doing and find out if she has any memory of our conversation. I'm quite sure that she does, but she may selectively decide not to remember just so it won't be discussed again." Hannah theorized.

"So, I guess he must have really hurt her badly if she wants to forget him." Martha said with concern.

Hannah looked away from Martha's troubled look. She still didn't want to believe that Joe would be such a dreadful man as to be so careless with anyone's emotions, let alone someone he was married to. But, she scarcely knows him. He could be the complete opposite of what he seemed to Hannah, or more truthfully, what she wanted him to be.

"It does seem that way, but you know, there are two sides to every story, and perhaps there are things we just don't know." Hannah said philosophically.

"I guess so." Martha mumbled, not seemingly convinced. "Well let's not try and figure that out, let's try and figure out what to do with these beautiful flowers. What vase should we use and where would you like them displayed?"

"I don't really care – you take them to your room and enjoy them."

"You don't care? I don't believe it. Just take one look at these beautiful gifts of nature, and tell me again you don't care!" Martha spoke with mock horror.

Hannah laughed at Martha's lighthearted mood and looked at the flowers and then back at Martha who was smiling broadly. "How in the world can you abandon these little babies?" Martha continued.

"Okay, put them in the living room. Would that make you happy?"

"Yes, it would." Martha buried her nose into the roses to take in their perfumed fragrance. "I'll put them in water just so they don't suffer being abandoned by their rightful owner. Poor things."

Hannah looked up at her sister as her eyes darted playfully away. "You're not making me feel badly and the roses can't hear you." Hannah said defiantly.

"Maybe not." Martha rationalized. "But just in case, I think it would be best if I let them know they're loved. You are welcome to visit them whenever you would like. Oh, and don't throw that card away. Whoever wrote it, and you know I have a good sense about these things, has to be just this side of wonderful." Martha announced as she walked her twelve new charges into the living room.

Hannah retrieved the card from Martha and read again the inviting chance of a reunion with Joe. Was he wonderful? Was Joe the Joseph that Kate talked about? Of course, he had to be. His picture was a younger version of the Joe she had met that wonderful day in the rain. What were the chances that she would meet a man that she felt so attracted to and that she had no hope now of having? And what of Kate? Her loyalty most certainly had to be with her dear friend. It made sense now that Kate's past was never discussed.

CHAPTER 17

Hannah fondly thought back to the day Kate had moved in across the road. For several years, that home had been occupied by Mr. and Mrs. Cassidy, an elderly couple who kept mostly to themselves. After a series of strokes, Mr. Cassidy had been moved to an assisted care facility and Mrs. Cassidy went to live with her daughter. Not long after, Kate moved in and for Hannah it was a relief to have someone closer to her own age as her new neighbour. Initially Kate kept to herself but Hannah made a concerted effort to welcome her to the neighbourhood. After a short time Hannah and Kate had become comfortable neighbours and then good friends.

Hannah's thoughts were interrupted by the shrill of the telephone and she ran into the kitchen to answer it, placing the card from Joe on the table.

"Hello?" Hannah asked as she brought the phone to her ear. "Oh, hey, I was just thinking about you." Hannah silently mouthed 'its Kate' as Martha popped her head around the door to see who was on the phone. "Sure, come over. I'll be here." Hannah placed put the phone back in its cradle and put her head in her hands.

"Not up for a visit from Kate?" Martha probed.

"Oh, no, I am. I just wonder if it will be awkward."

"She's a friend. There won't be any awkwardness." Martha rationalized.

"Maybe, but I feel I'm getting caught up in some emotional commitment with Kate's past and I think it may be more complicated than just a bad marriage gone terribly wrong. Now that she has confessed her past, there will be a responsibility on my part to keep my heart in it, and I'm not sure I'm up for it." Hannah pushed away from the kitchen table as if silently pushing away her concerns.

"It will all be forgotten, I'm sure. Don't forget, one of the reasons Kate came here was to forget." Martha stated as Kate burst through the door.

"HEY!" Kate yelled.

"We're in the kitchen. I'll put the kettle on or would you like some wine?" Martha offered.

"No thanks! I'm done with the *vino* for awhile. I need to give this old bean a break." Kate laughed.

"Tea it is then."

"Hey, nice flowers! Who are they for?" Kate asked wandering over to take a closer look.

"They're Martha's." Hannah broke in abruptly before Martha could say anything.

"Ah, yes, they're mine." Martha added but looked quizzically at Hannah.

"Are they from Adam?"

"Yes!" "No!" Martha and Hannah said simultaneously. "No!" "Yes!" They corrected.

"I didn't realize this would be such a tough question." Kate suggested.

"No, it's not a tough question, it's just...I misunderstood what you meant." Martha said unconvincingly.

"Okay, well they're beautiful, whoever gave them to you."

"They're actually from someone I work with. He sent them after he heard about my engagement to Adam." Martha explained.

"Wow, generous co-worker with excellent taste!" Kate beamed.

"Yes, I work with some very nice people." Martha agreed and then fixed a gaze on Hannah.

"Did I come at a bad time?" Kate asked.

"NO." Hannah and Martha shouted in unison.

"Really?" Kate stated, not really convinced.

"Don't be silly." Hannah scolded. "Come on, let's have some tea."

"Sure, just one cup, but I can't stay long. I just wanted to come over and thank you Hannah for taking care of me the night of the party and seeing me home. I know I must have ruined your night because I drank so much. I am sorry for my behavior especially on such an important night for you Martha."

"I had a wonderful time and you have nothing to apologize for. I must admit, I think those bartenders were a little heavy handed with the liquor that night." Martha offered hoping to ease Kate's conscience.

"Yes, I agree." Hannah chimed in. "In fact, Sally said she had a huge headache the next day and she thinks it had to be the alcohol."

"Well, that's sweet of you both but I am responsible for how many I should have, and clearly I had more than my share. I learned a long time ago that I couldn't hold my liquor because not only do I forget half of what I say, but even a little bit gets the better of me." Kate said and smiled up at Hannah as she placed a steaming cup of tea on the table.

"Just move all that stuff out of your way Kate, and I'll get you a piece of cake from Martha and Adam's party." Hannah instructed, referring to the clutter on the kitchen table, as she wrestled with items in the fridge to get to the cake.

"Is this what came with the flowers?" Kate asked innocently.

Hannah stretched her head around the fridge door, holding a carton of milk in one hand and the platter of cake in the other. 'What?" She asked.

"This. Is Zed the person that you work with Martha? The message sounds almost romantic. You'd better not show this to Adam." Kate said as she stretched her hand towards Hannah to offer her the tiny card that had accompanied the flowers. The silence was broken as the platter of cake smashed to the floor.

"Oh my God…" Hannah sputtered, as she fell to the floor to make an attempt to scoop up the cake with her hands.

"It's my card. Well, I mean I didn't write it, it's from Adam. He gave me flowers too and that's the card he sent with them. I wondered where it had got to." Martha declared as she gently released the card from Kate's grasp.

"You call him Zed?" Kate asked appearing confused.

"Sometimes, yes. It's a pet name I gave him." Martha said unconvincingly.

An awkward silence fell over the three women, clearly uncomfortable with the explanation over an innocuous little card. Sensing the deceit, Kate got up from her chair and walked into the living room to look for the card for the bouquet of roses.

"Where is the card for these flowers?" Kate questioned.

"I guess I lost that one too." Martha confessed meekly.

Hannah had still not moved from her spot, surrounded by the fallen cake, wishing that she could be absorbed into the fridge with the rest of its contents. She felt the threat of tears as she looked with embarrassment at Martha.

"I guess you had better put that card with the flowers then before you lose it again." Kate suggested.

"Yes, I will. They're upstairs in my room hidden safely away!" Martha laughed weakly.

"Hidden away?" Kate questioned.

"Well no, I don't mean hidden really. I meant that since they're special, I just wanted to keep them in my room."

"Okay, well that makes sense I guess. Look, I think I'd better get home." Kate stated turning toward the door, a mixture of anger and hurt on her face.

"I'm sorry." Hannah spat out, desperate to put things right.

"What are you sorry for?" Kate asked.

"For having ruined the cake. Why don't you have some tea?" Hannah asked.

"I think its best if I go. I have lots to do, and I really just wanted to come over and apologize and make sure that I hadn't damaged our friendship." Kate's words hung in the air as she waited for Hannah's response.

"No, you haven't ruined anything at all. If anything…" Hannah faltered but could not continue.

"If anything, I think someone might have a secret admirer." Kate muttered as she headed for the front door.

Kate and Hannah stared at each other until Hannah's eyes fell to the floor.

"I'll see you later, maybe tomorrow or the next day Hannah." Kate called back.

"Yes, of course, see you tomorrow or the next day." Hannah repeated softly.

"Bye Kate." Martha said walking to her sister and slipping her arm around her waist. Hannah's hand moved to meet the hand that had tightened around her, and gripped it as if she were afraid it would slip away.

CHAPTER 18

No words were spoken until the sound of the front door closing confirmed that Kate had left. Martha's hand left her sister's side and she finally spoke softly to her.

"Please tell me what's going on." Martha pleaded as she led her back into the kitchen. "Sit down and tell me."

Hannah followed Martha and sat down at the table while her sister sat opposite her.

"I've met Kate's husband, or should I say, her ex-husband. At least, I'm sure it's him. I met him quite by accident one day when I was running. It started to rain and that's how we met. Just because it was raining, and we both needed to find a place where we could keep dry. As luck would have it, we both ended up in the same place."

"So, the flowers are from Kate's ex-husband?" Martha leaned forward and grabbed Hannah's hand to get her attention.

"Yes." Hannah offered plainly.

"Do you think Kate knows who really sent the flowers?"

"I think she might have guessed, don't you? I'm just hoping the name Zed might have thrown her off."

"And this is supposed to explain why you didn't want the flowers in the house? I don't think I completely understand this. Who were you really trying to hide them from?" Martha asked impatiently.

"I just didn't feel comfortable having them here, and I really thought I shouldn't keep them. I guess I made a mess of it." Hannah confessed as they both looked to the floor where the cake had fallen in a ruined mess.

"And you decided that you needed to hide all of this from me? Was it so hard just to tell me the truth?" Martha offered incredulously.

"I know that's what it must seem like, but I would never try to hide anything from you. I was trying to hide my guilty conscience. The day I first met Joe, we spoke briefly. I have to admit there was an attraction between us, but there was no attempt from him to see me again."

Hannah hesitated briefly to take in her sister's tiny porcelain face. It struck her then how much she resembled their mother. Both had hazel eyes framed in long lashes that gave them a look of innocence. Often she and Martha were mistaken for twins, but despite the similarity in their looks, Hannah felt she was not nearly the beauty that her sister was. Martha's looks resembled their mother, and Hannah favoured their father. The memories of her mother and father during the years they were all together were sometimes difficult for Hannah to recall. Despite the years that had passed since their deaths, she tried to hold those memories clearly in her mind. It was unfathomable to have lost them when she and Martha were so young and she still missed them so much. She slowly opened her eyes and allowed her attention to be drawn back to Martha.

"You know Hannah. You say you're only trying to hide a guilty conscience, but I'm really not convinced. Why would you entertain a man who could be so awful to someone he was once married to? You must have known that this was wrong from the start. What were you thinking?" Martha demanded.

"Martha, I have done nothing wrong. I knew that Kate knew Joe but I didn't know how well. It was only at your party when I realized that the person she referred to as her ex husband was likely Joe, but she referred to him as Joseph. I've only seen him on two other occasions completely by accident, and both times, Kate was nearby. And still, both those times, I had no idea that they knew each other well. She never said he was her ex-husband!" Hannah exclaimed.

"You say that Kate was close by when you saw him, so don't you think you would make a connection?" Martha probed.

"I didn't pay attention and besides that, it seemed like a coincidence when they ran into each other. I wasn't even sure that they were friends. I was shopping with Kate one day and she ran into him and they had a brief and uncomfortable conversation from what I could see. The second time was at your engagement party."

"My engagement party?" Martha shouted. "Who invited him? Did you invite him?" Martha was incredulous.

"Of course I didn't invite him. I didn't know he was there until I went out to the garden and he followed me out there. Don't forget Martha, everyone was masked that night." Hannah was beginning to feel very tired and wished the conversation were over, but she could see that Martha was just getting started.

"Honestly Hannah, who could have invited him? Wait a minute, what did you say his name is?" Martha demanded.

"His name is Joe." Hannah felt relieved by the confession and a feeling of warmth saying his name out loud.

"Do you know his last name?" Martha pushed.

"Hastings." Hannah offered quietly.

"Never heard of him!" Martha exclaimed, as though Hannah had been making the whole thing up.

"Remember the event started out as a Halloween party so it would make sense that there were a lot of people there that you wouldn't know." Hannah hoped this would settle Martha down.

"Good point." Martha granted. "It seems so strange that Kate's ex-husband would know Joshua."

"True." Hannah agreed thinking there may be thousands of reasons anyone would know anyone. It would be pointless to raise this because she really had grown weary of the conversation and was hoping to bring it to a quick close.

"I'm sorry Martha. I didn't mean to hurt your feelings and I hope you can forgive me for not being more open with you. I'm really tired, so I'd like to have a bite to eat and then go up to bed but I want to make sure you aren't angry." Hannah said sincerely.

"I'm not angry with you and I'm sorry I was hard on you, but I think my feelings were hurt. It's as though you don't trust me."

"I understand. You had every right to be annoyed. I just have to figure out how to make this right with Kate, and convince her that I'm not encouraging anything." Hannah confessed.

Martha leaned over to kiss her sister's cheek. "Let's order something so we don't have to fiddle around with dinner. Why don't you go and have a bath and I'll call for a pizza. You relax and try not to worry. Kate needs to think this through too. Everything will be alright in the morning."

"I hope so. A bath sounds wonderful right now, but I want to give Josh a call and thank him for the party, and apologize for my quick exit."

"Oh, I know he would understand, but I'm sure he'd appreciate hearing from you. Adam and I are going to take him out to dinner tomorrow night as a way of thanking him."

When Hannah attempted to call Josh, her call went unanswered, so she made a mental note to call him the next day. Nothing further was said about the interaction with Kate that evening. Hannah and Martha ate their pizza and laughed about events of the engagement party that Hannah was not able to witness due to her caring for Kate. After a few hours and feeling happily sated, Hannah went upstairs to her bed.

CHAPTER 19

Despite her fatigue, Hannah had difficulty getting to sleep. Thoughts raced through her head over and over again. She silently reviewed her attempts in guarding her attraction to Joe. She realized, almost foolishly, that she had nothing to hide since she wasn't involved with him and the fact that Kate seemed so annoyed with her was ridiculous. Admittedly, she had felt a strong attraction to him but that was before realizing his involvement with Kate. Had she known, she would not have ever considered the possibility of a relationship with Joe. As her thoughts settled into a more peaceful nature, Hannah drifted off to sleep.

The next morning as she dressed for work, Hannah felt surprisingly refreshed and decided that before the week was out, she would make a point of sitting down and talking to Kate. She would not confess her attraction to Joe, but rather would focus on the fact that knowing Joe was simply a coincidence and there was nothing more to it. How though would she explain the flowers, when they didn't make sense even to her? This is where Hannah felt stuck and almost annoyed at the indecisiveness that Joe was displaying with his attempts to show an interest towards her. I'll have to think about this one, she thought. Perhaps, the flowers were a reminder of his request that they keep their encounter to themselves, almost as though to encourage her not to be tempted by any confession to Kate. That must be it, Hannah decided. Why then did she feel foolish and then disappointed with the possibility of only a friendship with Joe? 'Make up your mind!' Hannah said out loud to herself as she climbed into her car and headed off to work.

Hannah arrived at her office to be greeted by her boss 'Uncle' Paul.

"Good morning Paul, how are you?" Hannah smiled as she greeted Paul.

"Good morning Hannah. I'm very well thank you." Paul responded kindly. "Do you think that I could see you in my office once you get settled?"

"Sure. Absolutely." Hannah assured. "I'll just be a minute."

"No rush, bring your coffee with you." Paul offered and gave Hannah a fatherly pat on the shoulder.

"Be right there." Hannah confirmed.

Despite Hannah reassuring herself that all was well, she couldn't shake the feeling of discomfort she felt being summoned to the boss's office. 'Ridiculous', Hannah said out loud as she turned on her computer.

"Talking to yourself?'

"Oh, hi Sally. You scared me." Hannah laughed. "Yes, I'm finally going crazy and now I'm talking to myself which as I said earlier is ridiculous."

"Well, I enjoy talking to myself. I have very interesting conversations." Sally confessed.

"Actually Paul wants to see me in his office and it unnerved me a bit. Just the thought of being asked to see the boss throws me back to being a little girl in school and being called to the Principal's office." Hannah explained.

"I understand, but I'm sure that it will only be good news." Sally offered.

"I know I'm being silly."

"No, it's not silly at all. Go and have your meeting with Paul and why don't we have lunch together today at that new restaurant on Chancery Street?" Sally suggested.

"I'd love that. I'll pick you up at your office at noon."

"Okay, it's a date." Sally laughed. "And don't worry."

Hannah knocked gently at Paul's door, despite it being open. He seemed engrossed in something he was reading and Hannah felt intrusive even though she had been invited to his office.

"Come in, come in." Paul beckoned, his tender face breaking into a big grin. "Good, you've brought your coffee."

"Shall I get you one?" Hannah offered.

"No. I've decided to cut back on my coffee consumption, but thanks anyway. Come and sit down."

Hannah slid lightly into one of Paul's visitor chairs, while placing her steaming coffee onto his desk and resting her office notepad on her knee.

"All settled?"

"Yes, thanks Uncle Paul".

"So, before we get down to business," Paul began with a feigned business voice for Hannah's benefit. "How have you been?"

Hannah laughed and confessed that she was just okay, given the recent events at home with Kate. She decided not to give any detail since she was mindful that this was a business meeting and not a personal one.

"Anything I can do to help?"

"No, really, its just 'girly' stuff really. All drama and intrigue!" She joked suddenly feeling silly that she had even inferred a problem to Paul.

"Oh, no! Girly stuff, you say!" Paul laughed while making a sign of the cross with his two index fingers.

"That's right, and you don't want to go there if you know what's good for you."

"I will not go where any man would dare not go." He offered as his laugh settled into a gentle smile. "But you know, I would dare to go if it would help. You just say the word."

"No, I...I..." Hannah stammered.

Paul interrupted as he felt and knew that she was trying to be considerate of his time.

"Hannah, I love you like a daughter. Martha too. I know there are times that you will have the world completely under control and there are times you will feel lost. The last thing I want to do is insert myself into your life when I know that you have the capacity and wisdom to make the right choices under any situation."

Hannah looked straight into Paul's eyes as he spoke, feeling tears stinging her eyes. She tried desperately to calm them, but despite her efforts, a tear broke free and fell gently down her cheek, followed by another and then another. Without missing a beat, Paul lifted a tissue from his Kleenex box and offered it to her and continued speaking.

"I have watched you grow into a confident young woman who has had to deal with so much, and I have never felt anything short of pride and complete respect for you. You have handled an extremely difficult situation with the loss of your parents with grace and strength. Despite the years since their passing, it doesn't mean it gets any easier or the pain becomes less bearable. You have grown to accept it and you have handled your and Martha's fate with selflessness and without a word of complaint."

Paul waited for these words to settle in as Hannah buried her face into a new set of tissues that he had passed to her. He rose from his chair so that he could close his office door to offer Hannah privacy, and once again, continued.

"You are a complete inspiration to me Hannah, and it goes without saying and perhaps a bit cliché, but your parents would be so proud of you. Nevertheless, it doesn't mean that you need to be brave all the time and not reach out for help through the rougher times." Paul waited saying nothing more until Hannah had subdued her tears.

"Why are you telling me this?" Hannah said this in an unchallenging manner, anticipating that he was thinking it was time she spread her wings and left the firm.

"Why do you think I'm telling you?" Paul asked simply.

"Because you think I should leave the firm? Is my time up?" Hannah looked up at Paul, giving him an opening to take the pressure off what she thought he was about to say.

"Didn't you hear what I said? I think you are amazing. Never a word of complaint from you, and so to answer your questions, absolutely not, to both. This has nothing to do with work, it has everything to do with you and your wellbeing. I've just noticed that you seem a bit weighed down and just a bit distracted. And, so naturally, I am concerned. I just want you to have a place to fall, so to speak, if you need it. I'm offering that to you." Paul assured her.

CHAPTER 20

Hannah stared out the window and minutes passed before she spoke. Paul allowed the time for her to think about what she was going to say.

"I don't really know where to begin. I am so grateful for all you have done for me and for Martha. I think that I have never given myself time to stop and really think how the loss of my parents has impacted me. Maybe, for preservation sake, I haven't wanted to go to those emotional lengths. I miss them so much, but soon after they died, I realized that it was all going to fall to me to keep our lives going. I was terrified that I would blow it and I wouldn't be able to hold it together and then Martha and I would be torn apart too. I didn't want to take that chance. So, I didn't ever want anyone to see me falter. I didn't want anyone to think that I couldn't do it, that I couldn't keep our little family together. I couldn't risk losing Martha too. I think I've done okay."

"You've done more than okay. You've done everything you held yourself to. You've never faltered." Paul said sincerely and continued. "That's the thing about families. We all have to make sacrifices when dealing with those that we love. We do whatever we can to make our lives more bearable and functional despite the obstacles, and it's how we endure them that builds our conviction to keep going and little by little, we succeed. You are a testament to that. It's really remarkable."

"I feel resentful that I have missed out on my parents, and now I feel even more so because of Martha and Adam's wonderful news. They would have loved Adam, and they deserved to be witnesses to their marriage. Often I sit and wonder how such a tragic event landed at our doorstep. Why did it happen to us?" Hannah questioned.

"Sometimes life points a finger and says 'it's your turn' and there simply is no reason why, it just is. We often want an explanation to tragic events and we want someone to make sense of them when there is no sense. There is so little justification in such a tragedy and it is completely unfair, particularly when it was almost proven to be such a deliberate act. Your parents didn't deserve such a fate, and neither did you or Martha. But what you do deserve is a good life and a life that your parents would want for you. I will tell you a million times over that they would be so grateful and proud that you have kept good care of Martha and of yourself. But I know in my heart, they would want you to live a good life and to be happy in your own right."

"I understand but I think you're trying to tell me something else and I'm really not sure what it is." Hannah confessed.

"I just want you to be okay Hannah. You have a beautiful sister and we are all so happy to hear about Adam's proposal. Proposals are always so exciting and full of promise for the future. It reminded me of when I proposed to your Auntie Jane so many years ago. Those wonderful times have now become wonderful memories for Jane and me and not a day goes by when I don't feel so grateful for our life together."

"You are wonderful together. I remember when you used to come to our house when we were young and you and Auntie Jane would always bring us gifts each time you visited. I can always remember laughter in the house when you got together with Mum and Dad."

"Jane always insisted on buying something for you and Martha. She adores you both. We were unfortunate that we were unable to have children of our own, but you were the next best thing. Your parents were very patient with Jane and were gracious enough to share you both by fulfilling the need for Jane to be a mother when she couldn't have her own. Your parents, and particularly your mother, were very generous that way. She helped Jane through some very emotional and difficult times. It's not something I can relate to because I don't have a maternal instinct obviously, but I witnessed a very powerful instinct that existed even when it was denied by nature."

"I guess we all go through difficult times and we have to deal with them the best way we can." Hannah decided.

"When we have wonderful friends like your parents were to us, it always makes the difficult times a bit more bearable. They did more for us than you will ever know Hannah, and the best way I can honour their memory is to support you and Martha as I know they would have if they were still here with us."

"Martha told me that she had asked you to walk her up the aisle. I was so pleased to hear that." Hannah smiled.

"I am honoured." Paul said sincerely. "But, it's your time now Hannah. You have done your job and you have to give yourself an opportunity to live your life and regain the years you lost when you were getting Martha to the stage of life that she has now successfully achieved. I'm not just referring to her impending marriage to Adam, but to her every success. She is a well adjusted and flourishing young woman and you must take the credit for that. She is well on her way, and now it's your turn to live your life for you."

"Oh, not you too. Are you saying, find a man?" Hannah said incredulously.

"Absolutely not." Paul laughed. "I think you need to let go a bit, and not put so much pressure on yourself to be there for Martha. You need time for you. Fill your days with Hannah now."

"Oh so you think I will go into shock when Martha leaves?" Hannah said seriously.

"Not so much shock, but it will be an adjustment and you might find it difficult. I just want you to think about the possibility of easing your way into a new way of thinking about how to focus on you."

"You're right. I guess I never anticipated what it would be like when she left. I know she and Adam were concerned for me, but I shook it off because I wanted them to concentrate on their wedding plans. Of course, I would be helping them prepare, but I guess it will be after the wedding when everything settles down, it may hit then." Hannah realized.

"It's only natural. I just want you to be prepared." Paul advised.

"Okay I've got it now. I'm going to think better about my future and how I can plan to be an empty nester!" Hannah laughed, hoping to appear lighthearted, but honestly feeling a little uncertain.

"You know I won't leave you to face it on your own, and I wonder if I could help give you a taste of the other side of life by offering you a work related opportunity that I hope you will find exciting."

"I'm intrigued. What is it?" Hannah asked with curiosity.

"You remember Robert O'Shea, the owner of O'Shea National Emporium? We have a motion pending over stalled payments that are owed to him by Goodson and Sons while the primary lawsuit is being litigated. We require Robert to sign paperwork in support of the motion and we had set up a time for him to do this here. Unfortunately, despite numerous attempts to plan a trip here, he can't seem to make it happen expeditiously and get away from his business over in the UK. So, we looked into the possibility of using a firm over there to prepare the necessary paperwork and have him attend those offices for signature and it just got too over the top with extra fees and lining up times and dates that worked for everyone. So, leave it to Sally, she came up with a brilliant idea." Paul paused.

"Sally?" Hannah asked. "She knew why I was meeting with you?"

"She did." Paul laughed. "This is your choice Hannah, but she thought, and I agreed, it would be a wonderful plan if you were to go to London and meet with Robert, have him sign with you as his witness, and while you're there, take in a few of the sights. A working holiday, if you like."

"When?" Hannah said simply, trying to take it all in.

"We would have to line that up with Robert. Get some dates that were suitable to you both, and go from there. But soon, sometime in the next two months definitely."

"How old is he?" Hannah inquired suspiciously.

"What does that have to do with... Oh, I get it." Paul started laughing. "No, I'm not setting you up with Robert. He's almost seventy and he is happily married with seven grandchildren. No, don't worry; I'm not joining the 'Find Hannah a Man Club'."

"Okay, does he have sons?" Hannah still wasn't convinced.

"All daughters, believe it or not. But nice try." Paul offered. "Trust me Hannah; I'm not setting you up. You're getting a little paranoid in your old age. What are you now? Twenty-nine?"

"Yes." Hannah said, still suspicious.

"Ah, you're an old girl. You're past your prime and it's too late for me to do anything about." Paul grinned.

"Gee thanks. I thought you were trying to make me feel better." Hannah joked.

"I am." Paul said sincerely. "Do you want to sleep on this? I can wait for tomorrow."

"I am nervous and excited all at once. I've never been anywhere on a plane. I would love to go. My answer is yes, I don't need to sleep on it. But how would I get around? Where will I stay?" Hannah asked suddenly feeling unsure.

"We will have that all worked out for you. You will stay just outside of London, in South Kensington. You fly into London Heathrow, take the Heathrow Express to Paddington Station, and cab it to your hotel. It sounds a bit daunting now but don't worry we will have full written instructions for you and where to go, and transportation will not be any trouble. You will have full expenses available for your incidentals and all else you will charge to the firm using a credit card. Easy."

"It sounds too good to be true. Thank you." Hannah said gratefully.

"It is, but not too good for you. You deserve this. You will have only one afternoon or morning that will be committed to business by meeting with Robert, and the rest, you take in at your leisure. There is so much to see and do, that you won't be bored and you certainly won't be at a loss for things to do. Take your laptop home and research London and sightseeing, and get a feel for what you would like to do. It will be an adventure for you. I have some suggestions too, so we can put our heads together in a few days and see what you've come up with, and perhaps I will be able to give you some options that you may not have come up with." Paul said standing up and walking around his desk to where Hannah sat. Hannah realized this was her cue that the meeting was over and she stood and extended her arms to him for a hug.

"Thank you for this and everything in the past and everything that I anticipate you will do in the future. It is almost too much. Those words, thank you, are not nearly enough to express how grateful I am for your support and kindness Uncle Paul."

"I know you are grateful, and you don't need to find a way to say thank you more than you have. All I ask is you go and have a wonderful time and be good to yourself." Paul requested as he hugged Hannah.

"I promise. I will have an incredible time I know I will." Hannah assured.

CHAPTER 21

Hannah returned to her desk and sat staring at her computer as her mind raced about the prospect of going to England. Routinely she went through the motions of working, answering the phone to various client inquiries, checking certain files for the completion of documentation for upcoming court matters, but essentially her mind was elsewhere. The few hours slipped by until she was ready for lunch with Sally.

"I'm a bit early." She announced as she arrived at Sally's desk.

"I thought you might be, so I'm ready too. Let's go." Sally laughed knowingly at Hannah.

Hannah and Sally made their way to the restaurant they had chosen for lunch and settled on the day's sandwich and soup special.

"So, we have lots to talk about." Sally projected.

"Yes, we do, and you have a bit of explaining to do as well." Hannah smiled.

"I didn't want to ruin the surprise. Are you thrilled?"

"Yes, I'm thrilled and scared and excited, and… Hey, wait a minute." Hannah stopped talking.

"What?" Sally asked while looking a little startled.

"Here I am so excited by such a wonderful opportunity and I've just realized that I shouldn't be going on this trip, you should be going!" Hannah almost shouted.

"No, I shouldn't be going. I think this is a perfect opportunity for you. You deserve this." Sally concluded.

"I don't deserve it at all. I have done nothing to earn a trip to London. I come to work every day, just as you do, and you've worked at the firm longer than me. Oh Sally, this is ridiculous." Hannah sat back against the booth and put her soup spoon down.

"No, you're being ridiculous Hannah. Even if I wanted to go, I couldn't because I would have to leave the responsibility of looking after my mother to someone else and I can't do that. I wouldn't be able to relax and enjoy myself."

Hannah was silently kicking herself after realizing the pressures that existed for Sally with having to look after an aging parent who had recently suffered a mild stroke. It was decided in the best interests of everyone that Sally's mum go into a senior's apartment where she could still interact with people her own age, but have the benefit of assistance if she needed it. It offered Sally a great deal of comfort to know that her mother still had a quality of life and a sense of her own independence. Luckily, the stroke did not leave any existing limitations and Sally's mother was gradually finding opportunities within her new dwelling that offered her a bit of a social life.

"But you told me that your mother was doing much better and she was in an assisted living residence and was very happy there. I don't know. I'm not convinced that this is the right thing. I just can't feel good about going."

"Listen to me Hannah. You have to believe me, even if I could go, it wouldn't be a good time for me. Don't worry, my time will come. I'm not resentful that you are going and I think you should be happy about this and look forward to it. And yes, my mother is happy where she is, but she still relies on me emotionally, and I wouldn't be comfortable leaving her just now." Sally leaned into the table and held Hannah's gaze.

"Okay." Hannah said simply.

"You need to eat your soup before it gets cold." Sally said as she extended her hand across the width of the table to slide Hannah's spoon into her fingers. As she leaned forward, her reach caused the loosely knit sweater that she was wearing to slide from her shoulder. This simple movement involuntarily caused Hannah to divert her gaze from Sally's face to the exposed skin. Normally such a simple reaction would be fleeting in its importance, barely registering on anyone's radar. However, what made it different this time was the condition of Sally's shoulder that held Hannah's gaze; the expectation of clear creamy skin was replaced by interruptions of blue and deep purple bruises.

"Oh my God what happened to your shoulder?"

"What do you mean?" Sally looked startled, but grasped the sweater to rearrange it to its proper place thereby concealing her bruised skin.

"Your shoulder - what did you do to it?" Hannah repeated.

Sally remained wordless and stared back at Hannah as though she still didn't understand her question.

"It's bruised." Hannah clarified needlessly as though this would be news to Sally.

Sally's hand went to cover her shoulder as though to protect it from further inquiry. "I fell." She explained simply, although not convincingly.

"It looks so sore! How did you fall?" Hannah asked with concern.

"I wasn't paying attention, I slipped in the shower and down I went. It's not sore at all, and in fact, I completely forgot about it until you mentioned it."

"Well as long as you're okay and you didn't break anything." Hannah stated.

"I'm okay and you have nothing to worry about. I just have to be careful next time." Sally assured her. "Can we change the subject now?"

"Yes, of course."

The lunch wrapped up with the two friends laughing about some of the costumes that had turned up at Josh's Halloween party. There was no further mention of Sally's fall, but as Hannah sat at her desk later that afternoon, she felt unsettled by the presence of those bruises and wondered if it really was a slippery shower that was the true cause.

CHAPTER 22

Despite the concern she felt, Hannah wrapped up her day feeling energized and grateful to have a distraction with going to London. Arriving home, she flew in the door, laptop under her arm, and ran into the kitchen to where she hoped Martha would be waiting so she could share her exciting news.

"Hey Martha I'm so glad you're home!" She cried happily.

"Why are you so happy?"

Hannah excitedly told Martha about her trip to London. Martha was delighted for her and she offered to sit down with her to plan out her trip.

"You're all dressed up. Are you going somewhere?" Hannah asked after discussing the trip.

"We're going out for dinner with Josh tonight." Martha reminded her.

"Oh, I forgot about that."

"Would you like to join us?" Martha asked hopefully.

"No, I don't think so. I think I'll just stay home and search the internet for places to go to in London."

"Are you sure? It will be fun. We can interrogate him about how he knows Joe Hastings." Martha teased with a hint of seriousness in her tone.

"Then I will definitely say no to that. I don't want to be part of any interrogation about Joe." Hannah said sincerely while feeling a charge of panic run through her.

"Are you telling me that you aren't the least bit curious about how he knows him?" Martha prodded.

"It is interesting how they know each other, but I am in no way comfortable about making a point of discussing it over dinner. I would just rather not have the subject of Joe raised at all and please don't ask Adam about Joe because it would be embarrassing for me."

"I won't ask anything. I wouldn't do anything to upset you."

"You wouldn't be upsetting me really. I think right now it would be best if I focus on my trip to London and not give any attention to the subject of Joe because of Kate. That way I will just stay out of trouble and I won't have anything to feel awkward about."

"You haven't done anything against Kate and she should realize that."

"I just need to keep my distance from the whole situation. It's obviously a very sensitive topic for Kate and I don't think it would be to anyone's benefit to poke the lion and make the situation worse. It is already a sore spot and I think I owe it to our friendship to be gracious about not making it worse for her."

"You are a really good friend Hannah. I really hope that Kate appreciates you." Martha said seriously.

Hannah was saved the trouble of answering Martha as Adam broke through the front door calling out to them.

"Hello." He shouted down the hall. "Are you ready my little Marzipan?"

"Marzipan?" Hannah muttered quietly to Martha.

"It's his new name for me. Cute isn't it?" Martha laughed. "It was created the night of the engagement party after he had had a few too many. He thinks it's very clever."

"Well your life will never be dull." Hannah laughed shaking her head.

"Yes, my love, I'm ready. Is Josh still picking us up?" Martha asked.

"He definitely is and he should be here in about ten minutes. You look beautiful." He said as he bent to kiss her lightly on the mouth.

"Thank you Adam. You look beautiful too."

"It's a curse." He said offering his best 'handsome' pose to the delight of Martha and Hannah.

"I'm speechless." Hannah chuckled.

"My looks have that effect." Adam teased. "Are you coming with us Hannah?"

"No, she isn't, I already asked her." Martha cut in. "But she has very good reason to turn us down because Uncle Paul has asked her to go to London, England on a business trip and so she is going to start planning her trip tonight."

"That's amazing Hannah. Josh has been to London. You should ask him where all the hot spots are." Adam suggested.

"When was he there?" Hannah asked.

"He went with some buddies after University, so it was about nine or ten years ago. But I don't think things would have changed that much. He could give you some tips on how to get around and where to stay if you want me to ask him to help you out."

"That would be really nice of him if he could help me. I think once I've searched around and completely confused myself, I will have lots of questions for him."

"That's great, I'll..." Adam's words were interrupted by the doorbell ringing. "Oh that must be Josh now."

"Last chance Hannah, you could come for dinner and talk about London." Martha suggested as Adam went to the door.

"No honestly, I'll stay home and you too go out and have a nice time with Josh. This evening is about you thanking him for the party and not about me and my trip to London. I am being a bit selfish too because I want to absorb myself in planning my trip. I also have to return my costume this evening otherwise they will charge me for an extra day. And since I don't think I'll be using it tonight, I am just going to hop in the car and run it back to the costume place."

"I understand. Hi Josh." Martha said as she leaned up to kiss him on the cheek.

"Hi Martha. Hi Hannah." Josh greeted as he gave them each a brotherly kiss on both cheeks.

There was no doubt that Josh and Adam were brothers, despite the four years' difference in age. Both stood just over six feet tall, soft pale brown hair adorned their heads and their physical builds were lean and toned. The only distinction in the similarity of their looks was Josh had green eyes and Adam's were hazel. Not only were they brothers, but they were great friends to one another.

"I meant to call you Josh and thank you so much for the wonderful party the other night. I feel a bit rude that I didn't get around to it yesterday." Hannah confessed.

"Don't worry. I'm glad you had a wonderful time. Luckily I was able to have a peaceful day yesterday because I hired a company to come in and clean everything up and I took off for the day. So, you would have had a very hard time getting hold of me."

"Well you deserve a day off after all the work and effort you went to for the party." Hannah said kindly.

"It was a good party, I must admit. How's Kate by the way?"

"She's fine thanks. Just had a few too many." Hannah explained.

"Like about ninety percent of the people there." Josh laughed. "I understood you took good care of her that night. That was nice of you."

"She would have done the same for me, it wasn't a problem." Hannah said modestly.

"Well, as the party-giver, so to speak, I am grateful that you made sure she got home okay."

"I hate to be rude and interrupt, but we should get going. I think we made a reservation for seven thirty, and we're cutting it a bit close as it is." Adam said.

"Will you come with us Hannah?" Josh asked.

For the third time that evening, Hannah gracefully declined the invitation. After Josh offered to help her with any planning after she had searched the London sites, the three left to have dinner.

Hannah thought it would be best to take her costume back sooner rather than later, so that she could leave the rest of the night for herself and planning London. She ran up the stairs to retrieve the cat suit and its mask when she suddenly remembered the mask that Joe had left behind and went to rescue it from her purse. Despite her conviction to forget about Joe, she felt comforted by the prospect of a souvenir of that night and opened the purse to find it wasn't there. She sat back on the bed and thought she had to be mistaken and that her recollection of putting it inside her purse must have been wrong. 'But I clearly remember putting it in there.' She thought after mentally going over the evening. But then she recalled the cab ride home and in her efforts to quickly pay the cab driver, it must have inadvertently dropped out while she took her wallet out. 'I guess it is happily being stomped into the floor of the cab by other riders and it's now completely destroyed. That mask seems symbolic of my prospects with Joe.' She thought a bit superstitiously.

It took no more that forty-five minutes for Hannah to return the costume and come back home. She quickly made herself a bowl of soup and settled in for a peaceful evening of planning her way around London, and after locating her hotel in South Kensington on a map, she felt she had a better sense of what she would like to do and see. She was just closing the lid to her laptop when Martha and Adam came back. Adam kissed Martha goodnight and waved goodnight to Hannah and he left to go back to his own apartment.

"Did you have a nice time?" Hannah asked sleepily.

"We did. Nice food, nice company. How did your planning go?" Martha asked.

"I got a good sense of where I will be staying in relation to the heart of London, so I'm feeling a little more comfortable being in a strange place."

"That's good. Josh said he would call you and arrange a time when he could come over and give you some advice if you like."

"I think the more information I have, the better." Hannah confessed.

"I want you to know that the subject of Joe did not come up. I didn't ask him anything, so I don't want you to worry about your nosey little sister." Martha assured her.

"Thank you. I don't want any inquiries on my part to circle their way back to Joe. I'd feel really silly about that."

"A little bit like high school days." Martha agreed. "I understand completely. My lips are sealed."

CHAPTER 23

Two days later, Josh called the house and set a time that night to drop by and give Hannah some information on her trip. Martha and Adam had gone out for the evening to the movies, and so Hannah was looking forward to the company. He arrived promptly at seven.

"Hi Josh, come in." He followed her into the kitchen and placed a large folder on the table. "Here's all the reading on London. I can help step you through it if you like."

Hannah laughed and said, "Well, we better have a beer to help us get through it all. Would you like one?"

"I'd love one, thanks. I have to confess when you spoke about your trip to London, it brought back so many great memories for me and so I think I may have gotten a little carried away with all the information I've brought over." Josh said apologetically.

"Well, it was sweet of you. Adam said you were there about ten years ago?" She said handing him his beer.

"Thanks. It was about then, yes, just after I got my B.A. from University. A bunch of my buddies took a needed break and we went to the UK, but two of us in particular loved London. We both have roots there and I think we felt a special connection to England because of that. I think if I didn't have my immediate family and friends here, I would move there. That's how impressed I was with the place."

"I've only heard good things about it, and I'm looking forward to going, but I guess I have this vision that it's not easy to maneuver around. So that is overwhelming me." Hannah confessed.

"No, you won't be overwhelmed. It's not huge at all and I think you will fall in love with the place. In fact, when we went, my buddy

Jabber decided to stay for about six months and he had a really hard time coming back here."

"Jabber?" Hannah laughed.

"Jabber is a nick name. It seems at university we were blessed with nicknames based on personality traits or behaviours."

"Do you have a nickname?" Hannah asked.

"Oh yeah, I didn't escape that." Josh smiled.

"What is it?" Hannah inquired.

"Hollywood." Josh confessed and waited for her reaction.

"That's a nice nickname, but why Hollywood?"

"Well I thought I was pretty cool back then and I always wore sunglasses to fit the image. My friends teased me about it a lot because I always wore them – day and night. So one night they were giving me the gears about some new sunglasses that I had bought, and someone said that I looked like I belonged in Hollywood..."

"And then your name became Hollywood." Hannah finished.

"I guess I deserved that one, but I admit I always liked it. Did you have a nickname Hannah?"

"Only when I was in grade school and it was Hannah Banana, which I'm sure isn't a surprise to you. I hated it of course because I didn't think I looked like a banana. Maybe if I had gone to University, I would have had a more sophisticated name and one that didn't rhyme."

"Well, if it's any consolation to you, you look nothing like a banana." Josh assured her with a smile.

"Oh that's good because I was always worried about that." Hannah joked.

"How did your friend Jabber get his name?" Hannah asked hoping that Josh would not detect her disappointment in the decision to work instead of going to University. While listening to Josh talk about the friendships he made and his unique memories, she felt a twinge of regret.

"Jabber jabbered a lot about everything. He is an inquisitive guy, lots of questions, never taking anything at face value and always probing to get to the bottom of everything. He's a great guy and always good company because he always has something to say. Initially it got him into a bit of trouble in University because he liked to challenge the professors, but after they got to know him a bit and realized it was natural curiosity and he wasn't being a shit disturber they all grew to respect him and like him. Honestly, I think they liked that he challenged them."

Hannah was quiet for a moment and Josh misread her silence. "I'm sorry, I didn't mean to swear."

"No, that's fine with me, I can take it." She laughed. "I was just thinking about how much fun and how exciting it would have been to go to University. I think you form such wonderful friends and associations when you're there because you have career choices and goals in common. It's not like high school where you have to be there and you go because you have to go."

"True, but I do have great friends from my high school days too. I understand what you're saying and I have to admit it was an amazing time for me. It's not for everyone though, and lots of my buddies dropped out because they couldn't take the workload, or they simply lost interest. We all make our way somehow and the nice thing is it's never too late for you Hannah." He said pointedly.

"I couldn't go now even if I wanted to." Hannah admitted.

"Why not?" Josh asked simply.

"Because I have a job and I have this chance to go to London." Was her first excuse.

"True, but then you could go back to school after you go to London so you would start next September giving your boss lots of notice, or he could give you a leave of absence." He suggested.

"It's really expensive to go to University." Was her second excuse.

"Take out a loan and get a part time job." He suggested.

"I'm too old now." Was her third excuse.

"People of all ages go back to University. It isn't uncommon for senior citizens to get degrees, despite the fact that you don't look like a senior citizen."

"I'm not going to convince you am I?" Hannah conceded.

"I don't want to interfere, but Adam mentioned that you intended to go to University but gave it up so that you could look after Martha. That tells me that perhaps your intentions may still lean towards going back to school and don't forget, you only live once."

"You're right. I guess I'm a bit scared by the prospect — fear of the unknown." Hannah admitted.

"There really is nothing to fear and, at the very least, you need to go just to get a better nickname." Josh joked as he reached for the package that he had brought over. "Let's change the subject because I don't want to put you on the hot seat. How 'bout we take a virtual tour of London?"

Hannah and Josh poured over the contents and Josh suggesting sites and ideas that might appeal. Because Hannah was most concerned about how to get around, he suggested one of the best ways to see London was to take an open top bus tour.

"It might seem a bit hokey, but you can hop on and hop off at any of the stops and change routes depending on what you want to see. If you want to shop on Oxford Street, all you have to do is get off and shop and once you've finished shopping you might want to go and see Westminster Abbey. Your hotel is not too far from Harrods, and so if you want to go there, and who doesn't want to go to Harrods, you do the same thing. So, any site that you want to go and see, the bus will take you there. It was one way I got accustomed to finding my way around. It will give you a sense of where everything is and it won't seem so confusing."

"Are you going to travel outside London do you think?" Josh asked.

"I hadn't thought of that but maybe I should consider it if there's time."

"Well, if you do decide you want to visit other parts of England, and you don't want to rent a car, the next best thing is the train. They have a wonderful rail system over there that will connect you to just about anywhere worth seeing."

"You should be a travel agent or a spokesperson for seeing England." Hannah laughed, "But I really appreciate that you're taking the time to help me out, and you have made me feel a lot more comfortable."

"I've enjoyed it Hannah. It really has reminded me of a great time and I hope I'll be able to go back one day. It's a country with lots of history and there's so much to do and see. You should try and make the most of it." Josh said sincerely.

"I feel silly but I've never been on a plane so everything seems a bit overwhelming. Despite that, I'm excited and I can't wait to be there."

"Not silly at all and you will be fine. Maybe this will be the first in a long list of travels for you." Josh said kindly.

"Oh, wouldn't that be nice. I think I could get used to that." Hannah laughed.

"I should be going and let you relax and enjoy the rest of your evening." Josh suggested. Despite Joe's remark, Hannah felt his hesitancy to leave.

"This has been really nice of you to spend your evening helping me out with my trip. If there's anyway I can return the favour, let me know." Hannah offered as she got up to show Josh out. However, Josh remained in his seat.

CHAPTER 24

Hannah slowly slipped back into her seat, confused by Josh's resistance to leave.

"Is everything alright Josh?" Hannah asked simply.

"Yes, well no. Actually, I'm not sure. Could I ask you something before I go? Do you have a bit more time?" Josh asked as his face became serious.

"Sure, you can ask me anything you like." Hannah offered although bracing herself because of his somewhat grave expression.

"Its about your friend Sally."

"What about her?" Hannah asked caught a bit off guard.

"I wondered if you thought her relationship with her boyfriend was a safe one." Josh asked tentatively. "I witnessed something at my party that really concerned me. Its one of those situations where if you don't say something you feel badly, and if you do say something, you feel worse because you are supposed to mind your own business. Anyway, I thought about it for a few days, and I just didn't feel comfortable keeping it quiet, and since you and she are such good friends, I thought I would ask you. If you think I'm being an idiot, just say so, and I'll shut up and be on my way."

"Of course you're not being an idiot, but I guess I'm not sure how to answer your question. I've never thought about it until now." Hannah confessed.

"I'm only asking because of what I saw." Josh qualified.

"What did you see Josh?"

"It was later on in the party and I was just taking a bag of rubbish out to the garage, but instead of walking it through the kitchen entrance,

I decided to go the long way and circle around the backyard to the outside entrance. It's pretty dark back there and so I didn't expect to see anyone. As I got closer to the door, I could hear a man shouting. Up until that point, the music was so loud that it had been drowning out his shouts. Anyway, my instinct was to leave and go back because clearly this was an argument in full force. But the rage that his voice held was scary, and the only other sound I could hear was a woman crying, and softly repeating, 'no, no, it wasn't like that.' I dropped the bag of garbage and quietly walked as close as I could to get a better look at what was going on. I wasn't even sure that it was anyone from the party. But then I could see they were both in costume and the woman crying was Sally. The gate leading down the path was open slightly and I could see her very clearly."

"And the guy shouting was Grayson?" Hannah asked quietly.

"Yes, I'm pretty sure it was him, but I'd never met him before that night, and I just made an assumption because their costumes sort of complimented each other - he was wearing a football uniform and she was in a cheerleader outfit."

"Yes, that was Grayson." Hannah said shaking her head. "Sally told me he wanted to go as a football player because it's his favourite sport and he used to play it up until a few years ago. In fact that's how they met; he was a linebacker and she was a cheerleader."

"Look Hannah, I don't want to upset you, but there's more. Are you okay with this? Am I doing the right thing by telling you?"

"Yes, you're doing the right thing. Tell me." Hannah encouraged.

"As I said, I could hear her crying, and so I stepped closer to the gate to get a better look at her. This guy had her by the hair with one hand and his other hand was gripping onto her shoulder and you could see her wincing with pain."

"Her shoulder?" She asked.

"Yes."

"He grabbed her left shoulder, near the top of her arm, like this." She stated but this time it wasn't a question, but rather a fact, while she demonstrated the grip on Josh's shoulder.

"Yes, how did you know that?" Josh asked curiously.

"We were out for lunch on Monday, and she leaned forward and it caused her sweater to slip off her shoulder and I saw those awful bruises. It was from his hand and not from a fall." She said as much to herself as to Josh.

"She said she fell?"

"Yes, but I admit I wasn't convinced. Just the way the bruises looked and her reaction when I saw them. I could tell she was a bit shocked and tried to make light of it. I'm not sure what to do Josh."

"What would happen if you were to talk to her?"

"This is way out of my league. I know I have to do something, but I want to do it properly. I should get some advice, because I think if she wanted to tell me she would have had a perfect opening when I asked her about the bruises. But instead she made a story about falling and so she's protecting him." Hannah said disbelievingly.

"I think she is more likely protecting herself. I'm sure this type of relationship comes with a lot of shame. Do you think he's done this before?"

"I have to admit that I never suspected physical abuse, but I did suspect that he bullied her. I never witnessed it, but there were days when she would come into work and she was overly nervous. Her whole demeanor would be different from her usual happy disposition, and she would give unspoken signals that she just wanted to be left alone. I know that he is very possessive and very controlling. I have witnessed that the few times we have been out together as a group. It's as though she becomes a different person when she's with him."

"So he's emotionally abusing her." Josh concluded.

"As well as physical abusing her." Hannah looked at Josh with worry.

"I don't know Hannah. Maybe this was an isolated case. He may have had too much to drink and he may just be an argumentative mean drunk." Josh offered hoping to ease her concern.

"What was he shouting at her about?" Hannah unexpectedly asked, as though to make sense of his rage.

"He was accusing her of flirting with all the men in the room and trying to seduce some guy who asked her to dance. He was calling her all kinds of vulgar names; a dirty slut, a whore, and much worse. I would prefer not to repeat the rest. It was pretty ugly. And all she could do was deny it over and over again. But you could tell he wasn't listening."

Hannah shook her head in disbelief trying to understand why she should want to stay with a man like that. I can't think that way. She had to try and help her, but if she didn't want the help, what were the options.

"How did it end? He didn't hit her did he?" Hannah said tentatively.

"I didn't see him hit her. I was thinking about interrupting them just so he would stop yelling at her, and then one of my buddies, actually it was the guy I went to London with – Jabber - was leaving the party and he called out my name. Grayson realized someone was close by and it must have spooked him so he dragged Sally away by the arm. I guess they must have gone home because I didn't see them after that."

"So this was later in the night but long before midnight?" Hannah determined.

"Yes, why?" Josh asked.

"No reason really except that I was in the back yard with Kate and I would have seen you come out the back during the time you discovered them. A bit later when Kate and I left, Kate left by the side and I met her around the front, but she didn't mention seeing them. I ran inside to say goodbye and asked Martha and Adam if they had seen Sally so I could say goodbye to her too. They said they hadn't seen her. I was surprised that she left without saying goodbye, but then I thought, maybe she couldn't find me. "

CHAPTER 25

Hannah realized it didn't matter what time it happened, but she felt a sting of guilt that while her friend was being bullied and terrorized, it was likely the time she was in the willow tree's enclosure with Joe. She would have been close to discovering them herself if she had chosen to go for a walk around the side of the house rather than into the back yard. Instinctively she would have to come to her defense. But now if she were to approach Sally suggesting that she suspects that Grayson is mistreating her, she might easily become upset and their friendship could be lost. She would be prepared to lose the friendship if she thought she could help Sally, but it was too soon to risk losing her friend until she knew without a doubt that abuse was evident. Hannah sat seriously in thought, shaking her head.

"Why are you shaking your head Hannah?"

"I went for a walk in your backyard before coming inside to rescue Kate, and I wished that I had walked around the side of the house instead of going the other way. What an idiot I am!"

"This isn't your fault Hannah. If it didn't happen at my place, I'm pretty certain it would have happened at their home. All he was looking for was a quiet place out of earshot, so he found a temporary spot around the side of my house."

"I was so preoccupied with Kate that I didn't spend anytime with Sally and maybe if I had, this wouldn't have happened."

"Hannah, I don't want to sound harsh, but you aren't responsible for the well being of your friends if their choices aren't yours. You could never have predicted that this was going to happen. Even now with what you know, you're not sure what to do and neither am I. If you had interrupted them that night, it might have made things better or it could have made things worse. My guess, it would have made things worse. I think if he has been doing this a lot, Sally has figured out a way to manage him so that it inflicts the least amount of damage. Remember, if this guy is so volatile, you can never predict what he's capable of and what will set him off. I suspect Sally doesn't know either." Josh said astutely.

"You're right. I just can't stand to think that she is being mistreated, and maybe she wants to leave him, but she can't because she is terrified to leave." Hannah suggested.

"I think you're right about what you said before. I think we have to do some research on how to help her. This may be an isolated situation..."

"My gut is that it isn't isolated. If that's the case, time isn't on our side or hers. I honestly don't know what to do."

"Lets put our heads together and come up with a game plan. We have to promise each other if we can't help her or she doesn't want our help, we have to accept that our intentions were good."

"Okay, I'll agree to that. I just have to try and live with walking away. I hope I can."

"I'd better go. Its getting late and I feel like I've taken up your whole evening." Josh said apologetically.

"You haven't taken up my evening at all. You've made me comfortable about my trip to London but more importantly, you're so sweet to be so concerned for Sally."

"Something tells me she's worth it. I hate to think that she's being abused and my gut tells me she is, so I would like to help. She looked so terrified and so vulnerable. It made me almost sick to my stomach. I don't get guys who do that kind of stuff. I know they're cowards, but it kind of gives nice guys a bad rap." Josh said lightly as he started to walk towards the front door.

"I wonder who Sally was dancing with that caused Grayson to get so crazed." Hannah said almost as an afterthought.

"It was me." Josh admitted keeping his back to her. He then turned around to the look on Hannah's face. As he suspected, she was astonished.

"You're doing this because you feel responsible?" Hannah asked incredulously.

"Not really. I know anything or anybody could set this guy off, but I would be lying if I didn't feel that I innocently encouraged his rage." Josh confessed.

"But why would you think that?"

"I knew Sally was coming to the party and I have to confess I was really looking forward to seeing her, but it didn't occur to me that she was with Grayson. I only found out when we were dancing, and I asked her if she would have a drink with me at the bar, and she told me she came with her boyfriend. Up until that point, it was me who was doing all the flirting. He must have been watching and it must have been causing him to do a slow boil. She did nothing to encourage me. I was doing all the encouraging." He admitted.

"She would be far better off with someone wonderful like you. I hope I'm not out of line in saying that to you, but it's true." Hannah said simply.

"Thanks Hannah, I could only hope to be that lucky. Look, would it be okay if I called you in a couple of days to see if we've found something that might help."

"Absolutely Josh. I feel better about doing this together."

"Before I go, I'll give you my cell phone number if you want to get hold of me for anything."

"Sure, I'll key it into my cell phone."

"I'll admit to it being a bit self serving. I don't want to sound dramatic, but what I witnessed the other night may be a precursor to worse things to come for Sally. I would love to have the opportunity to be her hero." Josh confessed somewhat bashfully.

Hannah reached up and gave Josh a light kiss on the cheek and wished him a safe trip home and went back to the kitchen and put the kettle on. She needed a hot cup of tea to help her think. As she waited for the kettle to boil, she keyed in Josh's number silently hoping she wouldn't have to use it. A few minutes later, as she sipped her tea, she mentally went back over the past couple of years since Sally began dating Grayson. She remembered how excited Sally was that he had finally asked her out, admitting to Hannah that she had had an instant attraction from the moment she had laid eyes on him. She wondered if Sally had been blinded to his darker side from the beginning, or perhaps in the beginning it wasn't evident but he became violent once they began living together. Hannah decided it was best not to summon up the past. The best thing she could do now was to help Sally with her future, and so she spent the rest of the evening researching how to help victims of domestic abuse.

CHAPTER 26

The following morning Hannah did not go directly into the office as she was required to file some documents at the Court House, and being there first thing in the morning saved line-ups. After she had completed her filings, she was about to leave when her cell phone rang. 'That's unusual', she thought, 'I wonder who would be calling since Paul knows I wouldn't be in first thing.'

"Hello?"

"Hannah, its Paul."

"Hi Paul. Did you forget that I was at the Court House this morning?"

"No, I didn't forget. But I'm a bit concerned because Sally hasn't arrived yet, and I haven't heard from her. Did she tell you that she wasn't coming in today?" Paul asked evenly, but his voice was full of concern.

"No, she didn't." Hannah found that her heart unexpectedly began racing. "Did you try calling her at home?"

"I did." He said plainly. "No answer."

It suddenly occurred to Hannah, that despite the fact that she didn't know that Sally may be in a turbulent relationship, it was quite likely that Paul was well aware of it. "I'll be right there Paul. I'm just leaving the Court House now."

"Good."

Hannah literally ran back to the office, impatiently thumping the elevator's eleventh floor button as though it would speed it up. Finally, the elevator doors opened and safely deposited Hannah at the eleventh floor. She quickly ran past Deb who manned the receptionist's desk.

"Did Sally come in yet?" Hannah asked trying to sound calm.

"No." She answered without looking away from her computer. "But Mr. Peterson is waiting for you."

"Okay, thanks Deb." Hannah responded and then quickened her step to a full run. She literally threw her purse on her desk and without stopping ran down the hall to Paul's office.

"Hi." She said attempting not to sound out of breath as she stood at his office door.

Paul was gazing thoughtfully out his office window, his hands were folded gently in his lap, and his feet crossed at the ankles were settled casually on his desk, but despite the peaceful affectation of his pose, his face was full of concern. He turned almost in slow motion to face Hannah and pressed his mouth into a strained smile.

"Did you hear from her?" Hannah asked resolutely anticipating that the look on his face may be bad news.

"No. Come in please Hannah."

"Okay. I'll shut the door." Hannah suggested.

"Sure, that might be best."

Hannah sat down on the edge of one of his visitor chairs, feeling very anxious, and waited for Paul to speak. He gently lifted his feet from the desk and settled himself into a more business like pose. He began rubbing his face as though he had just woken up or perhaps to realign his thoughts in preparation for what he was about to say.

"I'm about to break a confidence, but I know or I hope Sally will understand." Paul looked at Hannah, not really expecting a response but rather to introduce what he was about to say. She really didn't have a choice but to listen and so she simply nodded without saying a word.

"About a year ago, I noticed that Sally was not quite herself, brooding and not spontaneously happy as she normally was. I decided it might be something temporary, but as soon as she would spring back to her old self, two or three days later she would be back to that broody state. I didn't know what to think really because her work was still excellent, and in fact, she almost became more productive at times. I must admit, I was conflicted. I wanted to ask her what was going on, but I didn't want to interfere. I thought I would wait it out and if it became a clear problem, I would say something. This went on for about one month or so, until one day she called in sick. Admittedly, it was rare for Sally to stay home because she loves her job so much that she hated missing even one day. Anyway, I thought nothing of it and I just assumed she had the flu or a bad cold. Two days went by and then on the third day she came back into work. Do you remember that Hannah? Do you remember when she called in sick?" His question to her was unexpected as she was completely mesmerized by the hypnotic rhythm of his dialogue.

"Yes, I remember she was ill, because I called her to see how she was."

It seemed he just needed to know that she was listening, because without acknowledging her answer, he continued.

"At first, she seemed okay. I asked her how she was and she said she had the flu."

"Yes, that's what she told me." Hannah confirmed, feeling compelled to be on the same page as Paul.

"She didn't have the flu." He said flatly.

"She didn't?" Hannah seemed puzzled.

He shook his head to indicate no. "She came into my office to get a few files from my cabinet, but you know how little she is. Well, she had to reach up on tip toes to wrestle a file out from the back of the file drawer. I would have helped her but I was on the phone. In any case, she was wearing this short top and it exposed her back as she reached forward."

Hannah didn't know if she wanted to hear what was coming, but she held his gaze, until his eyes fell away from her stare and he began to look blankly out the window. It was as though he couldn't look at her.

"Her back was covered in bruises. Now, I'm not a doctor, but I could tell they were fairly new, and they were excessive." He paused slightly as though to allow her to let this sink in. Hannah's hand rose to her mouth as she imagined what she must have endured.

"I was so shocked that I was unable to conceal it and as she turned to face me after she retrieved the file, she realized she was found out. I must have made a quick excuse to end my phone call, I can't honestly remember, but I asked her to shut the door and sit down. I could tell she didn't want to but she felt somewhat obliged. When she sat in front of me I noticed more bruises, a slight one on her face that she had tried to hide with make up, and then another one just slightly below her neckline. I'm sure they didn't stop there."

Paul turned back to face Hannah, wondering how his confession had affected her. Her hand was still covering her mouth, and her eyes were wide and fighting tears.

"I asked her simply what had happened and that she needed to tell me the truth. She hesitated for a long time until she finally told me that Grayson had gotten angry at her for something she had done. She looked terrified simply because she admitted that this creep was beating her, but assured me that it was her fault and she shouldn't have provoked him. I knew with this kind of thinking she was in deep, and I knew not only was he physically abusing her, he was emotionally abusing her. Nevertheless, I promised that I wouldn't tell anyone and I asked her if she was safe. She assured me she felt she was and I told her that in no way did she deserve that kind of treatment and she had every right to leave him. We talked for a long time and I gave her all kinds of options if she wanted to leave that I would help her. She tried to convince me that it was an isolated incident and she loved him and she didn't want me to be mad at him. She promised that if it happened again she would tell me and then she would do something about it. Although I haven't seen more bruises, I know it has continued but she hasn't said a word. Honestly though, I think she won't leave because she thinks he will come after her. I have handled some domestic cases, and I know that the general thinking among abused women is that they deserve the abuse and they have no where to run, and if they were to run, they would be found. It's a vicious cycle because no matter what they choose to do, they don't feel safe."

CHAPTER 27

After several minutes of silence, Paul seemed to have nothing further to say and he continued staring out the window. Hannah took this silent opportunity to collect her thoughts as she was unable to find the right words to try and make sense of his concerns. After talking with Josh last night, she knew that her gut instinct was right all along. It wasn't going to help sitting in Paul's office so she decided to take control and try to locate Sally.

"Paul, I think it might be best if I drive over to Sally's apartment and see if she is okay. Maybe she's asleep and can't hear the phone." Hannah guessed.

"Honestly Hannah, I don't know what to do. What time is it now?" He said looking at his watch as Hannah looked at hers.

"Its eleven thirty." They said in unison.

"I would feel better if I drove over to their apartment. If she doesn't answer, I'll call you. How would that be?"

"Okay."

"Don't worry Paul, everything will be fine. I'll call you when I get there." Hannah said feeling the same concern she knew Paul was feeling but felt she had to try and assure him. He smiled at her gratefully and told her to be careful. Her sense was that he was feeling somewhat responsible for not forcing Sally to get some help.

Sally lived about ten minutes from the office, but it seemed an eternity before Hannah arrived in the guest parking lot. When she arrived at the front doors, she entered the code for Sally's apartment and waited for a response. None came. She tried again. Nothing. 'I guess I'd better call Paul and give him the news.' Hannah decided.

"Hi Paul, I'm here and still downstairs in the lobby. Sally isn't answering her buzzer." Hannah reported evenly.

"What will you do now?" He asked evenly.

"I can wait until someone comes through the front doors and let myself in and go up to the apartment and see if the door is locked."

"I'm not sure that's such a good idea. It's not safe Hannah. I'm not getting a good feeling about this, so maybe we should just call the police."

"Well wait Paul. Before we start jumping to conclusions, I have an idea. I have a friend, actually its Adam's brother, and he recently witnessed an argument between Sally and Grayson that really unsettled him. He was concerned and offered to help. Would you mind if I called him?" Hannah was grateful that she had an opportunity to involve Josh since she was feeling all that comfortable about being alone in Sally's building.

"I would feel much better if you had someone there with you Hannah, so go ahead and call him. If you can't reach him, I think you had better come back to the office." Paul said cautiously.

"Okay, let me see what happens with Josh, and I will call you back."

Hannah signed off and then immediately called Josh. He picked up after three rings.

"Josh, its Hannah. Have I caught you at a bad time?" Hannah asked hearing impatience in his voice.

"Oh hi Hannah, no this is a good time. Has something happened to Sally?" Josh's voice sounded concerned after realizing why Hannah may be calling.

Hannah gave Josh a full explanation as to what led her to being at Sally's apartment and asked if he had time to go with her to Sally's apartment. "My boss would be very grateful to you if you could help too." Hannah reinforced.

"I'll be right there. What's the address?" Hannah was thankful Josh knew exactly where she lived, which saved time for him to get to her.

Hannah went back to the front doors and waited patiently for someone to leave the building. It was just before noon, and luckily, Hannah was able to gain access to the lobby with the arrival of school children coming home for lunch. Within fifteen minutes, Josh was at the door and Hannah ran to the doors to let him in.

"I'm so glad I could come and help you out Hannah. What do you think we should do?" Josh asked hurriedly.

"I think we have to go up to the apartment and see if the door is unlocked and go from there." Hannah suggested.

Hannah and Josh got off the elevator to the 5th floor and headed towards Sally's apartment.

Neither said a word, each silently anticipating what they may discover. Once outside the door, Hannah lifted her hand to knock but looked first to Josh for his endorsement. A slight nod of his head gave her the go ahead and she rapped very lightly. Realizing that this attempt would not do the trick, she tried again but this time more forcefully. Hannah's knocks were unanswered and she stared back at Josh as her hand fell to the doorknob. "Go handle of the doorknob, a gentle click indicated that it was indeed unlocked. As though to indicate her strength of mind, she thrust her hip to kick softly against the body of the door to propel it open. It rested fully open as if to invite entry into the apartment. Josh's hand went to Hannah's forearm to hold her back and he asked her to wait. "Let me go in first." Hannah nodded her affirmation quietly grateful for him to take the lead.

"Hannah, can you come in here?" Josh called. "I'm in the living room."

Hannah entered the apartment and went straight to where Josh stood in the living room. She was sickened to see that it was in a state of complete chaos. It was as though a hurricane had swept through the room. Hannah ran from the living room to the back bedrooms frantically calling Sally's name. Josh caught up to her and grabbed her arm to stop her.

"She's not here Hannah."

"We have to call the police. I don't want to wait any longer to see if she is in danger or not! If this place is any indication of what Grayson is capable of, then I can't bear to think what he may have done to Sally. This is horrible Josh!" Once Josh had called 911 and had connected with the police dispatcher, Hannah pulled out her cell phone to call Paul. She took a minute to calm down so she did not alarm him. Despite her attempt to be positive, once she heard his voice, her voice broke as she told him of her concern. He said very little except a request to promise to keep in touch with him. She said goodbye just as Josh was ending his call with the police.

CHAPTER 28

The police response took no more than fifteen minutes although it felt interminably long. Josh answered the buzzer so they could make their way into the lobby and before long, two uniformed officers – one male and one female – arrived at the door to Sally's apartment. Despite the fact that the door was still open, the officers knocked to indicate they had arrived. Josh greeted them and he led them into the living room where Hannah stood waiting.

The male officer spoke first to introduce his female partner, "This is Officer Burroughs, and I am..."

"Constable Barker." Hannah said interrupting his introduction.

"Sergeant Barker." He corrected.

"You've had a promotion." Hannah qualified.

"Three years ago. You look familiar, do I know you?" He asked.

"A long time ago, you came to my house with another officer, Detective Burgess, to tell my sister and me about a fatal car accident my parents were involved in." Hannah spoke as casually as she could but found it difficult to control the lump that rose in her throat.

"Of course it became a cold case because we were never able to find the driver of the other car. I remember now."

"It's a comfort to see a familiar face and I remember how kind and understanding you were. I hope you can help us once again with our friend Sally who lives here in this apartment." Hannah said not wanting to have the officers' time taken up reliving the events of her parents' car crash.

"So neither of you live here?" He asked.

"No, we're friends of Sally who lives here with her boyfriend. Sally and I also work together. She didn't arrive at work today and our boss had been trying to call her to find out where she was. Since she wasn't answering, we became alarmed and so I decided to drive over here. I called Josh to meet me here in case I needed help."

"Okay, I think I had better start with your names and contacts and Sally and her boyfriend's names and then we can get into the details of why you called us." Officer Burroughs suggested.

"My name is Hannah Hutton. Sally's proper name is Sarah-Anne, and her last name is Eaton. Grayson's last name is Burton." Hannah then offered her address and phone numbers as her contact.

"Thank you and you are?" Officer Burroughs asked looking at Josh.

"Joshua Hardcastle."

After taking down all the details that were required, Sergeant Barker began his questioning.

"How were you able to gain entry to the apartment? Do you have a key?"

"No, the door was unlocked and so we came in because we weren't sure if Sally was still inside." Hannah said.

"And you found it to be empty but disrupted as it is now." This was presented more as a statement rather than a question from Sergeant Barker. "You came here because you were concerned for Sally's safety?"

"Yes. Josh and I believe that Sally is in a dangerous relationship with her boyfriend, otherwise, we wouldn't even be here." Hannah explained.

"Sergeant, I hosted a party the other night and Sally and her boyfriend were there as well, and they were in a heated argument and Grayson was being quite rough with her." Josh added.

"Well, sometimes couples do fight and they fight a little more vigorously than the rest of us. Perhaps this is an indication that they had another fight, and she may not be hurt." Sergeant Barker offered attempting not to encourage alarm.

"My boss and I have seen bruises on her." Hannah said simply.

Sergeant Barker studied Hannah and Josh with an unreadable expression as though he was trying to absorb what she had said. "I'm going to have a look around." He said finally.

CHAPTER 29

As Sergeant Barker rose from his seat, he heard a soft voice call out from the hallway. He asked everyone to stay where they were while he went to see who it was. After a few minutes he returned to the living room and advised that it was the neighbour from across the hall. "Sally is with her in her apartment. She's been watching through the peep hole to make sure it wasn't Mr. Burton who had come back."

"Is she okay?" Josh and Hannah asked simultaneously.

"She's upset and scared, but her boyfriend doesn't know that she's there. I think it would be best if Officer Burroughs and I go across the hall first and ask a few questions to protect her privacy. The neighbour doesn't know where Mr. Burton went, or when he may be coming back so I recommend you not wait here in case he returns. I don't think he would be too happy if he found you here. I would suggest that you go for a coffee and I will call you when we're through. I have your cell phone numbers."

"Thank you." They both mumbled, not really wanting to go for a coffee, but feeling they should co-operate. They left the apartment gently closing the door behind them and took the elevator to the lobby, while the two officers crossed the hall to the neighbour's apartment.

"I hope we don't run into Grayson on the way out." Hannah said with concern.

"I do." Josh said without concern.

"Why do women shy away from aggression and men almost welcome it?" Hannah asked trying to sort out the difference in their reactions.

"Natures of the beasts I suppose. I'm actually not a fighter Hannah, but I do admit that if it came down to fight or flight, I would fight, unless I was up against a knife or a gun, and that's unlikely. "

"But if you did come up against a gun or a knife?" Hannah asked curiously.

"I'd run like a little girl on steroids." He admitted.

"Now you're talking. I'd do the same thing. Speaking of talking, I'd better give Paul a quick call while we get our coffees."

"Let's go in my car so you can make your call. I'll go through the drive thru and then we can come back here and wait in the parking lot. " Josh suggested.

"Good idea." Hannah said as she settled into the passenger seat and dialed Paul to let him know that Sally was safe.

By the time Hannah had got off the phone with Paul, Josh had ordered their coffees and they made their way back to the apartment's visitor parking lot.

"That was a long conversation, and you did none of the talking." Josh laughed.

"While we've been here, Paul has been researching domestic abuse and how to help its victims. He was giving me very clear instructions about how we can hopefully convince Sally to get help. The only problem is I don't know if Sally is going to agree with his plans."

"Why wouldn't she agree?" Josh asked, "Despite the fact I have no idea what his instructions were."

"First, he is insisting she not stay in the apartment because she is not safe." Hannah paused for Josh's reaction.

"That sounds about right to me. Why wouldn't she agree?" He repeated.

"If someone were to say to you that you can't go back to your home where all your things are, how would you react?" Hannah asked.

"If it wasn't safe for me to be there, I wouldn't have a problem with it." Josh stated as he sipped on his coffee.

"My guess is she won't like it. Paul has spoken with his wife and they have agreed to take her in. It may make her feel a little uncomfortable living temporarily with her boss, but she would be safe. If Grayson were looking for her that would be the last place he would look."

Josh was quiet for awhile and then asked Hannah what his other instructions were.

"He said if she's not comfortable staying with Paul and his wife, then he hopes she would consider going to a woman's shelter. I had offered to take her in, but he thinks that that would be one of the first places Grayson would look for her."

"I agree with that. I know its tempting for you to help her Hannah, but you shouldn't put yourself in that position."

"Paul also thinks she should be checked out by a doctor too and get some counseling – he'll pay for it if need be. He wants me to tell her that she has so much to offer and that she shouldn't waste her time with such a jerk. Those are my words, not his." Hannah offered.

"She doesn't have to go to a shelter Hannah, she can stay with me." Josh said quietly.

"Think carefully about that Josh. Everyone is high on emotion right now, so let's take time to think about what's best for Sally in the long run. She'll need time to think things through as well."

"She doesn't have time Hannah. No matter where she stays it will be uncomfortable for her but it will be better than the option she has now."

Just as he spoke those words, Hannah's cell phone rang.

"Hello?" Hannah answered. "Okay, thanks, we'll be up shortly." Hannah snapped her cell phone shut. "They've finished so we can go up."

CHAPTER 30

O n the way in the elevator, Hannah asked Josh a couple of questions and it was clear he was preoccupied with something since she had to repeat each question twice.

"Are you okay Josh?" Hannah asked.

"I wonder if you think it's a good idea that I be here. It may upset her." Josh said with concern.

"You couldn't possibly upset her Josh." Hannah assured.

"We still don't know what shape she is going to be in and my guess is she won't want an audience. I don't want to make it worse for her. Maybe I should reconsider that fight or flight conversation I had with you earlier, and take off, so to speak." Josh conceded.

"Josh, I don't want you to do anything you don't want to do, and I fully understand if you feel uncomfortable, but…"

Before Hannah could continue, the elevator doors opened onto the fifth floor and as they both stepped out they were greeted by Sergeant Barker and Officer Burroughs.

"I'm glad we were able to see you both again to thank you for coming. How is Sally doing?" Hannah asked.

"She was quite upset. Your feeling was right about her boyfriend." Sergeant Barker confirmed.

"Is she hurt?" Josh asked.

"She does have some injuries, but they aren't serious. We have suggested that she press charges, but she needs a bit of time to think it over. It's not unusual in these kinds of cases. There is always a fear of retaliation. Victims of abuse don't feel they have a safe place to go and so they feel very vulnerable. Fortunately, there are shelters for women where they are taken care of until they can get themselves on their feet again. We have lots of resources for her when she is ready."

"Thank you again for everything." Hannah said gratefully.

"We shouldn't keep you any longer. Sally wanted to see you both and she'll be wondering where you are." Sergeant Barker offered.

Hannah and Josh said goodbye and began to walk down the hall towards Sally's apartment.

"Well, it looks like she expecting us so I hope you've changed your mind about taking off." Hannah said.

"What do you honestly think Hannah?"

"I think she would be disappointed if you don't show up and I have a sense that it will make a big difference to her if you visit for awhile or for as long as you're comfortable. Think about it. If you were hurt and she came to see you, you would be comforted by the fact that she cared enough to make sure you were alright." Hannah said sincerely.

"Okay, I'm convinced. Now I wish I had brought flowers to cheer her up." Josh admitted.

"Why don't you do that next time you see her?" Hannah suggested as she knocked on the apartment door belonging to Sally's neighbour.

"Do women really like to get flowers?" Josh asked.

"I would guess that most women love to get them." Hannah confessed, thinking about the flowers she had received from Joe and the personal happiness they had given her. "I don't think I've ever known a woman who didn't love to have flowers given to her."

Just then, the door was opened by a young woman not much older than Hannah.

"Hello, I'm Gabriella. You must be Josh and Hannah, please come in quickly. I'm afraid Grayson might discover where Sally is. I'm going to speak quietly in case he comes to the door. I don't want him to know that I'm home." Gabriella explained pressing her index finger to her lips to encourage silence as she led them to a sitting room in the back of the apartment. "Sally is just having a shower. She's expecting you and she hoped you wouldn't mind if she got cleaned up a bit. She thought it would make her feel better."

Hannah and Josh settled on the chesterfield and declined the offer any refreshments.

"We've just had a coffee, but thanks." Hannah said softly. "Tell me Gabriella, what happened to Sally. How do you think she is?"

In a whisper, Gabriella recounted the events of the morning.

"She is very upset because she is blaming herself, which is ridiculous. I have lived across the hall from Grayson since he moved here and then just after Sally moved in, I could hear them fighting. I had my suspicions that he was being rough with her, but I couldn't bring myself to knock on the door and demand to know what was going on. So I decided I would just keep an eye on things and if I felt it was getting really bad then I would call the police. This time though, it happened so quickly."

"What do you mean it happened quickly?" Hannah asked.

"Usually when they argued, Grayson's voice was like a storm brewing with the thunder off in the distance and it would get closer and closer and louder and louder and suddenly it would be like the heavens opening and it would all come crashing down. Then it would be very quiet and the storm would be over." Gabriella said dramatically.

"And this time..." Josh encouraged.

"And this time, there was no warning. No thunder in the distance, no loud voices. But I knew somehow that it was worse, almost like a tornado silently building momentum. Initially, I don't think I would have heard a thing except I was leaving my apartment to go to work and I turned to lock my door and I heard a thud. Normally, I wouldn't have paid attention to it because I expected that Sally and Grayson would already have left for work. So I waited because I was pretty certain the noise came from their apartment. Then there was another thud, and this time it was followed by Grayson's voice and he was angry but he was trying to control it and not raise his voice. It was really strange because at that point his was the only voice I could hear. I was curious and so I went across the hall and pressed my ear to their door, and that's when I heard Sally. She was crying, no - she was whimpering really. It made me feel sick inside because I knew she was in trouble. She sounded so scared. I didn't know what to do because I thought if I disturbed them, it might make it worse, but I knew if I ignored them, it may be horrible. I could hear her saying she was sorry over and over again, but it just seemed to make him angrier. And then I heard another thud, and I heard her whimper." Gabriella's voice faltered and she looked away to give herself time to regain control.

Hannah gently placed her hand over Gabriella's. "If this is too hard, its okay, you don't have to continue."

"No, I just hated that sound." Gabriella shook her head as though to shake the thought away.

"We're so grateful that you waited. You saved her Gabriella." Josh offered.

"I hope I did the right thing. I hope this is the end of it for her." Gabriella wished.

"We do too. But Gabriella, how were you able to get her into your apartment?" Hannah probed.

"I decided I had to make up a story and hoped that it would work. I decided to knock on their door and say I had a really important meeting that I had to get to but my car wouldn't start and ask if Sally would give me a ride to work. I knew I risked the chance that Grayson wouldn't open the door to me, but I had to try something."

"Good thinking." Josh assured.

"Honestly, I was terrified that I wouldn't be able to pull it off. When I knocked on their door, there was silence. I knocked again and I said, 'Grayson it's just me Gabriella. I'm sorry to disturb you but I'm really in a bind and I need a ride to work and wondered if Sally could give me a lift'. I was right, he wouldn't open the door, but he answered me and said that Sally was ill and wouldn't be going to work. So I asked if he could give me a ride. He had no choice, this time he had to open the door. He poked his head out and said he couldn't give me a ride because he wanted to stay home with Sally since she wasn't feeling well."

"So, you were done." Hannah observed.

"I was, but I thought I have to keep pushing. So I begged him to come and have a look at my car in case I just needed a boost and then I could leave and not have to bother them. I really poured it on so he couldn't say no, and I think he thought he would be well rid of me if he could get my car started, so he agreed. He asked me to give him a couple of minutes and he would meet me down in the underground parking lot. Our cars are parked in the same section so he knew exactly where my car was."

"What happened when you met him at your car?" Hannah said.

"I didn't go down to my car right away. I ran down the hall instead and hid in the staircase with the door opened just enough so that I could see Grayson leave. I'm telling you, my heart was pounding so hard I was sure he would hear it. I was absolutely terrified. As soon as I saw the elevator door slide shut with him in it, I ran to their apartment and pounded on it calling Sally's name. At first she ignored me, but I pleaded with her to come to the door and that if she didn't, I would call the police. Finally she did and I was shocked when I saw her face because it was so swollen and that's when I realized the thuds were him hitting her." Gabriella looked at Josh and Hannah as they winced at the image that she had offered them, and she continued.

"I took her hand and pulled her to my apartment, and begged her to stay there and not say a word. 'Promise me Sally' I said to her. I pleaded with her to trust me to make sure that she would be safe in my place. She agreed, but only because I kept saying I would call the police if she didn't stay. I told her I would be right back, and under no conditions was she to go back to her apartment. I then ran downstairs as fast I could and met Grayson by my car where he was waiting with his car and the jumper cables. I apologized to him with the excuse that I had to go back for my car keys that I had left upstairs. I could tell he was annoyed but he had to play nice."

"Well at least he bought it." Hannah said.

"Yes, and all I cared about was she was out of that apartment and hopefully still in mine. I was just hoping it would work out. So I climbed into my car and put the key in the ignition and my car started."

"Oh no, of course it would start. Grayson must have been furious." Hannah realized incredulously.

"I just acted like he had fixed it. I jumped out of the car and hugged him and thanked him profusely for fixing it. I knew he thought I was crazy, but I think he was just happy to be rid of me and I jumped back in my car and I sped out of the underground as though I was hurrying off to my meeting. But instead I drove madly around to the front of the building, parked in the visitors' parking and bolted back upstairs and prayed that I would make it to my apartment without running into Grayson. The coast was clear and I quickly unlocked the door and went inside where Sally sat huddled on the chesterfield and I ran back to my door and bolted it shut. I waited by the door and peered through the peep hole and watched as Grayson finally appeared. When he put his key in the lock, it was already unlocked. I watched him hesitate because he likely would have locked it when he left. I could almost see the anger seep into the back of his shoulders as he realized Sally wouldn't be there."

"This is unbelievable!" Josh whispered incredibly, mindful of keeping quiet.

"I only beat him by maybe a minute because by the time he drove his car back to his parking spot and then walked to the elevator to wait for it to arrive - given that so many people were using it to go to work and school - I was making better time by using the stairs. I was just grateful that he didn't think to use the stairs as well."

"So what happened?" Hannah was riveted and had almost forgotten that Sally was in the apartment until they heard the soft hum of the hairdryer in the distance.

"I quietly said to Sally no matter what, under no circumstances was she to make a sound. I think she was so worn out that she was just prepared to agree to anything. I ran back to the door and looked through the peep hole just in time to see Grayson come out of his apartment. He looked panicked looking up and down the hall. Then he became furious and he started punching his fists into the wall and then suddenly he turned and stared directly at my door. I moved away from the peep hole in case he caught a shadow through it and I went into the living room and held Sally's hand. Then we heard him knock at the door, but I could tell it wasn't a convincing knock at first. Then, just as he did with the wall, he started punching at my front door. Sally started to cry and I buried her face in my shoulder so he wouldn't hear her. I felt sick and began to imagine that he was going to break down my door. Finally he stopped and there was nothing. We just sat and waited and waited. I think we were there for ten or fifteen minutes before we even spoke. We were both so afraid that he might hear us even though at that point we had no idea where he was. I decided to lead Sally into my guest room and told her to try and get some sleep so I could think about what to do next. She made me promise not to do anything until she had woken up.

I agreed but then a couple of hours later I heard you two at their door so I watched and waited to see what you would do. I didn't know who you were, so I wasn't going to show myself at that point. Then the two police officers arrived and I realized I would be able to help."

Hannah and Josh who, up until this point, were sitting bolt upright transfixed by Gabriella's story both fell against the back of the chesterfield relieved to have heard the end of Sally and Gabriella's ordeal. Both looked at each other and shook their heads in disbelief. The timing of the end of her report cued Sally's arrival into the living room and, while freshly showered, her face was red from crying and bruised from Grayson's fists. Josh and Hannah were briefly silenced by her appearance, but then quickly collected themselves and both stood to greet her. Hannah extended her arms to welcome her into a hug until she heard Sally mumble thank you for coming back. Sally leaned forward to hug Josh as he planted a friendly kiss on the top of her head and said he was relieved that she was okay. Gabriella had stepped out of the room to prepare a bag of ice for Sally's face to help calm the swelling. They all sat back down and Sally apologized for putting them through such an upsetting morning.

"We're just glad you're okay now." Hannah assured.

CHAPTER 31

Sally was so exhausted from her experience, but found the strength to relate what had happened to her. She admitted that she and Grayson had had an argument at Josh's party and while she didn't confess to the reasons leading up to their fight, she said that Grayson was not willing to let go of his anger from that night.

"He was just so convinced I was hiding something from him. I was so worn out from his questions and accusations; I just curled up and fell asleep on the chesterfield. This enraged him even more and he decided that I just didn't care about his feelings. He woke me up at about 6:00 this morning and started in on me again. I couldn't believe it. It was crazy. Instead of giving in to him so he would leave me alone, I became angry. I thought that the best defense was a good offence and I told him how he was so disrespectful and insulting. He was standing over by the kitchen with his back to me. I guess I thought that he was listening and finally hearing my side. But then, he turned around and I saw the look on his face – pure hatred and pure rage. For an instant I froze and then I realized that he was going to really hurt me. I tried to run, but he was so quick, he grabbed my hair and he hit head into the wall."

"That was the thud I heard when I was just leaving for work." Gabriella explained.

"I was terrified and I began to cry and begged him not to hurt me. He knew he had me where he wanted me. He pushed me again and told me to be quiet. I thought, this is the end, he's angrier than I've ever seen him and I wasn't sure how far he would go. I honestly thought in that moment that he was capable of killing me. I don't mean to be dramatic, but if you could have seen the rage that consumed him you would understand. I always thought that if I just tried to convince him that I was not what he accused me of, he would settle down and not be angry anymore. It was a vicious cycle and I know it must sound pathetic to you, but I just wanted our lives to be normal. No matter how much I tried to behave, be what he wanted me to be, it never mattered. I just wanted Grayson to be the Grayson I first met." Sally confessed.

"Maybe he was never that guy that you thought he was. He was probably always a volcano ready to erupt." Hannah suggested, realizing she was borrowing Gabriella's analogy style.

Sally nodded in agreement realizing that a normal life was in fact an illusion with Grayson. She was just about to say something when Josh's cell phone that had been placed on the coffee table vibrated to signal an incoming call. Josh excused himself and answered the call to discover that it was his old friend Jabber.

"Hi Jabber. What's up?" Josh said quietly. As Josh listened to his friend, his face went from a smile to a look of revelation as his gaze focused on Hannah, just as though he was seeing her for the first time. His look was so intense that it interrupted the quiet conversation the three women were having with each other. As he realized that he had unwittingly captured their attention, he quickly recovered by smiling and walking from the room to finish is conversation.

"What do you think that was about?" Hannah asked clearly confused by what they had witnessed.

"I don't know. Who is he talking to?" Sally asked.

"An old university buddy." Hannah explained.

"Do you know him?"

"No, I just recognized his name." Hannah admitted.

Josh returned to the living room after ending his call and greeted the three women with an innocent smile. They all stared blankly at him as though they were waiting for him to explain what the call was about.

"Is everything okay?" Hannah asked hoping to give him an opening to the reason for Jabber's call.

"Everything is great. Why?" Josh questioned seemingly confused.

"You were looking strangely at Hannah while you were on the phone with your friend." Sally explained.

"Oh, I'm sorry. I must have been focused on Hannah without realizing it, but the call had nothing to do with her. Honestly, it didn't." Josh reinforced.

An awkward silence fell within the room as Sally and Hannah exchanged glances since Josh's explanation was not very convincing.

"I think we have to come up with a plan for you Sally." Gabriella said breaking the silence.

"Yes, of course we do." Hannah agreed.

After several minutes of discussion, it was agreed that Sally would stay the night with Gabriella so she could get a good night's sleep. Gabriella was happy for her to temporarily stay with her, but they all agreed that she would feel vulnerable because of her proximity to Grayson. Surprisingly, she didn't feel uncomfortable with the prospect of staying with Paul and his wife, and agreed that it would be better than a shelter.

"Thank you so much for helping me through this." Sally said as she attempted to stifle a yawn.

"I think that should be our cue to go." Josh suggested.

"You will have to do that very carefully." Gabriella warned. "I don't want you to leave and run into Grayson on the way out.

Both Josh and Hannah looked at each other realizing that they hadn't thought of the threat this could offer should Grayson see them.

"I think I may have an idea. Where does he work Sally?" Josh asked.

Sally gave Josh the name of the car dealership that he worked for.

"Do you remember if he called in this morning to say he wouldn't be in today?"

"No, not while he was with me. But he didn't have to go in until noon, and I would be surprised if he didn't show up. He works on commission." Sally explained.

"Okay, if you give me the phone number there, I'll use my cell phone and give him a call." Josh said.

"And what will you say if he picks up the phone?" Gabriella asked.

"That's a good question – let me think about that." Josh proposed.

"Why don't you ask if he has a certain car on the lot?" Sally suggested.

"That's a great idea, I'll do that."

"How ridiculous is it that I feel awful fooling him like this, after everything I've been through?" Sally confessed after she recited the phone number.

Josh looked at Sally and stopped pressing the phone number into his cell phone. "Sally, your intentions for a healthy relationship were always good. I'm not surprised by your loyalty at all. Just because he was awful to you doesn't mean that you want to be the same with him. We're only doing this because we want to keep you safe."

"I know it doesn't make sense, but it makes me feel sad." Sally conceded.

"I'll go into the next room so I don't subject you to the call. Would that make you feel better?"

"It really would, thank you." Sally confessed as she lowered her head hoping to hide the tear that slid down her face.

A few minutes later Josh returned and confirmed that Grayson had answered the phone.

"I actually didn't get very far with the call because he was with a customer, so he asked me to call back."

Sally nodded silently still feeling conflicted about her loyalties. Despite her concern, Josh and Hannah assured her things were going to work out and left their phone numbers with Gabriella before leaving the apartment.

"Call me any time about anything no matter what time of day or night. The next few days will be crucial because we'll have to be very careful so that Grayson doesn't discover where she is." Josh insisted.

Even though they knew they were in the clear, Josh and Hannah decided to take the stairs instead of the elevator just as a precaution.

"Josh, I need to ask you something." Hannah said as they descended the stairs.

"Sure, what is it?"

"Was it my imagination, or was there something being said about me in your conversation with Jabber?" Hannah asked feeling completely ill at ease.

"Yes, it was definitely your imagination. Jabber doesn't know you. What could we possibly talk about?" Josh said defensively.

Hannah responded with a frown and a quick look in Josh's direction.

"I'm sorry Hannah, that sounded rough and I didn't mean it that way. Jabber was just sharing a personal concern with me and I guess I just focused on your face, it was nothing more than that."

"Okay." Hannah said simply, but her gut was telling her that he wasn't being straightforward with her. She hated to use the word lying because she just didn't want to accept that Adam's brother wouldn't be honest with her.

Once they arrived at the visitor's parking lot they said goodbye and promised to call each other if either heard from Gabriella.

CHAPTER 32

Hannah's drive back to the office was reflective, but not because of the events that had unfolded due to Sally. It was none of her business that Josh had a private conversation with his friend, but she was certain that he was hiding something from her. She would be grateful when she could go home at the end of the day and share a quiet dinner with her sister. Once she arrived back at the office, the receptionist informed her that Paul had been a nervous wreck for most of the morning.

"I'll go and see him right away. Thanks Deb." Hannah said gratefully.

As she ate a sandwich that Paul had ordered for her, Hannah discussed the morning and the arrangements they had made to keep Sally safe for the night and her agreement to stay at Paul's to avoid any possible retaliation from Grayson.

"She really does need to be where he will not expect her to be, and our house would be the last one he would check. If she is with you and Martha, he might not think twice about coming to your home, so I'm glad she will be staying with us." Paul stated.

"My friend Josh had also offered to take her in and Grayson doesn't know him."

Paul looked to Hannah and simply raised his eyebrows. "You don't say?"

Hannah laughed. "I think he's a bit smitten."

"I'm not surprised because she is a very sweet young woman. At least she knows we're all behind her."

"Without a doubt." Hannah agreed.

Before leaving the office, Hannah checked her messages and returned all of her calls, and decided that she would go home a bit early since there was nothing really pressing to deal with. She was just shutting down her computer as her telephone rang. The caller ID display indicated an unknown caller.

"This is Hannah Hutton, may I help you?" Hannah said into the phone as she slipped on her coat.

Her greeting went unanswered.

"Hello, may I help you?" She repeated.

"You'd better mind your own business." Said the caller.

"Excuse me?" Hannah demanded, barely hearing what was said.

"You heard me." Hannah then heard a click to signal that the caller had hung up.

Hannah stared at her phone trying to make sense of the call.

"Everything okay Hannah?" Hannah jumped as Paul had unexpectedly appeared beside her.

"I don't know. I just had the strangest call." Hannah repeated the exchange and confessed that she had no idea who called her.

"Let's go out to reception and ask Deb if she put the call through to you. I would hate to think that caller might have your direct line." Paul suggested.

"Good idea."

Deb confirmed that a woman with a raspy voice had asked for Hannah.

"I could hardly hear her because she was whispering. I asked for her name, but she said it was personal. Should I have insisted?" Deb asked a bit defensively.

"No, of course you did the right thing by putting the call through, especially if she said it was personal." Hannah assured the receptionist.

She and Paul walked out of the receptionist's range and back to Hannah's desk. "I wonder if this is connected to Sally."

"I suppose it could be." Paul said as he watched Hannah dial Gabriella's number on her cell phone.

"I think maybe...Gabriella? Hi, it's Hannah Hutton, Sally's friend from this morning. I was wondering if you've heard anything from Grayson."

Hannah listened while looking at Paul and shook her head to indicate nothing from Grayson. "Okay, thanks Gabriella, I'm glad you're both okay and everything has been quiet." Hannah signed off, snapped her phone shut and told Paul that Sally and Gabriella were watching a movie. They haven't made any calls or received any since we left.

"This doesn't make sense. If this is connected to Sally, then who else besides you and Gabriella would know about it?" Paul questioned.

"You're not suggesting that Gabriella is somehow involved?"

"I'm just looking at the..."

"Wait!" Hannah interrupted.

"You remember something?"

"Yes, but nothing to do with Gabriella. When I was at her apartment, Josh got a funny call from one of his friends."

"What do you mean funny call?"

"When Josh was talking to his friend, he was looking at me strangely and then when I asked him if they were talking about me, he denied it, but I didn't believe him."

"You're not suggested that Josh..."

"No, not Josh, but I wonder if he told his friend about Sally."

"Is this friend a woman?"

"No, a man."

"But you said it was a woman who called you." Paul reminded her.

"I think it was a woman. I've never met this friend of Josh's but maybe he has a light voice. Or maybe he had a female friend make the call. But then why the whispering? That bothers me." Hannah admitted to Paul.

"The whole thing bothers me." He declared simply.

"Yes, but my point is when someone whispers you can't detect who they are since it erases distinguishable or recognizable features because friction is eliminated from the vocal chords. So the tone that we recognize as someone's unique voice is gone." Hannah explained.

"Meaning, that if this person spoke in her normal voice, you would have recognized who was calling. So she was deliberately altering her voice by whispering."

"Exactly. She, whoever she is, is someone I know." Hannah said simply.

"I think I need to walk you to your car. It's probably not anyone you know but Grayson putting someone up to scare off anyone even remotely related to Sally. He's got to figure she is with someone she knows and trusts. I think it was meant to alarm you, and even if it hasn't alarmed you, it's alarmed me, so let's go."

CHAPTER 33

Paul and Hannah left their offices and took the elevator down to the underground parking lot to her car. Hannah thanked Paul and assured him she would be fine.

"Nevertheless, I'm beginning to think the earlier you go on your trip to London, the better. You don't need to be dealing with this." Paul said determinedly.

Hannah climbed into the driver's seat while Paul promised to firm up dates from Robert O'Shea in London so that he could fly her out sooner rather than later. She was grateful that he had raised the issue because she had been worried that, with the events surrounding Sally and her troubles, Paul may have wanted to postpone or cancel her trip. Given the likelihood that Sally would be taking some time off, it would affect the rhythm of the work going out the door should they both be absent from the office.

"Paul, I completely understand if the timing for me to go to London is out of the question right now." Hannah offered unselfishly.

"No, actually the timing is good and I really do need you to go so we can move ahead with Robert's lawsuit. This is a huge case and I can't risk upsetting him by delaying any further. Don't you worry, despite what's going on with Sally, my practice can't come to a grinding halt. That would be professional suicide." Paul said while closing Hannah's car door signaling the end of the conversation. "Go straight home and have a nice evening."

Paul's words offered a tonic to Hannah's peace of mind so that her drive home was filled with ideas of visiting London and the welcomed escape from the drama of recent events. After parking her car in the driveway, she drifted through the front door calling out to Martha.

"I'm in the kitchen making dinner and your timing is excellent because I've just made tea." Martha called back.

Hannah was so happy to be home. She was grateful for the comfort of her sister. She quickly changed from her work clothes and settled in to tell Martha about Sally and Grayson.

"What do you think Sally will do?" Martha questioned.

"We're hoping after a couple of good nights sleep she may consider pressing charges." Hannah confessed. She then told Martha of her surprise when Sergeant Barker had been one of the responding police officers.

"Wasn't it Officer Barker?" Martha asked.

"It was, but he has been promoted since we saw him last."

"That must have been difficult to see him again." Martha realized and turned to face her sister while leaning back against the kitchen counter.

"It was difficult but as strange as it sounds, it was also a comfort to see him." Hannah confessed.

Martha nodded silently perhaps conflicted by the idea of those memories being a comfort.

"Oh, speaking of police officers. You had a call from a Detective Hastings."

"Did you say Detective Hastings?" Hannah asked with surprise.

"Yes I did. Who is he?" Martha asked curiously.

"Joe." Hannah said pointedly.

"Joe who?"

"Joe Hastings." Hannah offered.

"Have I met him?" Martha stated while looking confused.

"Joe Hastings." Hannah repeated more emphatically.

"Still not connecting." Martha insisted.

"Joe who sent the flowers - Kate's Joe. Well, her ex I should say." Hannah bumbled.

"Oh, that Joe." Martha realized.

"Yes, that Joe."

"He's a detective?" Martha asked.

"Yes." Hannah responded simply.

"Interesting."

"Did he say why he was calling?" Hannah asked attempting to ignore Martha's last comment.

"No, he just asked for you and I said you would be home at about five. He said he would call again."

"That's it? That's all he said?" Hannah asked.

"That's all. Short and sweet." Martha said looking at Hannah steadily.

"Okay, thanks." Hannah returned her steady gaze.

"Did you do something wrong?"

"What?"

"You said he was a detective. So, I'm wondering if you did something wrong."

"Come on. Of course I didn't."

"Good. I thought that's why he was calling." Martha suggested.

Hannah decided not to play along with Martha and sat back, crossed her arms, and stared at her without expression.

Martha's face broke into a wide smile. "Stop staring at me like that!"

"You started it!" Hannah replied as though she were six years old. They started laughing until there were tears streaming down their cheeks.

"Oh, I needed that." Hannah confessed, wiping the tears from her face.

"That was fun." Martha exclaimed trying to stifle a huge grin for fear that she would start up again. "Thank you Joe for unknowingly making us laugh."

"Thanks Joe." Hannah joined in as she raised her cup of tea as a salute in the air.

They were suddenly interrupted by the phone that for no reason at all, started them laughing again. Martha squatted down in an attempt to answer the phone and stop herself from laughing.

"Hello?" She peeped muffling her laughter. She looked up at Hannah and covered the mouthpiece and said that she could hardly hear them.

"Hello?" She demanded.

"I can't hear you." She insisted into the phone. "Did you say you want to speak to Hannah?" Martha listened a bit longer and looked at Hannah with an expression that erased the smile from her face. She then stretched her arm out to extend the phone to Hannah.

"I don't know who it is. They're whispering."

"Whispering?" Hannah questioned disbelievingly and took the phone. Martha simply nodded and watched Hannah put the receiver to her ear. "Hello." When she heard her name whispered, she slammed the phone down.

CHAPTER 34

Hannah pressed the caller display button to review the last call but it came up as blocked. While her hand rested against the phone, she lifted her other hand to her forehead pushing her fingers through her hair. She closed her eyes and tried to make sense of this and the earlier calls, and as she contemplated what she should do, the phone rang again. Rather than answer it, she pulled her hand away from the phone.

"I can't answer it Martha."

"I'll get it." Martha said as she jumped to answer the phone. "Who is this? What? Oh, I'm so sorry. I thought you were someone else. I'll put Hannah on." She handed the receiver to Hannah. "It's Detective Hastings called back".

"Hello." Hannah said into the phone.

"Hannah, I'm sorry to be so formal. It's me Joe."

"Is there something wrong?"

"I hope you won't think I'm stepping out of line here, but your name came across my desk this afternoon, and I just wanted to make sure you were okay."

"I'm fine, but why would my name come across your desk?" Hannah said feeling a bit alarmed.

Joe explained that he had read a report that included her name with the incident involving Sally and Grayson.

I thought this couldn't have been easy for you." Joe confessed.

"I was worried for Sally but hopefully now she's out of danger." Hannah offered.

"Well, you can never be too sure because domestic incidents can be unpredictable. Just make sure you keep yourself out of harm's way." Joe said sincerely.

"I will." Hannah said simply. "Thank you for being concerned."

"Hannah, I am sorry that I have to stay at a distance right now, but that doesn't mean that my thoughts for you take the same position. You just have to trust me."

Hannah didn't know how to respond and so she said nothing. After a moment of either of them speaking, Joe spoke again.

"I know this is confusing and I don't have a right to ask anything of you except believe that my intentions are sincere. I wouldn't do anything to hurt you."

Hannah was still conflicted and wanted so much to say something, but she couldn't bring herself to speak. This day had been a day of confusing and disquieting calls, and this one was no different. As though he read her mind he broke the pattern of his conversation and changed the subject.

"Hannah, has someone been bothering you?" Joe questioned, snapping her out of her silence.

"Why do you ask that?"

"The woman who answered the phone when I called just now seemed agitated and demanded to know who I was. It seemed a strange way to answer the phone."

"That was my sister Martha. A mysterious caller phoned me today at my office and then here at home tonight. I hung up on them and you called right after. Martha thought they were calling back." Hannah explained.

"Was it a man?"

"No, it was a female and she was whispering."

"What did she say?"

"She told me to mind my own business."

"Do you have even a clue who it might be?" Joe .

"No, not at all. The only thing that may make sense is the guy who was involved in the domestic incident this morning may have decided to scare me if he thinks I know what's going on. Maybe he had a friend of his call me. He may think that I'm hiding his girlfriend here because not only do we work together but we are really good friends."

"Hannah, could you take my number? I want you to have it just in case you run into trouble. You can call me anytime."

"You don't have to be concerned. I really appreciate..."

"Please Hannah, just do as I ask. Do you have a pen handy? Better yet if you have a cell phone and you can programme my numbers into it." Hannah retrieved her phone from her purse and remotely entered Joe's desk phone and his mobile phone.

"I'm feeling a little silly about this."

"Don't feel silly. This is just to be on the safe side." Joe admitted.

"Do you think something bad is going to happen?"

"Probably not, but I don't like the sound of this guy and honestly Hannah, I've seen so much that I just can't say for sure what he would and wouldn't do. And the fact that you and Sally are close, if he can't find her, he'll go where he thinks she might be. You might be an obvious choice."

"You're scaring me." Hannah laughed nervously.

"I don't want to, but I do want you to be careful."

"Thank you." Hannah said simply, although she wasn't really sure she felt thankful.

"I loved seeing you the other night. I've thought of little else." Joe suddenly admitted.

"I loved seeing you too. But Joe, I..." Hannah hesitated not quite sure how she could say that anything more than a friendship would be out of the question because she still wasn't convinced she could accept that prospect.

"Hannah, don't say anything. I know what you're going to say to me and I understand that you are unsure, but all I ask is to give me some time and appreciate my reservations right now." Joe insisted.

Hannah was silent once again and considered what he had said.

"Just a little more time, that's all I ask." Joe repeated hoping to prompt a response from her.

"Joe, more time isn't the issue here. I think we can both agree that no matter how much time goes by, it will not erase the past or who's involved in it." Hannah admitted, thinking of Kate.

"Hannah, I can't get into a protracted discussion about this and I know I am appearing very selfish, but if you feel compromised by my requests in any way, I will understand and leave you alone. Just say the word and I will walk away."

"I'm not feeling compromised, I'm feeling confused. I just don't see how this can ever work because it just seems so complicated." Hannah sputtered trying to calm her uncertainty.

"Look how about if you give me some time to prove that I'm asking you to wait for very good reason. Hannah I know we feel something for each other – obviously we do."

"Yes, I admit that but I don't want to hurt anyone."

"Hannah, I'm going to have to go, but I promise you I am doing this for you not for me. I'm not so insensitive that I would want to make things uncomfortable for you. So I will let time decide. Is that a deal?"

"Yes." Hannah said simply refusing to say anymore.

"But you'll call me if you need me?" Joe reminded her.

"Yes."

"Okay good. Remember to call me any time of the day or night." Joe insisted.

"Yes."

"Uh oh, we're back to those one word answers again." Joe teased and then he heard her laugh so that he felt sure that they could leave things on a lighter note.

"Sometimes you render me completely speechless." Hannah teased.

"I'll take that as a good thing. It was nice hearing your voice again. Good night Hannah."

"Good night."

CHAPTER 35

Hannah placed the phone back in the cradle and despite her earlier unsettling call, a feeling of calm and contentment settled in after their conversation.

"Have you finished your call?" Martha asked a few moments later as she descended the stairs from her bedroom.

"I have." Hannah called out.

"How did that go?"

"It was okay."

"Just okay huh?" Martha smiled.

"Well, you know what I mean. I can't put that Joe together with the Joe that Kate described. They almost seem like two different people." Hannah went on to relate the whole conversation to Martha who listened intently with her chin resting casually in her hands. Hannah finished her explanation with Martha offering her a sleepy smile.

"Don't start with that again." Hannah warned.

"With what?" Martha laughed pretending not to know what she was talking about.

"That smiling stuff and trying to make me laugh, that's what."

"I don't know what you're talking about." Martha replied innocently but still grinning.

A knock at the door interrupted the banter as Martha jumped up to answer it.

"Are you expecting someone?"

"No, I'm not, so make sure you see who it is before you open the door." Hannah warned.

"Oh, it's Kate." Martha announced as she opened the door.

Kate walked into the house and pushed past Martha demanding to know where Hannah was. Hannah, hearing the agitation in her voice, ran from the kitchen and into the hall to meet her.

"Kate, what's the matter?" Hannah said and opened up her arms to comfort her.

"Are you telling me you don't know or are you hoping I wouldn't notice?" Kate demanded.

"Notice what?" Hannah responded with bewilderment as her arms dropped vacantly to her sides.

"The police car that's parked outside your house! I thought we were friends. It's not enough that I poured out my heart to you the other night. It's as though you didn't hear a word that I was saying." Kate spat irrationally.

Hannah ran past her to the front door and looked out to see a police car parked opposite the house. She reeled back around clearly confused.

"I have no idea what that car is doing out there and I also have no idea why you are shouting at me. What does a police car have to do with the conversation we had the other night?" Hannah demanded.

"Do you want to play this game Hannah? Is that what you want?" Kate tested.

"What in the world are you talking about? I'm not playing any game and I really don't appreciate you barging into my house and raging at me without telling me why." Hannah said disbelievingly.

"So you're just going to keep up this charade by pretending to be a friend while you are sneaking behind my back." Kate alleged unkindly.

"Kate, I'm going to try and not be offended by your terrible accusation and I will give you one more chance to tell me what you are talking about." Hannah said evenly.

"Well let me put it into a term that will make sense to you."

"Go ahead."

"Joe." Kate sneered.

An uncomfortable silence fell between the two women. Hannah didn't know whether to laugh or cry and continued to look disbelievingly at Kate. Martha stood between both women looking from one to the other as though she were watching a tennis match.

"What about Joe?" Hannah prodded through gritted teeth.

"You know very well about Joe, so why can't you leave him alone?"

"Now wait a minute Kate…" Martha interjected. "You walk into this house just because a police car is parked on the street and that somehow gives you the right to come in here and accuse my sister of not being a good friend to you."

"You got upset the other night Hannah because someone was sneaking around your house and so miraculously a police car turns up outside. Obviously you decided to appeal to Joe to protect you." Kate spat, completely disregarding the fact that Martha had spoken to her.

"That police car has nothing to do with the other night and it has nothing to do with Joe. I have no idea why its there." Hannah snapped back, incensed that she was even continuing the exchange but feeling that she had to defend herself.

"It's there for you." Kate offered confidently.

"What do you mean its there for me?" Hannah said feeling a suddenly deflated by the air of confidence exhibited by Kate. Why did she suddenly feel like a lamb being led to the slaughter?

"I wondered why there was a cruiser parked outside and so I walked up to it, told the policeman who I was and where I lived, and asked why he was there. Because, stupid me, I thought maybe he was there for me, but he said no he was watching another house on the street. He said he wasn't able to disclose which one, but based on where he was parked, it was pretty evident to me that it was you he was protecting."

"You're playing a guessing game. This is really about your frustration over something you had conjured up in your mind and since it didn't play out in your favour, you got upset and decided to take it out on me." Hannah said incredulously.

"Nice try Hannah, but no, I think we both know what this is really about."

"I don't want to continue this conversation Kate. I think you are out of line here and maybe we should just end it now." Hannah offered trying to calm her inner anger and remain cool.

"Well that makes it easy doesn't it? No explanation which leaves me to go home with my tail between my legs. Then you can feel happy knowing that you manipulated me to believe your lies." Kate suggested unkindly.

Hannah was lost for words and acutely hurt by the exchange. She looked to Martha not necessarily for her to come to her defense but to see if Martha was reacting to the exchange in the same way.

"Look, if I can attempt to be the voice of reason here Kate why don't you do what Hannah suggests and end the conversation. I think you're overly upset and you need to go home to calm down." Martha suggested.

"Are you kidding? I don't need to calm down at all. I think I have a right to know why Hannah, as my friend, could be so deliberately selfish. I confided a very hurtful experience to Hannah, trusted her, and believed she was someone who cared about me, and I ended up being deceived and betrayed."

"That's enough Kate." Hannah warned.

"No, this is enough." Kate reached into her pocket and pulled out a black mask, the memento of Hannah's encounter with Joe.

"Where did you get that?" Hannah said momentarily stunned by what she thought had been lost was now found and in Kate's possession.

"You left it in my house the night of the party. But don't think that I wasn't aware of what led up to why you had this mask in the first place."

Hannah said nothing. She felt trapped and sick at heart. While she didn't feel Kate had the right to invade her home and treat her with such disrespect she also knew that Kate had correctly connected her to Joe. She felt completely leveled.

"At first, I didn't recognize Joe at the party because of the Zorro outfit, but I had to admit I was a bit intrigued by his interest in you, and so I watched to see what kind of move he would make. You were pretending not to know who he was, but something told me that you knew all along."

"I had no idea who he was but what's more incredible is that you were actually spying on me." Hannah said in disbelief.

"You call it spying and I call it protecting my interests, but the bottom line is I think what you were doing was far worse." Kate presented.

"This is ridiculous Kate." Hannah suggested with alarming concern.

"No it isn't. I was actually just looking for you that night and someone said you had gone outside so I went to find you. I walked out to the backyard and I saw the object of your affection walking through the branches of the willow tree which I thought was a bit strange and so I waited to see what he was doing. I realize now that you had arranged to meet him."

"I didn't arrange anything." Hannah said defensively. Her hope to remain cool had dissipated and was being replaced with fury.

"But you didn't tell him to go away did you?" Kate charged.

"No." She admitted feeling uneasiness in her stomach.

"Well, it disgusts me now to think what took place behind those branches because when they parted again, who should come back out without his mask but my ex-husband. I was so shocked that I couldn't say a word to him. After he walked away with this big beautiful smile on his face, I went to see what had captured his interest. I pulled the branches to one side and there you were with your eyes closed leaning contentedly against the tree trunk. You were so self-absorbed that you never saw me."

"And then you went back into the house and decided to drink away your sorrows and bait me into being so concerned about you, and I bought it hook, line, and sinker. Did it occur to you Kate that up until that point and really to this day, you never told me that Joe was your ex-husband?" Hannah offered feeling a bit mollified that this fact had just popped into her head.

"I didn't have to tell you, you knew." Kate snapped.

"I guessed and even then I wasn't sure. In fact the few times I have spoken to Joe, and I emphasize few, he has not mentioned you to me in that context or any context for that matter."

"Are you trying to make me feel better or are you trying to make me feel worse with that remark?"

"Neither actually. I'm trying to impress upon you that I have done nothing wrong except innocently becoming tangled up in your troubles and being demeaned for not playing your guessing game very well." Hannah stated with impatience.

"Well that's convenient to say it's a guessing game. I didn't owe you anything in the way of sharing my personal life." Kate defended somewhat weakly.

"This is crazy talk. You're going round in circles. One minute you want me to know everything about you and the next you want me to stand back as though I haven't the right to know anything. What's it going to be Kate?" Hannah demanded.

CHAPTER 36

The fact that Kate hadn't an appropriate comeback to Hannah's reasoning didn't prevent her from backing down. As she continued her criticism, her fingers unwittingly toyed with Joe's mask, repeatedly pulling and letting go of its elastic strapping so that it snapped rhythmically against the inside of the mask. It was the only evidence of any uneasiness Kate may have been having with this whole exchange. Hannah's glances scuttled back and forth from Kate's eyes to Joe's mask, silently hoping that she wouldn't pull so hard that the elastic would break.

"I don't think we need to split hairs on what's fitting and what's not Hannah. I find it a bit offensive that you are trying to protect yourself and that makes it even harder for me to accept that you have ever had my back." As she offered her final verbal slight, Kate pulled extra hard at the elastic so that it stretched beyond its limit and, to Hannah's horror, tore from its stapling.

Oh!" Hannah cried out as she watched the elastic fall from Kate's fingers and silently hit the floor. Kate seemed unaware that Hannah's reaction was focused on the injured mask rather than on her stinging words as she spun on her heels to leave still clutching the remnants of Hannah's keepsake. Hannah began to protest Kate's right to take the mask but something stopped her as she knew this would just invite further abuse.

Despite how ridiculous it seemed, she felt saddened to see it taken from her like an innocent hostage. As Kate slammed the front door on her way out, Hannah stood bewildered by the abruptness of her departure. She looked once again to the abandoned elastic and stooped down to gently rescue it as though it were a wounded child. She walked to the chesterfield where she sat down and tenderly laid the elastic across her lap. Up until that point, she hadn't realized that Martha was no longer in the room with her, but rather than go look for her, she simply waited. After a few minutes the front door began to open and Hannah slid forward in her place anticipating that it might be Kate again. To her relief, it was Martha accompanied by the police officer.

"Are you okay Hannah? I thought I would go and get the officer here because I wasn't comfortable with the way Kate was behaving." Martha explained.

Hannah simply nodded as though she didn't dare speak for fear of losing control of her emotions. She kept her head bent as she gently toyed the elastic band that lay limply across her knee, and despite her attempts to hide them, Martha witnessed the tears swell and fall from her eyes. Quietly, Martha made her way to Hannah and sat beside her and gently laid her hand on her sister's.

"Miss Hutton is there anything I can do for you?" The officer asked from across the room.

"I don't need anything, thank you. I think I'm just a little shell shocked, but otherwise, I'm fine." Hannah said simply.

"Did she threaten you in any way?"

"No." Hannah said halfheartedly. She thought he wouldn't be interested to know that Kate had threatened her with not being a good friend.

"Okay, well, I'll be outside if you need me." He offered kindly.

"Officer, I don't want to appear ungrateful, but why are you parked outside our house?" Hannah inquired.

"I was assigned to watch your home as a preventative measure because of a domestic issue that you were involved with this morning. It's just for tonight."

"But you don't have these types of assignments routinely just because there's a domestic dispute somewhere do you?"

"No, this was a specific assignment, but if you find it bothersome, I can request that it be called off."

"If it's just for tonight that should be fine. I don't think there will be a problem but I suppose its best to be safe, don't you Hannah?" Martha broke in since she was certain Hannah would insist that he leave.

"I suppose." Hannah hesitated as she was clearly not convinced.

"I'll be outside." The officer reiterated and left the house, pulling the front door closed behind him.

"Kate's behaviour was beyond awful Hannah." Martha said quietly. "I'm so sorry."

"I don't know what to say, what to think, or how to even begin to process all of this."

"What you need to think is that she was so out of line and had no right to come in here as though she owned the place and accuse you of complete nonsense."

"That whole exchange was exhausting, but I stand guilty on some of what she said. It wasn't all nonsense."

"I don't care how guilty you are! She does not have a right to treat you that way." Martha charged. "Come on Hannah, you aren't going to sit here and try and convince me that any of that was the least bit okay."

"No, I'm not trying to convince you of anything. I haven't done anything to deliberately hurt Kate and so I can't lose sleep over our friendship because I believe it's damaged beyond repair. I don't expect that she shouldn't be upset with me, but it's the way she handled the whole thing that really offends me. Why would I want to be a friend to anyone who imposes their reality on you and cares nothing about your perception? She wasn't even remotely interested in giving me the benefit of the doubt or in hearing my side of things. If I were that upset I would want to make it better, not worse, and the only way that can be done is to talk it out sensibly. But, she continued to assault me with her opinion and her accusations. I don't say this conveniently to get me off the hook, but I just don't think Kate had any interest in preserving our friendship."

"Why do you say that?" Martha said with surprise.

"None of this needed to happen if she were honest with me from the very beginning. It's as though there's still something she's not telling me. As hard as it was to take her abuse, I was hoping we could get past all the craziness and get to the truth."

"So what do you think it was really about?"

"Peripherally I think it is about Joe. Joe is what gives her the reason

171

to stomp around and behave so territorially. But directly I don't think it is about him. From the very moment she realized I knew Joe, she continued to keep their relationship hush-hush. So I have to ask myself why she would do that. She thought Joe was interested in me, so why not simply say that they were once married."

"Because he was her ex-husband and she doesn't have a right to him anymore."

"I don't think so Martha. I believe there is something more to this, something that she isn't prepared to tell me."

"So you think she's holding back something that she doesn't want you to know?"

"She said she had witnessed Joe secretly meeting me the night of the party, but she didn't react nearly as aggressively as when she saw the police car parked outside our house. If you think about it, what would distress you more?" Hannah offered logically.

"Of course, his meeting you at the party would have." Martha admitted.

"When I think back to the night of the party, despite her being drunk, she was very controlled and systematic about what she was saying, almost as though she knew exactly what she was going to say. That police car seemed to trigger something for her. That's what I think she is hiding." Hannah presented as she picked at the elastic and then took it in her hand. "I need time to think this through and try and make sense of it. But right now, I need a break from it all and I would like just to go upstairs and take a long hot bath."

"Good idea Hannah. Try to relax and not to think anything more about Kate."

Hannah kissed her sister gently on the cheek and made her way out of the living room up the stairs to her bedroom. She opened her cupboard door and reached up to an old tin box that she kept on the top shelf. It was a tin that visually held no charm, but she held onto it because it used to belong to her mother. What once held thread, needles, straight pins and buttons was now used for Hannah's keepsakes and special mementos mostly related to her parents. As silly as she felt, she wanted to keep the elastic in a safe place and thought that this was the best place for it. As she nestled it into the tin, she closed the lid and slid the box back into its usual resting place.

CHAPTER 37

The week that followed was quiet and as the days wore on the absence of Kate in Hannah's life was palpable. The season turned from autumn to winter seemingly overnight when one morning Hannah woke to a delicate sifting of snow that had fallen and coated the ground. On this morning, she shivered against the wind as she made her way outside, her footprints stamping the frosty ground evidencing her path to the car. After unlocking her car door, she slid into the driver's seat and turned the ignition. As the car began to warm, she watched the icy skin on the windows slide away offering her a better view outside.

Her eyes fell to the rearview mirror that reflected the houses across the road, and in particular Kate's home. It appeared ordinary in its existence, but Hannah felt empty as she looked to that house now with discriminating eyes. It no longer reflected a place of comfort and familiarity but one that was now uncomfortable and strange. Despite her conviction not to be adversely affected by Kate, she felt emotionally bruised by her accusations and sad to feel that a friend could turn on her so easily. She wondered how she would function as a neighbour to someone she now had to turn away from and pretend wasn't there. As though to escape these thoughts, she put the car into reverse and gently rolled the car out of the driveway and made her way to work.

Once she had arrived, Paul had been waiting for her and pleased to confirm that he had spoken with Robert and firmed up preferred dates for Hannah to travel to London. She was even more grateful now with the prospect of traveling overseas to put some distance between her and Kate. To her surprise, the dates were sooner than she expected and Paul asked if she could get her itinerary together to travel in a week's time.

"Yes, I can finish putting together an itinerary." Hannah assured.

"Okay, I think the best thing to do is look at some flights and give yourself a day or two before your meeting with Robert so you can get your bearings and rest up a bit. I'm sorry Sally isn't here to do this for you, but I think maybe you would prefer to plan your own flights." Paul suggested.

"That's fine with me and it makes sense. I meant to call Sally last night to see how she is and let her know I haven't abandoned her."

Hannah avoided any explanation about her experience with Kate since it would upset Paul. She felt it was enough that he was looking after Sally and she didn't want to add to his concerns. Sally had been comfortably installed in Paul's home once they had moved her from Gabriella's. It took some doing because they were worried that they would leave the apartment at the wrong time and run into Grayson. It was left to Gabriella to put a plan in place.

Acting as though she were leaving for the day, she accompanied Grayson down to the underground parking lot and followed him as he drove out of the neighbourhood. Calling from her cell phone, she gave the all clear to Josh whom she had enlisted to escort Sally out of the apartment, a task that Josh was only too pleased to accept. Just to be sure, Sally was disguised wearing a dark red wig that transformed her from a natural pale blonde. She was then successfully transported from the safety and somewhat vulnerable surroundings of Gabriella's apartment to Paul and Jane's home on the outskirts of town.

"She knows that you haven't abandoned her Hannah. She has told me many times how grateful she is to you for getting her out of a terrible situation. She seems much happier and she is stronger in her conviction to break away from her relationship with Grayson. It doesn't hurt either that Josh has been a frequent visitor to our home and calls daily to make sure she is okay. I think everything will work out for her, it just may take a little time to get used to." He offered practically.

"Sometimes life can offer us chances to make better decisions for ourselves, and I guess we have to be brave enough to believe in those decisions."

"It does Hannah but that sounds like wishful thinking rather than conclusive thinking."

"Well actually it's a little of both. I think when we can't see our way clear to make the best decisions for ourselves, opportunities or situations come along that almost force our hand."

"And sometimes we don't take those opportunities because we're more comfortable with what we know." Paul suggested.

"Yes, but its only when we know better that we do better but getting to that point is hard because sometimes we have to do it alone and that makes it scary."

"Fear of the unknown."

"Yes fear of the unknown. And about taking chances and having the courage of your convictions." Hannah stated and looked at her Uncle Paul with a smile but it was an unconvincing one. He now realized that Hannah was referring to herself and looking for reassurance.

"Well Hannah if I were a betting man, I would bet my life that you have the courage within you to stay true to your convictions. Don't let anyone or anything sway you."

Hannah simply smiled at her uncle and offered him a grateful hug. "Thank you for being an unwavering presence in my life. You offer sensibility to my life when even I can't see it for myself." He returned her hug and held her until he knew whatever thoughts were haunting her had subsided to a more manageable level. "Go book your flights." Paul offered encouragingly.

She retreated to her office where she focused her attention on finding flights to London. Before leaving for the day, she had booked a return ticket with her departure scheduled in one week's time. Her thoughts were crowded with the anticipation of London as she made her way down the elevator to her car in the underground parking. When she attempted to start her car, the engine was dead and after a few more attempts, she decided to call Paul from her cell phone.

"Does it turn over at all?" Paul asked after she explained her dilemma.

"No, not at all. Should I wait here and see if someone can give me a boost?" Hannah asked.

"I don't like the thought of you being down there waiting around for someone to come along. Why don't you come back up here to wait while I call a tow truck? They can either boost you or tow you."

Hannah was relieved to get out of the underground and went back up to her office where Paul met her to let her know that help was on its way.

"Give me your keys and I'll go down and wait for the tow truck. This shouldn't take too long." Paul assured.

Approximately half an hour later, Paul arrived back at the office and reported that they had towed her car because they suspected it was the starter.

"Unfortunately you are without a car for the evening, so I will drive you home."

"Don't be silly, you live in the opposite direction to me. Martha won't be home until late otherwise I would ask her to come and get me, so I'll call a cab instead." Hannah insisted. After a bit of arm twisting, Paul finally relented and agreed that Hannah would take a cab home.

CHAPTER 38

The taxi arrived and Hannah settled into the back seat and peered out the window to watch as a moderate snow began to fall. Hannah remembered the weather reports in the morning predicting a heavy snow fall for later in the day. Evening was closing in as the darkness offered a backdrop to the falling snowflakes that were illuminated from the headlights of oncoming traffic.

Within half an hour Hannah was safely home. The snowfall was now so heavy and accumulating on the ground so quickly that by the time Hannah walked from the taxi to her front door, her footprints had been completely obliterated. 'Like I wasn't even here.' Hannah thought as she pushed her key into the lock.

Safely inside she locked the door, hung up her coat, and kicked off her boots and placed them on a mat inside the hall closet. Hannah left the ground floor in darkness and ran up to her bedroom to change from her workday clothes. Feeling more settled in a cozier outfit, she ran back down the stairs to the living room and set some logs in the fireplace. She struck a single match and held it steadily against a pre-set bundle of paper and kindling and waited for the paper to catch. The fire threw a gentle light into the room casting subtle shadows that danced against the walls. The projection of reflected light off the snow outside dominated and overruled the light inside. Hannah made her way into the kitchen and turned on a small lamp and began to prepare a salad for her dinner. She looked out her window as the blizzard continued to build a snowy covering in her backyard. The tranquility of her surroundings was broken by the phone ringing. She faltered briefly wondering if it would an unwelcomed caller, but to her relief it was Martha.

"Hi Hannah, I just wanted to check to make sure you had made it home safely in the storm."

"I made it home safe and sound but my car didn't." Hannah explained that her car had been towed to a local shop and she was hoping to hear that evening of the damage.

"Well, Adam and I were just saying it might be better to stay downtown in a hotel tonight rather than make our way home. We're here for at least another three hours and by the looks of it, the snow is not going to let up anytime soon. Would you be okay with that?"

"I'm definitely okay with that. It's probably best if you just stay put and enjoy some extra glasses of wine. I'll be fine." Hannah talked for a few brief moments with Martha before saying goodbye and then placing the phone back in its cradle. It was then that she noticed that the living room was shrouded in darkness. She realized that the fire had gone out and so Hannah grabbed the matches from the kitchen counter in order to relight it. She made her way into the living room and as she gingerly negotiated her path, her attention was captured by someone passing the living room window.

'Not Again!' She thought as she quickly lowered herself to her knees to hide behind the chesterfield. A wave of déjà vu washed over her as she watched the form turn to look in through the frosted window and then continue its path towards her front door. Hannah quickly rose to her feet realizing that her reaction was ridiculous since this could not be the same mysterious figure that visited over a month ago. As then, she expected to hear a knock at the door but instead she heard a key slide into the lock.

'That's strange,' she thought. No one had a key to the house except Martha and Adam. Logically she knew it would have been a miracle for Martha to have made it home so quickly. Given this, Hannah's instincts were to resume her earlier position and lightly kneeled down again to hide herself behind the chesterfield. The house remained in complete darkness with the exception of the small lamp that offered a gentle glow from within the kitchen. Whoever had placed the key in the lock had been successful in entering the house as Hannah could now hear the distinct sound of the rustle of a ski jacket. Hannah remembered that Martha wore her long black coat to work that morning, and this further confirmed that the person in her home was not someone who Hannah would expect to have a key. No words were spoken, no one called out to announce their arrival, and so Hannah waited. Her vulnerability and exposure were the only two things that were protected by the darkness that encircled her.

The rustling of the jacket became louder as the figure entered the room and unsuspectingly came into Hannah's line of vision. Because of the darkness that enveloped the room, Hannah could see that her visitor was waiting for their eyes to adjust to the surrounding darkness. Ideally, turning on a light would instantly solve this problem, but it was clear that this was not a choice that this trespasser was willing to take. Hannah was unable to distinguish any facial features because of the oversized hood on the ski jacket. She hoped that once the hood was pulled back it would expose the intruder's identity. Her hopes were extinguished as she watched the hooded form turn and run in heavy winter boots up the stairs to the second floor.

Hannah's mind raced with a flood of actions she thought of taking, but stalled in choosing any of them since they would all put her in a vulnerable position. She realized that any attempt to move from the place that masked her presence would invite the intruder's notice and possibly put her in uncertain danger. As her thoughts collided crazily in her head, Hannah could hear the heavy footfalls overhead that confirmed the intruder was securely busying themselves upstairs. 'I might have time to leave the house without being noticed.' She thought, but then realized that she would have to put on her boots and coat which most certainly would steal precious time. And then the realization hit her that she would not be able to go anywhere without her car. To her horror, it then occurred to Hannah that with the house shrouded in darkness, no car in the driveway, and no dinner cooking in the oven it offered the intruder the belief that no one was home. Since this was most certainly someone breaking into her home, she had no choice but to leave and solicit help.

The weather was so bad that if she set out on foot, it would with all certainty persist in making any progress nearly impossible. It then occurred to her that she had no other choice but to swallow her pride and enlist Kate's help. She hoped that Kate would overlook their terrible fight and shelter Hannah in her time of need. Hannah cautiously made her way to the front entranceway and slipped on her boots. She waited briefly and listened for sounds upstairs that would ensure her extra time to execute her escape. She recognized the sounds of rifling through drawers and almost instinctively Hannah wanted to run up the stairs and stop the intruder from invading her privacy. Determinedly shaking the thoughts from her head, she reached for her heavy coat from the hall closet and bundled herself inside it before quietly opening her front door.

Hannah pushed against the door as the wind blew furiously as she attempted to make her way outside. Despite her instinct to run in a straight path to Kate's house, she decided to make her movements less obvious and skirted the front of the house and moved across the side lawn to her next door neighbour's driveway. The blizzard aided her escape by obliterating all traces of footprints that would otherwise implicate her. After having made her way down the neighbour's driveway, she now only had to cross the road to where she hoped she would be welcomed. She huddled against the wind and biting cold, looking back only briefly to her house. It held her gaze for only seconds as she thought about how deliberate this person's intentions seemed to be. The snow assaulted her face as she steeled herself against returning home and seconds later arrived at Kate's door.

"Kate, Kate!" She screamed as she banged her gloved fists furiously against the door, but there was no answer. Hannah pulled back and looked to see that the house was partially lit. 'She must be home.' Hannah thought and then realized that her gloves must be muffling the sound of her knocking. She tugged at the gloves to pull them off when it occurred to her to try the doorknob. With one jerk to the right the door unlatched and Hannah pushed hard against it. She stepped inside Kate's front hall, pulled the door shut against the storm, and continued calling Kate's name, but there was no answer. Stooping down, she pulled off her boots and deciding not to leave them in the front hall, carried them inside and once again called out Kate's name. Still no answer.

CHAPTER 39

Hannah thought that she must be possibly upstairs bathing or lying down. Before she went to check upstairs, she stepped into the living room to look out the front window where she had a perfect view to her own home. She was hoping that there may be an indication that the intruder had left, but given the short amount of time that had passed, Hannah felt sure they were still there. Just as she was turning away from the window, she noticed as her front door open and the hooded figure cautiously made its way outside and into the blizzard.

As though following in Hannah's footsteps, the figure followed her path to the next door neighbour's house and ran down the driveway. Hannah watched as it made its way across the road heading in the direction of Kate's home. Feeling vulnerable and likely in full view at the front window, Hannah ran upstairs hoping she would find Kate in her room. As she reached the top of the staircase, she heard the whoosh of the front door causing a gust of icy wind to race up the stairs as if to hunt her down. She wasn't quite sure who had just made their way into the house, so to be safe, she slipped quietly into Kate's room and sought shelter in the clothes closet. The louvered doors offered her a protectively obscured view into the room.

Hannah sat awkwardly in amongst Kate's shoes hugging her knees tightly to her chest. Her pulse thundered in fear as she listened to the sound of footsteps approaching. Within seconds the bedroom was flooded with light, and although the vantage point from where she sat did not offer her a proper view, she could hear the distinct sound of the rustle of a ski jacket. With its back to her, the figure came into sight and stopped at the foot of Kate's bed. She heard a clattering as the figure threw something on the bed. Hannah peered through the wooden slats as it shrugged out of the ski jacket and let it drop to the floor disclosing the intruder's identity.

Hannah felt revulsion knowing now that the hooded figure that had been rummaging through her home was Kate. She now wondered if the silhouette that had passed her window just one month ago was Kate. And then she remembered Kate's call that same evening and wondered if she was checking to see if Hannah had recognized her walking past her window. Reasoning and confusion crashed in Hannah's head as she tried to make sense of it all. She watched as Kate settled onto the bed sitting side saddle and began looking at the items she had casually thrown there. Kate lifted a framed photograph and studied it closely. Hannah had to repress a cry of alarm as she recognized it as a picture of her parents.

Kate casually threw the picture on the bed and then picked up another. Again, Hannah recognized the frame as one featuring a picture of her with Martha and her parents taken shortly before her parents died. Hannah felt violated and panicked by the intrusion as she tried to come to terms with Kate's need to take them. The next in her repertoire of stolen items was the tin box that Hannah kept in her bedroom cupboard's top shelf. Hannah felt a tear slide down her cheek as she watched Kate pull items out one by one and examine them with rapt interest. The one that seemed to capture her curiosity to the greatest extent was a newspaper clipping that reported the events surrounding the tragic deaths of her parents.

With every bit of conviction she held within her, Hannah remained steadfast to her spot agonizing over her impulse to explode through the louvered doors and rescue her possessions. Finally Kate's attention was broken from the items splayed out on her bed when she walked to the window to look out across the street seemingly studying Hannah's house. As she pensively watched, the snow slammed against the window, sticking and then sliding away as though trying but not able to shield against further intrusion into Hannah's life. Kate turned away from the window with tears slipping down her face as her fingers tried hopelessly to wipe them away. Hannah was fascinated by this display of raw emotion. How could these items even slightly have this affect on her? Despite her confusion, she was fascinated by the performance.

Kate walked back to sift through the tin box and pulled out a necklace that Martha and Hannah had bought for their mother for her last Mother's Day gift. Kate held it up against the bedroom's light as the single diamond dangled from the platinum chain and flickered radiantly. Placing it delicately around her neck, she secured the clasp so that the chain fell securely against her chest. Her fingers played tenderly with the diamond where it rested as though to assure herself that's where it belonged. She then picked up the fallen ski jacket and walked out of her bedroom flicking out the bedroom light as she left.

Hannah sat quietly in the darkness feeling worn out with the events that had played out before her. Distress was the least of what she was feeling as she reflected on and dissected each action in which Kate had involved her over that last few months. She had only scratched the surface of knowing who this person really was and who she was professing to be. Hannah was certain now that whatever had driven Kate's antagonism was indirectly related to Joe but directly related somehow to the items that were now left abandoned on Kate's bed. Feeling resolute in her determination that Kate's intentions were beyond Hannah's control, her next course of action was to try and leave the confines of the closet and return home.

Working quietly within her cramped quarters, she grabbed a cotton shirt that was hanging in the cupboard and wiped dry the soles of her own boots and slipped them on with little effort. She marveled quietly to herself why she had thought of not leaving them at the front door when she arrived. They most certainly would have been a conspirator to revealing her presence in the house. Not only would she then have been at Kate's mercy, but she would not have discovered the proof behind Kate's clandestine intentions to break into her home and take her things. Stealing them was one thing, but why she was stealing them was what truly mystified Hannah. They should mean little or nothing to anyone else. It did shore up her resolve that Kate's strange behaviour was focused on Hannah and she was determined to find out why.

Hannah perched on all fours in the cupboard and listened carefully for sounds from downstairs in order to try and position Kate. She thought of ways to leave the house without notice, but despite knowing exactly where Kate was, she was determined it had to be a sensible escape. She even entertained the option of casually walking down the stairs and straight out through the front door but then realized how self defeating that would be. She had to keep her wits about her and be smart about how to execute her getaway. The worst scenario was to stay hidden in the closet and wait until Kate went to bed and fell asleep, but that could take hours. The good thing was that Martha wasn't home and she wouldn't be missed at all. Luckily, Hannah would not have to wait that long as another opportunity presented itself when Kate came upstairs and went into the bathroom to draw a bath. Once again, the bedroom was flushed in light as Kate came in to grab her night clothes and retreat once again leaving the room in darkness.

CHAPTER 40

The wait for the bathtub to fill seemed interminable and Hannah felt a swell of impatience filling her. Finally she heard the tap being turned off and sounds of water swishing signaling Kate climbing into the tub, but admittedly, Hannah wasn't sure. Two minutes went by and Hannah decided that she at least had to try and get to the bedroom door to get a better sense of Kate's location. Slowly and quietly, she pulled back the closet door. It swooshed almost silently on its tracks and Hannah slipped out from her hiding place.

She crept methodically to the door and peaked out to where the bathroom was positioned down the hall. The vantage point gave her no benefit at all except she could see the bathroom door was slightly open. The only way she would locate Kate was is if she actually took the chance to look through the opening. Taking a deep breath and silently encouraging herself, she stepped out into the hall and tip-toed haltingly the few steps to the bathroom. One creak in the floor would give her up and so each step was like anticipating a land mine. She finally arrived at the bathroom and held her hair back against her head so it wouldn't drop into full view. Slowly she edged her face closer to peer into the steamy room. Her eyes took in Kate reaching her hands up to shampoo her hair and Hannah leaned back and pressed her hands in relief to her face. She retraced her steps to move cautiously back towards the top of the stairs.

It was so difficult for her to walk past the bedroom that held her possessions, but she needed to leave them undisturbed just as Kate had left them. Despite knowing that Kate was busily preoccupied with her bathing, Hannah's heart was hammering in her chest in anticipation of being discovered. Finally she made it to the front door and opened it to be greeted by a welcomed blast of the winter storm that she had left only two hours ago. As cold as it was, it signaled her freedom. The safety and comfort of her home awaited her and she bolted through the heavy snow to her front entrance and turned the door knob. To her horror, it was locked.

Hannah realized with absolute dread that she had left her house without a key, forgetting that Kate had used a stolen key to unlock and relock the door. She had no choice and little time but to run back to Kate's to see if she could find the key to her own house. She turned back and ran painstakingly through the heavy snow to the house that only minutes before she was so grateful to have left. She opened the front door and made her way back inside as her heart thumped crazily once more in anticipation of running into Kate. She wasn't even sure where Kate was at this point but she hoped that she was still lazing contentedly in her bathtub. Hannah crept into the living room and searched quietly but frantically for the key. As though to break the silence, a door shut upstairs signaling that she didn't have a lot of time.

She then spotted Kate's purse that had been left by the coffee table. She pulled the zipper back on the soft burgundy pouch and dug her fingers through its contents until finally she felt the distinct shape of a ring of keys. The ring held about six keys all similar in size and shape to each other, but one appeared much newer than the rest. Perhaps the newer one was just cut, Hannah thought. New or not, she had at least six opportunities that one key belonged to her house. Hannah edged her way to the front door and out into the cold night as the biting wind greeted her once again. Just as she was pulling it shut behind her she heard Kate call out.

Her call was an inquisitive hello, the kind when one senses that someone may be nearby without actually seeing them. Hannah waited pressing herself against the outer wall of the house, and despite the biting cold, she was not prepared to run down the driveway in case Kate was at the window waiting and watching. To make headway and to assure she was out of Kate's range of sight, she decided to cross to the neighbours' homes directly to her right. She felt exhausted as she trudged painstakingly through the snow stalling for time before she felt it was safe to cross the road to her house.

She overshot her house by two so that if Kate were watching, it would look as though Hannah had walked from another direction to her home. She walked the length of her driveway to her front door resisting the temptation to turn in the direction of Kate's home to see if she were under surveillance. She pulled the keys from her pocket and slid the newest one first into her lock and turned. It didn't budge. Hannah stalled only briefly before trying another and then another. Finally on the fourth attempt, the chosen key slid smoothly into the slot and with nearly frozen fingers, Hannah turned it easily to the right until she heard the welcomed sound of a click. Without looking back, she pushed her door open and stepped gratefully into the entranceway and locked the door behind her.

Without taking a chance to advertise that she wasn't home, Hannah went from room to room switching on lights but closing curtains and blinds so as to safely obscure her from Kate's inspection. Her thoughts cluttered her mind confusing her so that she wasn't really sure what to do next. Disturbing Martha and Adam at this point would only distress them and they would only want to come home which, given the weather, was next to impossible. She mentally went through a list of people whom she could call but she realized all would be in the same situation as Martha and Adam – impeded by the weather. She knew it would be reckless to let the evening's events go without advising authorities and she knew that all those on her list would insist on the same action. She would have to call the police.

CHAPTER 41

Hannah ran upstairs to her bedroom to look for her purse hoping that her cell phone was still part of its contents. It was Hannah's habit when she got home to slide her purse under her bed while Martha would laugh and call her paranoid, but she would say she did it to keep the threat of bill collectors at bay.

While it could be put down as simple superstition or simple security, Hannah was thankful that her daily ritual was going to pay off. Reaching under the bed she found her purse where her cell phone still nestled in its individual compartment. She flipped its silver facing open and scrolled through her contact list until Joe's name was highlighted. She stared at his name and her thoughts ricocheted between whether to call him or not to call him. What was stopping her was her attraction to him and while she knew she had good reason to call, it suddenly now seemed feeble in its import.

For one or two minutes she repeatedly flipped the phone's cover open and shut depending on her comfort level in making the call. The solitude of her home offered her a sense of calm until she heard an indecipherable sound from outside. It propelled her out of her sense of doubt and without hesitating she flipped open the phone and once again found Joe's number. She pressed send and watched the phone's panel indicating that his number was being dialed. Her heart thumped unreasonably as she waited for him to pick up. To her disappointment, her call went to his voicemail and while her instinct was to hang up, she knew he would likely have call display and so she decided to leave a short message.

"Hi Joe, it's me Hannah. I'm sorry to bother you, but I wonder if you have a minute could you please call me? I know this may sound strange, but I've had a break in of sorts and I didn't want to call the police before talking to you first. It's a bit complicated. Thanks Joe. Bye."

Hannah flipped her phone shut. 'God, what was I thinking? I should never have called him. How in the world am I going to explain that his ex-wife broke into my home?' Hannah thought as she mentally reproached herself. She decided that she would soothe her conscience by preparing a light meal and then she would turn in for the night.

Half an hour later, Hannah had turned out all but two lights downstairs and retreated to her bedroom where she got ready for bed. Once tucked under her covers, the full impact of the evening hit her as she was struck with overwhelming fatigue. She flipped out the lamp on her night table and turned to watch the snow continue to fall and dance past her window hypnotizing her into peaceful slumber.

Another half hour passed by and as a deeper sleep and dreams took hold, a quiet melody began to play over and over again in Hannah's head until she was forced into full consciousness. She realized it was her cell phone ringing and she immediately grabbed it from her nightstand.

"Hello?" She said sleepily.

"Hannah, its Joe. Are you alright?"

"Joe! Yes, I'm fine, thanks. I'm sorry I was just asleep and didn't realize that my phone was ringing."

"I'm sorry it took so long to call you, but I only just got your message and wanted to call you back right away."

"What time is it?" Hannah asked still feeling a bit disoriented.

"Its midnight. Hannah you said you had a break in. Are you too tired to tell me what happened? " Hannah was exhausted, but decided she had better explain the events that had unfolded. He listened intently without saying a word until Hannah had completely finished speaking. The only detail that she couldn't bring herself to offer to him was Kate's name, but instead she referred to her simply as a neighbour.

"Did you call the police when you couldn't get hold of me?" Joe asked plainly.

"No, because it was my neighbour and I must admit I was really unsure what to do." Hannah admitted.

"Hannah is there a reason that you are protecting your neighbour? Because, under the circumstances, you shouldn't be."

"No, not really."

"Not really?

"No, its not really my neighbour I'm protecting." Hannah offered.

"Then who are you protecting?" Joe asked quizzically.

"You." Hannah offered.

"Me?"

"Yes, you."

"Hannah, what in the world are you talking about?" Joe insisted gently.

"Joe, the neighbour who broke in to my house tonight is Kate."

"Kate Robinson?"

"Yes. Look, Joe, I didn't call you to upset you. I know this may seem like an incredible coincidence, but Kate lives across the street from me."

"Are you certain it was Kate who broke in?" Joe probed.

"Yes." Hannah offered simply. An uncomfortable silence fell between them as Hannah waited for a response from Joe. When none came, Hannah thought that perhaps she lost her connection with Joe's phone.

"Are you still there?" Hannah asked softly.

"Yes."

"I've upset you."

"No, you haven't upset me at all. It's you who should be upset. But I have to admit that I'm a bit confused by something you said earlier."

"What was that?"

"You said that you were trying to protect me."

"Yes of course. Even though you and Kate are no longer married, I'm not so insensitive to think that it would be hard to hear me accuse her of breaking into my home."

"What did you say?" Joe said with an edge to his tone.

"I said..." Hannah faltered.

"You said that we were no longer married." Joe broke in.

"Yes."

"Hannah. Kate is not my ex-wife."

"What do you mean she isn't your ex-wife?"

"Well, I don't know how to say it any differently. She is not my ex-wife or any wife for that matter. I've never been married."

CHAPTER 42

Seconds went by although it seemed hours before anyone spoke. Hannah felt certain that she had offended Joe but wasn't sure why.

"You've never been married to Kate?" Hoping if she said it a bit differently it may clarify the confusion she was feeling.

"No. Don't you remember the night of the party I told you I wasn't married?"

"Yes, I remember." Hannah said quietly.

"But you forgot?"

"No, I thought…"

"You thought that I was trying to hide that from you? Why do you think that I was married to Kate?"

"Kate said you were married." Hannah was now fully awake, sitting upright in her bed and feeling very uncomfortable.

"It has never even existed as a simple thought to date her let alone marry her."

"Joe, I'm sorry, but she told me you had been married to her. After I met you that night under the willow tree at my sister's engagement party, I went into the house to find her and she was so drunk and upset. I took her outside to try and sober her up and she told me how much she still loved you and that she just couldn't seem to get over the fact that her marriage with you was over. Up until that point, I only thought the two of you were friends. Then when I took her home, I saw a photograph of the two of you which made me think she must have been telling me the truth." Hannah explained desperately.

"Well, she's good, I'll give her that." Joe said almost laughing, but clearly not amused.

"Why do you say that?" Hannah said with confusion.

"I met Kate during my university days and one night a group of us went out to a bar. We were all sitting around having a few drinks and all of a sudden she became really flushed and began complaining about her heart beating wildly and she felt sick to her stomach. She then started having trouble breathing. The only reason I remember this is because someone finally called 911 and we were all pretty scared. We thought she was having a heart attack. Anyway, one of her friends went with her to the hospital, and after they did some tests, they concluded that she had an intolerance to alcohol."

"You mean she's allergic to alcohol?"

"No when the doctors examined her they said that alcohol isn't an allergen but she has an intolerance to it. Apparently it's quite rare and varies from person to person but the affects can be horrible. So, even if she was drinking that night with you, and I suspect she wasn't, she would have had a severe reaction to it. My guess is she was pretending to be drunk so she could lure you into believing her confessions and convince you that I was a monster so you would stay away."

"But why the act? She could have easily told me the same thing without pretending to be drunk."

"A lot of people believe that drunken minds speak sober truth. You could call it drunken poetry. I suspect she hoped to plant a seed, and then hope you would think that because she was drunk she was speaking the truth."

Hannah was speechless, feeling foolish and betrayed. Joe took advantage of this silence to fill in some of the gaps that hopefully would convince Hannah of his truth rather than Kate's.

"Hannah I don't want to sound boastful but when I first met Kate she pursued me very aggressively. She was and still is a very determined woman. At first I was tempted and enthralled by her because she was not only beautiful, but willing and able. Those were the discovery days of freedom, booze, and sexuality with little regard for the consequences. Like all my buddies, I joined in for all the temptations. My mistake was giving in to her, but I was young and naïve and I treated the whole thing very casually. I'm not proud of this Hannah but I used her. I never gave her any reason to believe that I had any other interest in her other than a sexual one. I never asked her out and I never wanted to be with her on a full time basis. I didn't realize that this must have really hurt her. Despite that, I kept my distance. The exception was when we were out together as a group of friends."

Hannah thought back to the evening of the party when she took the tea up to Kate's bedroom. She remembered that the only photograph of Joe with Kate was the group one and if she were to look at that photograph again, it would qualify what Joe was saying as being the truth.

"I honestly believed that she had gotten past her obsession and I am so sorry you have been dragged into this unnecessarily." Joe stated resolutely. "Are you still there Hannah?"

"Yes, I'm here. I'm listening and trying to put everything in order from my perspective. I'm sorry that I questioned what you were saying and thought you may have been misleading me. Kate had told me that she moved here to start a new life and then you reappeared in her life and it just seemed to make sense that she was telling the truth." Hannah said faintly. "When Kate finally told me that you were married, I wondered why you would simply not tell me."

"I know this is hard Hannah, but she has been lying to you." Joe stated carefully.

"I have come to the realization that Kate has been lying to me for a long time, and this may sound strange, but I think there is more to her lying than a woman being infatuated with a man. I hope that doesn't hurt your feelings when I say that."

"I'm not offended in the least and actually I agree with you."

"You do?"

"I do, but I'm curious to find out why you think so."

"I have had some unexplainable things happen recently involving Kate, but I wouldn't say they link to you. Soon after I met her, Kate asked me about my family and I told her that my parents died ten years ago in a car accident."

"How did she react?"

"She was sympathetic and asked if I kept any special memories of them or saved anything related to the accident. I told her that I kept those sorts of things in my room because I felt they were protected there. And then she asked if she could see them. I remember feeling hesitant but excited because after so many years having passed it was rare that anyone asked about my parents."

"So you showed her those things?" Joe prompted.

"I didn't show her anything related to the accident explaining that it was personal and also very hard for me to look at, let alone show anyone else. So I only showed her a few photographs thinking that she might have been curious about what my parents looked like. She seemed only mildly interested which is understandable since she never knew them. But I do remember that she seemed really drawn to one photograph of my mother and father taken about a month before they died and then out of the blue she asked what had caused their car accident. For whatever reason, I didn't give her any details."

"Maybe it was because you sensed her disinterest." Joe concluded.

"Yes that may have been it. In any case, I just told her their car hit an icy patch on the road. She seemed genuinely sympathetic and said that at least I had saved some very special memories of them. So I find it incredibly upsetting that she would break into my house to steal those memories. When I watched her rummage through all my personal things, she started to cry. At first I thought she was suddenly struck with a conscience and was feeling badly about taking my things. But now I believe that those tears were not from guilt or concern but from relief."

"Why do you say that?"

"If she were feeling badly about what she had done she would have put everything back where it belonged and closed the lid. Instead, she took out a necklace that we gave to our mother and she put it around her neck as though to console herself with it. I don't know why she was even remotely interested in that box, but she clearly felt entitled to it, and wasn't the least bit concerned that I would be missing it."

CHAPTER 43

As Hannah spoke Joe heard the anguish elevating in her voice and decided it was best not to prolong the conversation.

"Hannah, do you remember what I asked of you that night under the willow tree?"

"You asked me to not say anything to anyone about our encounter."

"I am going to ask you once more to trust me and let me take care of things from here. If you can, try not to have any contact with Kate. Can you do that please?" Joe proposed.

"I can quite easily because she is angry with me and I haven't had any contact with her for over a week now."

"Well, if she has an ulterior motive, she may realize that it isn't serving her well not to be talking to you. So, in case she has a change of heart, please try and steer clear of her."

"I will be going to London, England on a business trip early next week, so I won't have a choice but to be out of sight."

"I feel better knowing that. What day do you leave?"

"Next Wednesday, very early in the morning. That's the only part I'm not looking forward to." Hannah said laughing.

"Have you already arranged to get to the airport?" Joe asked simply.

"My sister and her fiancé are going to drive me."

"If that plan falls through, I can offer you a full police escort." Joe teased.

"I thought I was supposed to keep a low profile. You're not helping the cause."

"You're right. I'd better let you get some sleep. You've got to be exhausted."

"I am tired, but I'm really grateful that you called me back tonight. You've put my mind at ease. Oh, and just one more thing before you go."

"What's that?"

"I never thanked you for the flowers. They were absolutely beautiful." Hannah said sincerely.

"My pleasure Hannah. I'm going to make you a promise okay?"

"What's that?"

"I'm going to get your things back for you so I don't want you to worry." Joe offered sincerely.

"You will?"

"I promise."

"Thank you." Hannah said quietly as tears welled in her eyes.

"You're welcome. Get some sleep and if I don't speak to you, have a wonderful trip."

Hannah hung up the phone and slipped back under the covers and rested her head gently on the pillow. Despite her fatigue, she wasn't able to sleep as her mind played the conversation with Joe over and over again in her head. She watched as the storm continued its intensity and despite it being nighttime, the skies were brightened almost to that of daylight by the reflective abundance of snow outside.

Her thoughts shifted to Kate, and in spite of her earlier anger, she had to admit a sense of sadness over the loss of a friendship. She realized that friendship means different things to different people. Some valued it and protected it at all costs and some threw it away with little concern for the damaging affects that the abandonment would leave. She had no doubt that Kate was faithful to the latter way of thinking. Hannah wasn't sure how things would play out but what she was sure of was the truth would betray Kate and most likely because of her inability to keep her own counsel.

CHAPTER 44

Hannah woke the next morning feeling tired and weighted with thoughts of the past evening. Her night's sleep offered her a welcomed escape, but now as the sun shone brightly to introduce the new day; discomforting thoughts assaulted her as she prepared her breakfast. She spilled icy cold milk over shredded wheat and methodically sliced a nearly ripe banana overtop, each slice featuring almost identical tiny faces.

It was nearly eight o'clock in the morning and she decided that after eating her breakfast, she would call the repair shop to find out about her car. It was unlikely that she would be going into work today given the weather and no method of transportation. Just as she anticipated, the service desk at the shop confirmed that they were unable to complete the repairs on her car and it wouldn't be ready until at least noon that day.

Her next call was to Paul on his cell phone thinking he would still be in transit. He picked up on the third ring and insisted that Hannah work from home since the roads were unplowed. The only reason he was venturing out was because he was scheduled to be in Court at nine o'clock.

"I feel really badly that you have to be out in this weather Paul."

"Don't feel badly. Over the years, I've gotten used to driving in this." Paul assured her. "Its actually quite nice because there's hardly anyone out in it. Just us crazy people."

"Well drive carefully and call me when you get to the office."

"I will call you even if you do sound like my mother." Paul joked.

"You can tease me all you like but I'll only worry if you don't call me."

"Okay, shouldn't take me more than an hour to get there."

After Hannah ended her call, she decided to go upstairs to shower and get ready for her day. Half an hour later she came downstairs dressed casually in blue jeans and a powder blue sweater with her laptop tucked under her arm. Deciding to break the silence, she turned on the radio just in time to hear the news reports on road closings because of whiteouts or unplowed streets. The weather report followed notifying their listeners that although the snow had stopped, it would start up again later in the day making rush hour almost unbearable. Hannah acknowledged that her car breaking down was a blessing in disguise and was now grateful for the inconvenience.

As the clock edged closer to nine o'clock, she wondered if Martha and Adam would stay downtown or attempt to venture home. 'I'll give them another half hour or so before calling them.' Hannah thought as she put on a pot of coffee and turned on her computer so she could check her email. 'It's going to be a quiet day.' She admitted to herself as only one message appeared and it was of little importance. After pouring a cup of coffee she carried it carefully into the livingroom to sit at the front bay window. She propped her feet up and leaned back sipping her steaming coffee and looked out on the winter's snowy offering. Its glossy patina reflected hundreds of icy crystals that were spotlighted by the emerging sun. The quietness and serenity of the morning now betrayed the previous evening's ordeal as though it was only imagination that had been captured in Hannah's mind. Hannah's attention was pulled towards Kate's house to contemplate and even validate all that had happened. As her attention held, the door to Kate's home opened as though to invite Hannah to draw her in more closely. She considered ducking away but she was compelled to watch. Within seconds Kate made her way out onto the front step, her eyes squinting against the sun's intensity. Her hand reached up to her face and arched it over her eyes to offer a shield against the glare. She turned in the direction of Hannah's house and focused then to where Hannah sat and despite the distance between them, each was now aware of the other. Their gazes held for no more than ten seconds but no other familiar recognition followed with either a smile or a wave of the hand. Thoughts of each one's betrayal defied the luxury of a gesture of friendship or forgiveness. Simultaneously their gazes fell away as Kate made her way towards her car and Hannah got up to answer the phone.

She picked up the receiver to hear Martha's light but somewhat groggy voice. "We're on our way home Hannah, but we're not sure how long it's going to take because the roads are awful."

"Well take your time."

"I don't think we have a choice." Martha laughed.

"That's true, but you know what I mean."

"Yes, I know what you mean, but Adam loves driving in this kind of weather."

"I always knew he was a little bit crazy." Hannah laughed.

"He wants to know if you want us to pick up your car for you. That way you don't have to go out in this later on."

"No, because then you will have to drive and I would just be happier if you didn't, but thank him for me."

"Okay, well hopefully it won't be long before we see you. Bye Hannah."

Hannah hung up the phone and had to admit she loved being at home but felt at loose ends so she decided to work on putting the file together for her trip to London. She had worked for quite awhile until she realized that almost two hours had passed and she still hadn't heard from Paul. She dialed his cell phone but there was no answer. 'He must be in Court now and he obviously forgot to call me.' She sat down once again to work on her file, but admittedly was distracted by the fact that he hadn't phoned because it just wasn't like him. 'I'm being silly.' She thought and resumed putting the file in order. Finally the phone rang.

"Paul?" Hannah anticipated. "Oh, hi sorry I was expecting someone else." Hannah listened for a minute and then confirmed with the auto repair shop that she would be in as soon as possible to pick up her car. Another half hour passed, and she tried once more to call Paul to no avail. She thought of calling Auntie Jane, but didn't want to alarm her unnecessarily. Hannah began to scold herself for not being able to keep her thoughts of apprehension under control and to stop worrying. She remembered that her father would tease her for being a worrier even at a young age. 'Don't worry until you have to.' He would say. But, in spite of his wisdom, she could never adjust her way of thinking. The phone rang again.

"Hello?" Hannah said less confidently. "Oh hi Sally, I've been meaning to call you, how have you...What?" Hannah listened as alarm swept through her. Hannah began to fire questions as tears spilled down her face. "Where's Jane?" "How is she?" "Wait, I'll grab a pen." Hannah began to write down the information that Sally was giving her, but her hand was shaking so badly, she could hardly keep the pen in place. "Okay, okay, yes I will." After she hung up the phone she hurled the pen across the room and let out an anguished scream.

CHAPTER 45

Martha was just coming through the door just as she heard Hannah's screams and ran into the kitchen. She found Hannah crouched down rocking back and forth with her arms tightly cradling her knees. Martha stooped down and placed her hands on her shoulders.

"Hannah, my God, what's happened?" Martha said gently knowing that she was going to hear terrible news. She gently lifted Hannah's chin so that she could make eye contact. "Tell me please Hannah. You're scaring me." The years rewound to the time that she said those very words to her sister just before hearing of her parents' deaths. A cold wave of fear pierced her heart.

"Paul. It's Paul. He's been in a terrible accident. I just...they don't think..." Hannah faltered through her tears.

"Hannah, he's alive. He's okay?" Martha urged hopefully.

"No. Yes, he's alive. They don't think..."

"They don't think what?" Martha said gently shaking her sister's shoulders to continue her thoughts.

"I can't say it." Hannah sobbed. "I didn't want him out in this weather. I can't bear this Martha. Not again."

Martha looked back to Adam who was standing in the doorway looking equally upset. For once, he was completely lost for words and was at a loss for what to do. Martha realized that she had to find out as much as she could but she knew that it would take time coming from Hannah.

"How did you find out? Who called you?" Martha demanded gently.

"Sally."

Martha turned to Adam and asked him to call her, and she put her arms around her sister and gently rocked her. Adam left the room and Martha heard his soothing voice speaking into his cell phone. After about five minutes he returned to the kitchen and stooped down to both women.

"Come on now. I want you two to get off this cold kitchen floor."

Remotely, Hannah and Martha got to their feet and followed Adam into the living room. Adam decided to light a fire to keep the atmosphere as soothing as possible. He went back to the kitchen to make a pot of fresh coffee and to make another call. This time it was to his brother Josh. They spoke at length and he signed off and then poured mugs of steaming coffee for everyone and returned to the living room. Martha looked at him expectantly hoping for some news.

"Paul has been a serious car accident. He was making a left hand turn and there was a truck coming from the other direction and it couldn't stop because of the icy roads. The truck slid into the passenger side of Paul's car and pushed it up against a traffic light standard. Paul had his seatbelt on but the impact threw him sideways and his head hit pretty hard against the car door. "

Martha cringed visualizing the collision and then nodded to Adam to encourage him to go on.

"I think what Hannah was trying to say is they don't think he's going to make it." Adam said quietly as tears welled in his eyes. "He's in a coma right now. The doctors are conducting tests to find out the level of the coma and to assess the severity. A lot depends on these tests and what they find, so we just have to try and be patient and hope for the best."

"Where is Auntie Jane?" Martha asked suddenly realizing the impact this must have had.

"She's at the hospital. Josh took her. Sally thought it was best if she stayed home in case people called."

"Thank God for Josh." Martha said.

"I spoke with him too. He said he will wait there with Jane until they get some results from the doctors." Adam assured. "What do you want to do Hannah?"

"I don't know what to do. I think I should probably go and be with

Jane. But I don't know if I can handle seeing him so vulnerable like that." Hannah offered honestly because she felt crushed with emotion and fear. She recognized that while Martha was very close to Paul, Hannah's relationship with him was much deeper not only because she worked with him every day but she had come to depend on him as a father figure.

"I think you'd feel better if you go and be near to him. We'll all go together." Adam offered.

The ride to the hospital was a relatively quiet one. From time to time Adam commented on the conditions of the road or the amounts of snow banked on the curbs. Hannah sat silently in the back seat and wondered with each minute that passed if it was a critical one in Paul's life. The weather stole precious travel time that on a normal day would have taken only twenty minutes. An hour later they arrived at the hospital's reception desk and were directed to the trauma unit. They stepped out onto the 4th floor and walked soldiered together until they saw Jane in the distance. Martha and Hannah both broke away from Adam to run towards her. Jane greeted them with a comforting smile and a long warm hug for each.

"How is he Auntie Jane?" Martha finally asked.

"He's still in a coma, but I believe he will pull through, so I don't want you girls to be upset. He would hate that." Jane said reassuringly.

"Have you had any updates from the doctors?" Hannah asked.

"They just moved him up here from emergency and they want to run tests today."

"What kind of tests?"

"One test is to find out the level of severity of the coma using what they call a Glasgow Coma Scale. It measures levels from one to fifteen, with one being severe and fifteen being normal. So of course we want to hope for the highest level possible."

"Can the test tell if someone is going to come out of a coma?" Hannah asked hopefully.

"I don't think so. It really didn't occur to me to ask because I just know he's going to pull through." Jane said resolutely.

"Are you really sure you feel good about this Jane?" Martha asked realizing she wasn't completely convinced.

"Yes because I'm not ready to lose him. He doesn't deserve this to be the end because he's worked so hard all his life and he has so many wonderful clients who rely on him. And of course there are his girls - for you Martha and Hannah, and now of course for Sally."

"I know he worries about Sally, but I think she will be okay." Hannah assured her. Jane was about to say something but stopped and simply smiled at Hannah.

"Can we see him?" Martha asked.

"No he's still in intensive care and so we can only wait. But you should go home because it could be ages before we know anything." Jane suggested.

"We're not going to leave you Jane until he shows some positive signs of change." Adam insisted.

"Thank you Adam, but I can't expect you all to take time away from your day to wait here. Your brother is already missing work today because of us."

"This is more important than work Jane, so don't think anything of it." Just as Adam spoke, his brother arrived with coffees for everyone.

"I heard you were on your way, so I thought you'd like coffees. Why don't we go and sit down the hall." Josh suggested after he had handed out the coffee and had given Adam a brotherly hug. They all walked silently to the waiting lounge and sat as comfortably as the hard vinyl chairs would allow.

"Your brother has been wonderful Adam; I don't know what I would have done without him this morning. He was at the house to pick up Sally when I got the call." Jane said gratefully.

"Ironically it was going to be Sally's first day back to work since being off and I offered to drive her since the weather was so awful. We were just about to leave when the hospital called. So Sally stayed put to make some phone calls and I drove Jane here." Josh was interrupted by a nurse who asked Jane to accompany her to Paul's room where the doctor was waiting to speak to her.

CHAPTER 46

They all fell silent as they watched Jane walk like a shrunken figure alongside the nurse. She turned back once to offer a weak smile, but her eyes belied fear. Their instincts were to go with her but held back because they new she had to do this alone. Twenty minutes passed silently before they caught sight of Jane again walking alongside the doctor. He spoke with her briefly before she left him to rejoin them in the waiting lounge. As she sat down, all four slid forward on their seats to offer her their undivided attention.

"He's hooked up to a lot of machines but they assure me he's comfortable. They've restrained him because he's moving. He's also making some sounds. I spoke with the doctor and they've determined that he has some swelling of the brain but there's no internal bleeding. So, that's a relief." Jane said sounding completely unrelieved.

"But if he's moving and making sounds, doesn't that mean that he's not in a coma?" Martha asked hopefully.

"No, the doctor explained that he is having reflex activities. For him to regain consciousness, he said that both inborn and learned movements have to be present. I think he called them reactive and perceptive movements. The doctor said examples of those might be a reaction to pain and if he began speaking again coherently. I think I've got that right, but he was giving me so much information all at once." Jane said apologetically.

"It's a lot to take in and I'm sure it's all very confusing." Josh affirmed.

"You're right Josh. I feel really muddled and not sure if I'm asking the right questions so I hope I understood everything the doctor was saying."

"Did he say that anything about the possibility of recovery?" Hannah asked.

"Only that if he were to recover he would wake up bit by bit over time and then eventually he would wake to full consciousness. The doctors will have a better sense once they know the outcomes of the tests."

By the end of day, they all left the hospital to get some rest. Josh insisted on driving Jane home and staying with her and Sally for the evening and promising to pick her up in the morning to take her back to the hospital.

Over the next few days, Paul was waking up intermittently and for longer periods of time which prompted the doctors to be hopeful for a full recovery. During this time, his small support group took turns arranging to visit him in shifts each day. Hannah split her time between the office and visiting Paul typically at the end of the workday just before going home. Normally, she would just sit by his bed and hold his hand and chat lightheartedly about work and life in general.

Sally had returned to the office and stopped in each night to visit Paul usually after Hannah's visit and always accompanied by Josh. Grayson had not been successful in his attempts to find her, but to be safe Josh insisted that he escort her to and from work and the hospital. He was determined for now to keep an emotional distance so that she could heal from her relationship with Grayson. He was equally determined to keep a physical presence so that she could grow to trust him.

On the fourth day, the nurses allowed Paul's request to have a longer visit with Hannah because he was fretting about work. Jane called Hannah at the office and asked her to come by the hospital at three o'clock rather than later in the day.

"He's feeling a bit stronger today Hannah and he would like to discuss some files with you."

"Are you sure Jane? Is this really good for him?" Hannah asked with concern.

"Yes. I spoke with the doctors and they seem to think it will settle him down a bit because he feels as though he abandoning his clients. He also wants to make sure that you're set for London."

"Well, I wasn't sure if I should go ahead with that right now or go later when he's better. I called Robert O'Shea in London, and he completely understands if we need more time."

"Paul is expecting you to go and he will be upset if he thinks it's not going to go ahead. The doctors are assuring me that the less stress he has the better. As long as he knows that his practice is running smoothly, he will rest easy."

"Okay, that makes sense. Did he tell you what files I should bring?"

"Yes, if you could bring Robert's file and the Sandra Eaton file."

"The Sandra Eaton file." Hannah repeated. "I don't think I know that one, it must new."

"He said it's in his desk drawer that he keeps locked. The key to the drawer is in the silver cigar box on his desk."

"Okay, I will bring the files and I will see you and Paul at three."

Hannah went into Paul's office and retrieved the desk key from the cigar box. She had admired this box as a simple desk ornament and never thought anything more about it. Now it held the means to unlock the drawer that held Paul's personal files. He had once told her that she had full reign in his office with the exception of this particular drawer which was off limits to all staff. She felt intrusive and if Paul hadn't invited her to unlock the drawer, she would not have wanted any part of it. She flipped mechanically through the tabs on all the files in the drawer until she found the Sandra Eaton file. She held her temptation to look in the file and placed it in her briefcase to be included with the Robert O'Shea file.

Hannah arrived at the hospital promptly at three where she was greeted by Jane.

"Hi Jane, how's Paul?" Hannah asked brightly.

"He's so much better today Hannah. I'm so grateful for the doctors and nurses here. They've been remarkable."

"That's wonderful and so reassuring for you to have him in such capable hands."

"Yes, I must admit I sleep well at night because I know he's well cared for." Jane admitted. "So Hannah, I've spoken to Paul and he would like the O'Shea file to look over on his own, and he has asked me to review the Eaton file with you."

"Oh, okay." Hannah said hesitantly wondering why she would be reviewing a file with her boss's wife.

"I know this is out of the ordinary Hannah but you'll understand soon enough."

"Okay, I'm intrigued." Hannah laughed pulling the O'Shea file from her briefcase to hand to Jane.

"I'll take this to Paul and I'll be right back." Jane promised leaving Hannah standing in the hallway outside Paul's room. During the five minutes while she waited, Hannah felt unusually ill at ease and out of her element with the prospect of discussing a file with someone other than Paul, even if it was his wife. Despite her discomfort, Hannah greeted Jane with a warm smile once she emerged from Paul's room.

"I've asked the nurses if we can use a private room down the hall." Jane advised.

CHAPTER 47

Hannah followed Jane silently down the hall wondering how this was going to play out. She was being silly as she realized that Jane was likely just sharing the workload with Paul. However, she knew that Jane knew nothing about his practice because so many times she had told Hannah that she refused to let Paul bring his work home. This is very confusing, she thought. Jane made her way into a small room that hosted a coffee table and two settees. On the other table there was a coffee maker with a freshly brewed carafe of coffee.

"Well this is very civilized." Hannah remarked laughing.

"Yes I wanted something comfortable. Shall we have a coffee?" Jane asked graciously.

"Sure I'll have a coffee thanks, but I must admit Jane you're making me a bit nervous. Is there more to this than just discussing a file?" Hannah asked seriously.

"I don't want you to be nervous and I'm sorry if I'm making you feel that way." Jane apologized.

"This is just out of the ordinary and that's what I'm reacting to. I also know that you're trying to help Paul so let's discuss this file." Hannah suggested.

"You're right, I'm trying to help Paul, but not in the way you think." Jane said handing Hannah her coffee.

"Well now I'm really curious." Hannah said pulling the Eaton file from her briefcase and pushing it toward Jane. Jane's response was to push it back to Hannah.

"I wonder if I could ask you to open the file and look through it before we start."

Hannah looked from the file that now sat in front of her to Jane who was expressionless. Their eyes held briefly until Jane nodded prompting Hannah to open the file. She did and leafed through it robotically as one would when reading documents that were completely unfamiliar. She began to read the first lines of each document that appeared to be related to a paternity claimed by a Sandra Eaton.

"Okay, I've got a sense of the file. What else do I need to know?" Hannah asked innocently.

"You've missed a document." Jane stated.

"I have?"

"Yes, there is one tucked in that brown envelope."

"Oh, I didn't see that one." Hannah realized as she pulled the document from its wrapper. "It looks like a birth certificate for a Sarah Eaton."

"Yes." Jane said simply.

"Oh, Sally's proper name is Sarah, so this is her birth certificate." Hannah said almost proudly as though she were making sense of the file.

"Yes it's her birth certificate." Jane confirmed.

"I'm sorry Jane, I'm not following."

"Look at the parents' names."

"Birth mother is Sandra Eaton and the birth father is..." Hannah stopped clearly taken aback by the name that was typed onto the official document. She looked disbelievingly at Jane who again held her gaze with an expression that pleaded understanding.

"And the birth father is?" Jane prompted.

"Paul Peterson." Hannah said distantly unable to drag her eyes from what was written before her. Jane slid her hand across the table to grasp Hannah's hand as a show of comfort.

"I don't understand Jane. The mother's name is Sandra Eaton. Who is she?"

"She is a woman who worked with Paul years ago as his secretary when you and Martha were just babies."

"But I remember that you and Paul just celebrated your thirty-fifth wedding anniversary a few months ago."

"Yes, we were married when Sandra came to work with Paul."

"Are you saying that Paul had an affair with this woman and the result of that affair was Sally?"

"Yes."

"And you were okay with that?"

"To say I was okay with it isn't actually accurate Hannah." Jane admitted solemnly.

"Okay, then what would be accurate?" Hannah challenged feeling impatiently annoyed that she was discovering yet another deception.

'Try not to be upset Hannah, this is not easy, but let me explain."

CHAPTER 48

Hannah realized that her tone was harsh and that she was being impatient with Jane. She needed to put her feelings and frustration aside.

"I'm trying not to be upset but it seems to me that I have been living in a bubble lately. Everyone I thought I knew seems to be not who I thought they were, and the very person who I exemplify to be the epitome of truth does not possess that quality at all."

"Hannah I understand how you feel because believe me I know all about shattered trust, but I don't think there is any point in telling you what I have to say until I can assure you that Paul is everything you've always known him to be and more. I know that he would understand your doubts and not challenge your opinion, but I feel it's my duty to defend his honour and so if you would give me a chance, I would like to explain. No matter what you see written on that paper, Paul loves you and Martha like you are his daughters."

"It's not about what's written on a piece of paper, it's about trust. I understand that I am not his daughter but we had a relationship that was almost as close. So at what point in a relationship does it become worthless because the truth has been just a lie. It changes everything when you don't have trust because to me it's the basis of every relationship. After all these years, was there a point not to tell me until now?"

"Yes, there was a point because Paul didn't find out until just before Sally began working for him, so he's only known of her existence for a short time. I know this is hard to hear but it's been a very difficult time for Sally and her mother and for me and Paul. I don't mean to dismiss your feelings, but before we could announce it, we had to work things out between the four of us so that we were all protected emotionally. It wasn't easy for me to know that Paul had had an affair and then to have it confirmed by a child, especially after I was not able to conceive. Or for Paul to know that he had a daughter whose whole childhood he missed, or Sandra to make a decision to hide Paul's child from him because she genuinely believed it would destroy a marriage that she had no interest in destroying."

"I'm sorry Jane. This is all so much to take in and I don't mean to be selfish. Obviously this has been awful for all of you."

"It could have been awful, but it's turned out to be really wonderful. A lot of women in my situation would have been angry and bitter, but I've forgiven Paul and I've accepted Sally since she is really the innocent one in this situation." Jane offered sincerely.

"Is that why Paul is so protective of her and why she is living with you?"

"Yes, in a way. For all those years, Paul was not involved because he simply didn't know that she even existed, otherwise he would have supported her financially and emotionally."

"So how did he find her, or how did she find him?"

"Well, actually it was Sandra who contacted Paul. She had suffered a stroke and she realized that if something happened to her, Sally would never know who her father is and it unsettled her. She only wanted to offer Paul and Sally the opportunity to know each other. Sandra knew that she was taking a huge chance because she had never disclosed the identity of Sally's father to anyone, not even to Sally."

"I don't want to be insensitive but how was Paul sure that it was his child?"

"He had a paternity test. But he only decided to have one for my benefit and not for his. He didn't tell me anything until after that test had been taken and it proved positive. Sandra said she would respect his decision to accept Sally or to walk away. "

"Of course he couldn't walk away." Hannah realized.

"He was excited and concerned because the next step was to tell me and Sandra to tell Sally. There was so much at stake but they knew they had no choice."

"But what about you Jane, how did you accept his affair and then his child?"

"I accepted it because I wasn't really surprised. I'm not saying it was easy and I would be lying if I said I wasn't upset, but when I look back to those days when the affair happened, Paul and I had become different people to each other." Jane admitted.

"Why?"

"We had tried to have children for so long. All our friends, including your parents, were having children of their own and with each new birth, I felt a terrible loss. I became completely obsessed with the prospect of having children and I was determined to become a mother. When each month would come and go without a pregnancy, I became more and more desolate. I was really insufferable Hannah because I let it completely consume me. I could feel no joy in anything and I began to take little pleasure in anything or anyone including my husband. There were many times that he tried to assure me that life would be just as fulfilling without children but that almost made it worse for me. It told me that he accepted it when I couldn't or wouldn't and so the resentment began to set in. I began to think that Paul was the reason I wasn't able to conceive, so we stopped trying all together and subconsciously I behaved as though my marriage were over. Then Paul began to spend more and more time at the office because he didn't want to come home to a miserable wife. When I look back, I realize how selfish and insensitive I was."

"Are you trying to tell me that Paul's affair with another woman was your fault?"

"Paul was responsible for his actions and it was clearly his choice to have an affair, but I believe I contributed to that decision. I do think we get into situations where we can't see our way clear to do the right thing. So the wrong thing becomes the solution and we really don't mean to hurt anyone but usually that's the end result. I like to think of it as misguided judgment during misguided times. We are all human and we all do things that we aren't proud of but I think we should be forgiven if the circumstances behind those indiscretions force us to behave out of character."

"I suppose there's a certain amount of irony in all of this if you think about it." Hannah realized.

"Yes of course. I was blaming Paul for not being able to conceive a child and it was me all along who wasn't able to have children. He didn't have an affair to prove that because as we know this fact was not known to him until recently, but I think he was desperate to escape and feel that there was more to him than just producing babies. I behaved as though he was of no value to me if he couldn't father a child, and the irony is that he could."

"Are you telling me all this now because Paul is in a similar situation to Sandra's because of his coma?"

"When Paul first came to the hospital, you asked me if I thought he was going to make it and I said yes because of you and Martha and then I mentioned Sally. Your reaction was because of her recent misfortune with Grayson and that's when I realized that you didn't know that she was Paul's daughter."

"Was I supposed to know?" Hannah said incredulously.

"We all decided recently that it was time to tell you and Martha. Sally was terrified because she thinks so much of you and she worried you wouldn't feel the same way about her. Paul and I were convinced that you would feel the same way no matter who her father was."

CHAPTER 49

Hannah said nothing because she actually wondered if Jane was giving her more credit than was due to her. She had to question herself and wonder why she was feeling so vulnerable to the prospect of Sally taking a place in Paul's life that she earned simply by a biological connection and not yet an emotional one. Sensing Hannah's hesitation, Jane continued.

"Paul wanted to wait for the right time and he tried to tell you one day in his office. It was the day he invited you to go to London." Jane stopped to allow Hannah to recall that conversation. Hannah nodded to indicate her recollection and Jane continued.

"He decided against it because he became concerned that if he were to tell you about Sally, you may feel an emotional loss that he felt you weren't prepared to deal with at the time. I know it may seem as though he was trying to hide something from you Hannah, but really he was trying to protect you. I think and he agreed that you have a right to know no matter what you are going through. It has been very hard on him keeping this from you and Martha, but it was only because he didn't want you to be upset. He was concerned that once you knew that Sally was his daughter, you would step aside and allow his rightful daughter to take your place."

"He's right, I would certainly do that, but not because I was upset but because I would give him that respect and Sally too."

"Well it doesn't have to be that way and he certainly doesn't want it to be that way. If he had the strength right now, he would tell you the same thing. One of the most imposing thoughts that Paul has had to deal with since this discovery was how it was going to impact you. He doesn't want anything to change between you two and he wants to be sure that you know that no one can replace you in his eyes."

"Nothing will change between us and I think if you're okay with this, then I should be too." Hannah offered kindly.

"I know this will take time to sink in Hannah, but all we can ask of you is to try and accept this in the most positive way."

"And how do you go about accepting those things Jane?" Hannah asked simply.

"I look forward to the prospect of grandchildren, and I know that even though my blood may not be running through their veins, Paul's is and that's enough for me."

Hannah leaned over and gave Jane a long hug.

"Thank you for telling me Jane. I realize that this has to have been hard for you but I am glad that Sally is authentically part of the family." Hannah offered.

"I am grateful for your understanding because Paul is concerned for you and although he agreed that you should know given his current situation he's been fretting. I didn't want another day to go by without you knowing the truth behind Sally's parenting."

"Can we go and see him now?" Hannah stood up and reached for Jane's hand. They walked the length of the hall to Paul's room.

"Why don't you go in and see him on your own?" Jane suggested.

Hannah agreed and went in to Paul's room to find him lying peacefully against his pillow. His head turned slightly in response to the sound of the door opening. His eyes were unsure but he smiled warmly. Hannah sat gently on the side of the bed and tenderly held his hand and looked into his tired eyes. Never before had she seen such raw vulnerability.

"Jane and I discussed the Sandra Eaton file and I want you to know that I have a renewed respect for you for so many reasons. For what it's worth, I can honestly assure you that you are more remarkable than I thought."

"Thank you." Paul's voice was weak but squeezed Hannah's hand with a strength that surprised her.

"And congratulations too." Hannah added.

"For what?"

"You have a daughter and if anyone deserves that, you do."

"I see you and Martha as my daughters. Please don't see this as a replacement." Paul said looking a bit worried.

"No, actually I see it as an addition."

"Good." Paul sighed.

"How about when you get out of here, you and I go out for a beer?" Hannah said lightheartedly.

"I would like that very much."

"Me too. I know that you're tired and I don't want to take time away from Jane, so I'm going to go and let you rest."

Paul agreed but went through with a few last minute instructions before Hannah took the O'Shea file from him. She stood up and leaned across the bed to kiss his cheek.

"I'll see you soon Paul."

"You will." He assured with a tired smile.

Hannah left the room to go home and despite the contentedness she felt, the vulnerability reflected in Paul's eyes lingered in her mind. She realized that while their relationship wouldn't change, adapting to assure its stability would take time. She wasn't convinced that Paul felt comfortable with what Hannah now knew. And while Hannah was pleased with the addition to Jane and Paul's family, instinctively she would want to stay in the background for a time so as not to appear territorial over Paul. She had to admit that while Paul was Sally's father, a sting of fear pierced her that she recognized as a feeling of loss. In a moment of weakness, Hannah had been concerned that Paul's presence in her life would fade away. She wanted to protect herself from those thoughts and knew that it would take patience and confidence to sustain her through the delicacies of adjusting to Sally in Paul's life. She decided not to anticipate distress but rather an opportunity to support Paul as he had done with her over the years.

CHAPTER 50

Once Hannah arrived home, she made her way up to her room and after changing her clothes, she decided to pack for her trip to London. She would be leaving in two days' time and to distract her from over thinking the day's news, she felt a completely mindless task would help. As she contemplated the best approach to tell Martha the news of Sally, she heard the front door open and close and Martha call out her name.

"Up here." Hannah instructed.

"Packing?" Martha said stating the obvious.

"Yes, but I'm almost finished, so lets go downstairs and start dinner." Hannah suggested.

"Okay, I'll change and I'll meet you down there."

Martha arrived at Hannah's side in the kitchen about five minutes later. They chatted casually about nothing in particular and then sat down to dinner when Hannah raised the subject of her visit with Paul. She carefully offered Martha the details of the invitation by Jane to sit down and talk over Sally's mother file. As the story unfolded, Martha gently placed her knife and fork on her plate and gave Hannah her full attention. Her expression was unreadable, neither sad nor happy. Hannah finished her report and waited for a reaction from Martha, but no words fell from her mouth. Instead, she continued to stare at her sister.

"What do you think Martha?" Hannah finally asked.

"Honestly I don't know what to think. I suppose I have to allow it to sink in, but I'm not really surprised."

"You're not surprised? That's amazing because that's the last thing I would have ever imagined."

"This is going to sound a bit strange, but I did wonder why Paul was so willing to take her in after her experience with Grayson. I know that he is very kind, but I felt that there was more to it. He seemed overly concerned about her well being than expected, well beyond a secretary and boss relationship. He became protective just as a father would be."

"Well, I've always said that you have a perception about people that never ceases to amaze me." Hannah admitted.

"Maybe I just have a suspicious nature." Martha suggested. "But I hope you won't worry that this will adversely affect your relationship with Paul."

"And with you…" Hannah added.

"You know as well as I do that he has a stronger connection to you, and I've always been comfortable with that. In fact, I was always grateful when we were younger because I think he gave you a lot of support when Mum and Dad died that I could not have possibly given you."

"I suppose so." Hannah said unconvincingly.

"You know Hannah, I've never told you this, but you had a lot of responsibility then and don't think for a minute that I thought that was fair for you." Hannah began to interrupt her, but Martha held up her hand for her to stop. "Just listen to me. I know you would not have had it any other way than for us to be together and for you to take care of me. But you were only nineteen and look what you took on. In an instant, you became my mother, my father, and thrown in there for good measure, you continued to be my sister. I leaned on you for everything, but I knew you needed someone to lean on too, and that was Paul. You need him more than I did. As long as I had you, I didn't need anyone else."

"I needed you too Martha."

"Not in the same way. You gave up everything for me." Martha admitted.

"No I didn't. Please don't think that." Hannah pleaded.

"I don't say it to make you feel badly. I say it so you realize that everything you did has been appreciated and I'm just grateful for all of it."

Their conversation maneuvered in other directions with the odd relapse back to the subject of Paul and Sally. Other than that Hannah was pleased and a little surprised that Martha didn't seem more interested in this new discovery. It encouraged Hannah to think that while this was indeed news, it wasn't enough to express concern from Martha. Even though Hannah was older than her sister, she often relied on Martha's sensibility to direct her thoughts. Hannah realized her next task would be to talk to Sally, but she felt she would wait until she could meet with her face to face rather than speak to her on the phone. That opportunity would not present itself until she was back from London.

Two days slipped by quietly and quickly with Hannah readying herself for her trip. Hannah had committed to her promise to Joe and had not mentioned a word to Martha about her ordeal with Kate. It was unnatural for her not to share such a critical event with her sister, but she felt compelled to do as Joe asked. Finally, early Monday morning, Hannah was on her way to the airport. Adam and Martha offered to drop her on their way to work and she was grateful for the company since her stomach was in knots. Her excitement was only slightly spoiled because despite saying that he might be in touch before she went to England, Joe had not phoned her. She realized that she was feeling silly and that she had no right to expect that he should contact her and convinced herself that he had simply didn't have time.

Half an hour later the car pulled up alongside the curb to the airport. Hannah climbed out and assured her sister and Adam that she didn't need to be escorted to the check in desk.

"Do you have everything Hannah – your passport and your itinerary?" Martha fussed.

"Yes, everything's in my purse. I've checked and rechecked at least a hundred times."

"Give us a hug and have a safe and wonderful first flight." Adam said. Hannah returned his hug and noticed a tear slip down Martha's cheek.

"Don't cry Martha. I'm only going for a short time. I'll be home before you know it." Hannah assured sweeping the tear away with her fingers.

"I know, but I'm not used to you being away at all let alone out of the country." Martha explained.

"It will go quickly, you'll see. Please check in on Paul for me Martha. I feel awful being so far away from him."

"I understand and I knew you'd be concerned about Paul, so Adam and I are going to stop in at Jane's on our way home from the airport."

"Are you sure you don't mind doing that? It's not out of your way?"

"No, we practically have to pass Jane's place on the way back, so it's definitely not out of the way."

Hannah reluctantly left the comfort of their company and walked into the terminal stopping about five times to wave back at Martha and Adam. The last one with Martha blowing kisses and waving as Adam shook his head and laughed.

CHAPTER 51

Hannah arrived at the baggage check in, claimed her boarding pass, and then made her way to the departure lounge. After a two hour wait, Hannah boarded her first plane. She was excited and slightly nervous by the prospect of flying for the seven hours it would take her to get to London. She watched as other seasoned passengers settled into their seats all of whom seemed to look much more comfortable than Hannah felt.

A man who looked to be in his late fifties sat in the empty seat beside Hannah. She watched as he pulled his cell phone from his shirt pocket and shut it off. He turned to smile at her and explain how he had to live without his cell phone for the duration of the flight, a practice he wasn't used to.

"Why are you shutting it off then?" Hannah asked.

"You can't leave cell phones on during a flight. I think it has something to do with interfering with the communication frequencies of the plane. Personally, I don't believe a word of it." The man explained with a slight British accent.

"Oh." Hannah said as she scrambled in her purse to look for her phone.

"Is this your first flight?" He asked kindly.

"Yes it is." Hannah answered almost guiltily.

"Don't worry, you'll love it. It's like a flying hotel complete with movies and refreshments. The flight attendants work hard to keep us all happy. You'll settle in in no time." He assured as the plane pulled back to taxi into position for take off.

Hannah smiled back at the man and extended her hand to introduce herself. He accepted her hand and introduced himself as Michael Janes. He explained that he had to make a quick trip 'over the pond' to see his mother who had recently fallen ill.

"I'm sorry." Hannah replied genuinely.

"Thank you. I know this kind of news shouldn't be a surprise considering she is well into her eighties, but it's upsetting nevertheless. I don't have a lot of chance to see her now that we live on two different continents, so this gives me an excuse to make an extra trip. I'm hoping I might be able to lift her spirits a bit."

"What about your dad?" Hannah inquired.

"Oh my dad died about six years ago and that was very hard for my mother. She is a strong woman, but you know at that age, they get into their routines and they really depend on each other. For our elderly parents, the time they really need each other is the time they are more likely to lose each other. Luckily my mum lives in a small village and has done so for a very long time, so she is very well connected with other neighbours and family who look out for her."

"It must be so difficult for you being so far away."

"Yes it is, but I have two brothers and a sister who still live in England, and they have had the lion's share of care and support. I try and fly over about four times a year and that gives them a bit of a break. It's not much, but when you have your own business, sometimes it's hard to take more time away."

"I'm sure that you visit more than a lot of people whose families live in the same town." Hannah qualified.

"You know, I never thought about that but you may be right. What about your parents Hannah? Do they live close by?" Michael asked.

"No, unfortunately my parents died in a car crash about ten years ago."

"That's so incredibly sad." Michael remarked with genuine shock. "The prospect of your parents having died never even crossed my mind since you're so young."

"Its okay, most people are genuinely surprised and as much as I miss them, I have gotten over the terrible emptiness that their deaths left. I have a wonderful sister who I am very close to and so I'm not alone."

Hannah's words were left hanging as the pilot's voice came over the loudspeaker requesting the flight attendants to prepare for take off. Her heart began to pound with excitement and a bit of fear as she realized that there was no turning back. This was it – her first flight.

"The take off is the best part." Michael assured. "You'll feel and hear the power in the engines. It's really quite exhilarating."

Hannah realized that Michael wanted to warn her once she heard the roar of the engines and she felt grateful for his thoughtfulness. As she thanked him his face crinkled into a smile. She took in the fine lines etched into his face and the soft graying of the hair at his temples. She averted her gaze to look out the window as the plane made its determined ascent slicing through the billowing clouds. Hannah's thoughts were occupied with the realization that Michael must be about the age her father would have been had he lived. She realized that when someone dies they stay as they were in the minds of those they leave behind. It would be unlikely or even difficult to imagine them any other way. It is more natural to accept reality as it was carved out before you. Until she met Michael, she had never thought to imagine what her parents would look if they hadn't died. She had left them as she last saw them, young and healthy. Perhaps it was kinder to leave them as they were before any of life's harsh realities could take hold. In her mind's eye, her parents were perfect and represented health and happiness to her. Time and aging may have altered that nearly idealized vision she had of them. Hannah's silent reasoning was interrupted by the flight attendant asking her what she preferred for breakfast.

"I'm sorry, I didn't hear the choices." Hannah apologized.

"Cheese omelet or ham and mushroom quiche." The attendant repeated.

"I'll have the omelet please." Hannah requested reaching for her purse.

Michael watched as she began to look through her wallet for payment and he reached his hand to place it over hers. "Its okay, you don't need that." He said without the attendant noticing.

"But I have to pay for my breakfast." Hannah explained.

"Meals are included in your flight. They will let you know if anything is extra, but meals are usually complimentary on transatlantic flights."

"Really? I assumed it was like any other restaurant and I would have to pay for it."

"It's only natural that you should expect to pay for your meal, just not this time." Michael laughed.

"There's a reason I was put next to you. I think you're here to stop me from making a complete fool of myself."

"You're being much too hard on yourself. You remind me of my daughter. I enjoy helping you because if she were in the same position as you, I would like to think someone would help her."

"Well, you'll have a lot of practice with me, so I'm glad you don't mind."

"Not in the least."

"It's funny you should say I remind you of your daughter because I think if my father had lived he would be very much like you. I have never imagined my parents getting older. It's as though they were frozen in time. But my father would be almost the age you are now had he lived and you remind me of how I think he would have been. And like you, he always looked out for his daughters."

Their conversation was momentarily halted as they started in on their omelets. Hannah realized how hungry she was as she pulled back the cellophane on her meal and took her first bite.

"Oh, this is good." Hannah said approvingly.

"This truly is your first flight." Michael laughed. "No one likes airplane food."

"Really? I think it's very good, but then, I like to be fed." Hannah qualified.

CHAPTER 52

Soon after coffee and tea was served, Hannah felt wonderfully relaxed and sated after her meal. Headphones were then handed out to all the passengers and after Michael had given her full instruction on how to use the viewing screen, she settled in to watch a movie. After it was finished she pulled off her headphones and placed them on her lap.

"How did you enjoy the movie Hannah?" Michael asked.

"I thought it was really good. Not a movie I would have ever chosen at home, but I have to admit it was enjoyable." Hannah admitted.

"We're about to have lunch soon, so I think I'll pop down to the loo." Michael announced as he unbuckled his seatbelt and stood up. He looked down at Hannah who had slid forward on her seat and looked back to see where he might possibly go to complete this task. It occurred to Michael that Hannah may have resisted sourcing out the possibility of using the washrooms, either out of shyness or not wanting to embarrass herself.

"Wanna come with me?" He said as though he were a teenager.

"Sure, I could probably use a trip to the loo too." Hannah said gratefully.

Michael escorted her to the washroom, gave her some quick instructions on locking the door, and said he would meet her back at their seats. Within minutes Hannah had returned and settled back into her seat.

"Feel better?" Michael asked.

"Yes, much better thank you."

As the flight progressed Hannah realized how comfortable she was with Michael's company. She also felt a freedom of mood or spirit

– she wasn't sure which – but it was one that she felt unaccustomed to. For once, she was literally and figuratively escaping from years of being weighed down from responsibility and accountability. After her parents' deaths, whether by design or her own decision, Hannah's life had fast-forwarded into assuming an adult role, the years skipping like a stone over the time of natural development for a young woman. She had no measure in understanding that loss until now.

"Tell me something Hannah." Michael said interrupting her thoughts.

"What's that?" Hannah asked gently.

"You were so young when you parents died. How were you able to get through those days?"

"It's almost a blur now, but I remember being terrified and trying very hard not to let it show. I was only nineteen and Martha was seventeen. I was so determined not let anyone think that I couldn't cope because I was afraid we might lose our home and be separated."

"Was there a threat that that might happen?" Michael asked curiously.

"The threat only existed in my mind. I know now that no one could actually make that decision because I was legally an adult at the time. It was probably a good thing that I didn't realize it since it motivated me not to become complacent." Hannah explained.

"So essentially you were not only coping with the loss of your parents, but you were living on fear. That seems incredibly unfair."

"It was, but I didn't have a choice." Hannah said simply.

"I'm being insensitive and I really don't mean to be."

"I know you don't and you're not being insensitive. I've had similar conversations with lots of people and I know it's hard for anyone to understand the impact of what my sister and I went through. But, if you think about it, living independently with only each other to rely on became our new normal."

"It would seem to me, knowing you for the short time that I have, that you managed your new normal very well."

"I think eventually we did and it helped that our parents provided well enough for us so we were able to stay in our house. I had to learn a lot very quickly in the way of finances and providing for my sister and me. Even though Martha was old enough, I had to assume a parental role because she was at an age where I believed she could lose her way, so to speak. She never seemed to truly mourn the loss the way I expected she would. She never cried. It was almost as though it didn't happen and I think that it must have been her way of coping. I think she recognized the responsibility that fell on me because I was older and I'm sure she thought if she fell apart it would just put more on my shoulders."

"Did you not have any family members like uncles or aunts or grandparents that could step in and help you out?" Michael asked as he started in on his lunch.

"Both my parents didn't have siblings and my grandparents had died long before I was born, so of course I never knew them. I guess you could say we became orphans of orphans. Luckily though my parents had very close friends who assumed the roles of aunt and uncle and they became our emotional support. In fact, I work for my uncle now. He's a lawyer and he trained me to be his assistant. The work I do is similar to a paralegal." Hannah explained.

"How do you like doing that?"

"I actually enjoy it. It wasn't what I had ever expected to do, but after my parents died, he offered me the job and so I was very grateful for that." Hannah said unconvincingly.

"Is it time to fly the coop?" Michael prodded.

"You mean get another job?"

"Yes, try something different, or are you happy there?"

"I've never really thought about whether I was happy there or not. I suppose it was an opportunity that I shouldn't ever question and I've never considered leaving. But…" Hannah hesitated.

"I'm not suggesting you should, but you're so young and I just wondered if there was something else in your future."

"It seems that my future is focused on others right now, so I'm not sure I could even consider a change for myself. My sister is getting married and my uncle was in a serious car accident just before I left for this trip."

"I'm sorry about your uncle. Is he going to be okay?"

"He's been out of a coma for a week now and he's stable. But who knows what the long lasting affects will be. I can't help but wonder how that is going to impact his ability to continue at the pace he has been working. And then there's Sally." Hannah offered.

"Sally?" Michael repeated hoping for an explanation. Hannah explained the unfolding of the past week's events from Sally's unfortunate experience with Grayson to the discovery that Paul is her father.

"And you had no idea that Sally was Paul's daughter?"

"Not a clue."

"That can't have been easy finding out."

"No, I was a bit upset when I first found out because I felt like I was the last one to know. But when I sat down with Paul's wife, she made me understand that sometimes life throws a curve ball at you and you just have to accept it."

"I guess no one knows that better than you." Michael suggested.

"Yes and that made me realize that I wasn't in a position to judge."

CHAPTER 53

Their conversation was interrupted by the flight attendant who began clearing their trays and offering coffee and tea. Both she and Michael declined the offer and relaxed to enjoy more lighthearted conversation. It was Hannah's turn to ask about Michael and his family. He spoke fondly of his wife and told her that they had been married for thirty years. He admitted that he would be lost without her because they had been almost inseparable since they were in high school. Not only had they been married for that length of time but they had decided to go into business together after their children were old enough to be a bit more self-sufficient.

"It sounds like you have a perfect life together." Hannah suggested.

"Not always perfect, but I wouldn't have it any other way."

Their conversation continued until finally the pilot announced their proximity to London and they would be making their descent into Heathrow within the hour. Hannah's heart bumped in excited anticipation mixed with trepidation as the plane began to cut through the clouds. Hannah watched out the window as her hands gripped the armrests in preparation for the landing.

"The landing is the best part." Michael chimed brightly.

Hannah looked a bit surprised and reminded him that that's what he said about the take off.

"Did I say that?" He said pretending to have completely forgotten his sentiments during their departure.

"I believe you did." Hannah said returning his smile.

"Huh! I don't recall saying that. I must have been confused." Michael said avoiding her look.

"I believe you were probably trying to be nice." Hannah offered.

"I really don't know what you're talking about, but I'll take the compliment as offered."

Suddenly there was a bump, a lurch, and a screeching of the plane's tires. Hannah turned with a startled look towards Michael, her eyes large with fear.

"It's okay. It's supposed to feel like this when we land." Michael assured.

"Really?" Hannah said feeling sick with fear.

"Yes, it's just the tires hitting the pavement. Its all good – you'll see."

CHAPTER 54

As if on cue, the plane settled smoothly onto the runway and taxied toward the terminal. Hannah rested her head back against the seat so as to calm her nerves, grateful to have finally arrived in London.

"I wonder if I will ever get used to flying. I must admit that was a bit nerve wracking." Hannah confessed.

"It's only because you're not used to it. I used to feel the same way."

"I don't know how I would have coped alone on my own through my first flight."

"You would have been just fine. Where do you go from here Hannah?"

"I have to take the Heathrow Express to Paddington Station and then I have to grab a cab to take me to my hotel in South Kensington."

"Why don't we get our baggage together and I'll show you where you need to go for the Heathrow Express. It's straightforward from there."

Both Michael and Hannah made the long trek through the terminal, claimed their baggage, and then made their way to the boarding area for her next destination.

"Hannah, it's been a pleasure and I hope you enjoy your stay in England."

"Thanks Michael, I will and I want you to know how much I appreciate all your help. You've made this trip so comfortable for me."

"It was nothing. Are you sure you're okay from here? I have rented a car and I can easily drive you to your hotel." Michael offered.

"I shouldn't take any more of your time or your kindness Michael. I think I should try and find my way from here on my own."

"If I remind you of your dad, let me do what he would do if he were here. I know he would want you to get to your hotel safely. I feel responsible for doing that and then you can go off on your business trip and do what you need to do."

"Are you sure it won't be out of your way?"

"It's not out of the way at all. Follow me."

Michael and Hannah made their way to the car rental kiosk and after registering his reservation with the desk; they were soon loading the car with their baggage and making their way out of the airport terminal.

"What street did you say the hotel was on?"

"It's on Harrington Road in South Kensington. There's a map on this." Hannah said handing Michael the reservation confirmation sheet from the hotel.

"It's near to Cromwell Road. I know exactly where it is."

As the made their way through the narrow streets, Hannah was distracted and somewhat unnerved by driving on the left side of the road rather than the right.

"Are you're alright Hannah – you're very quiet." Michael asked after the silence became conspicuous.

"I feel as though someone has dropped a huge mirror in front of me. Everything seems not as it should be."

"The driving you mean. Of course, it's an adjustment from what you're used to. You also have to be careful when crossing the road because your tendency will be to look to the left for oncoming traffic rather than looking to the right."

"I wonder why some countries drive on the right and others drive on the left."

"I believe it goes back to feudal times. Horse mounted riders traveled on the left side of a road or pathway because since most people were right-handed, they could keep their right hands free if they had to defend themselves with their swords. Later, freight wagons that were pulled by teams of horses were introduced in the United States. The freight wagons had no seats so it was easier for the riders to sit on the left rear horse of the team so they could use right hands to whip the other horses. So, I suppose the choice to ride on the right side or the left side evolved through the most sensible and common use of travel. Now I understand about three-quarters of the world drives on the right side, and the rest drive on the left."

"Then why did Britain not change to the right side?"

"Their horse-drawn wagons were made with seats so the riders either sat centrally or to the right side of their wagons. So, no need to change."

"So I have to blame the type of wagons they used for my confusion."

"Very simply, yes you do." Michael laughed. "Don't worry, just let everyone else do the driving for you and relax and take in the sites."

"Agreed, but my sense of independence is being challenged."

"I think you should accept that as a sign of a good thing. You've been independent for so long that you should allow yourself to be catered to while you're here."

"It all seems so foreign to me in more ways than one."

"Push yourself out of your comfort zone. You might enjoy it." Michael added.

"Advice taken and accepted." Hannah conceded.

CHAPTER 55

It took no longer than half an hour before Michael had wound his way from Heathrow to Queen's Gate and pulled up alongside Hannah's hotel. Many of the buildings entering the South Kensington area including her hotel were stately, elegant, and iron gated. Hannah felt overwhelmed by the grandness of the architecture.

"Here we are." Michael announced cheerfully.

"I think we must have the wrong place." Hannah said disbelievingly.

"No, this is right. This is Harrington and this is the hotel you're staying at." Michael said rechecking Hannah's confirmation sheet making sure he had read it correctly.

"Are you sure?" Hannah said staring out the window at the hotel.

"Yes quite sure. Is there something wrong?" Michael asked with concern.

"No, it just seems too nice. There must be a mistake."

"Come on Hannah. Let's get your bags and we'll go in and speak to the desk clerks. I'm sure you will find your reservation and your room waiting for you."

As Michael retrieved her bags from the car, Hannah stood on the sidewalk and waited still in awe of her surroundings.

"Ready?" Michael prompted.

"Yes of course, let's go inside."

The desk clerk greeted them with a warm hello and Michael stood behind as Hannah gave her name.

"Thank you Miss Hutton. Yes, here we are as the clerk entered her name in the computer. If I could just make an impression of the card you will be using?" The clerk asked as she handed Hannah a message that had been waiting for her." Within minutes she had registered and been given the pass to her room. As if still in a state of disbelief, she quietly thanked the clerk and turned to face Michael.

"This is all too much to take in." Hannah said to Michael as they stepped out of earshot of the reception desk.

"I hope you enjoy it." Michael offered.

"I will once it all sinks in. Thank you so much for everything. I don't know what I would have done without you." Hannah said as she extended her arms to hug Michael.

"You would have been fine. I am happy to have been a bit of a support to you." Michael said as he released Hannah from her hug. "Have a wonderful stay. I know you will fall into a rhythm here and you'll feel at home in no time."

Hannah simply nodded her head anticipating a final goodbye with someone she now considered a friend. As though reading her mind, Michael reached into his jacket pocket and pulled out his business card.

"Would it be okay if I gave you my card Hannah, just in case you ever need anything? I may even check in on you in a few days time just to see how you're making out."

Hannah gratefully took his card and without reading it slipped it into her purse. "Thank you Michael, but you shouldn't take time away from your family."

"Not at all, it's the least I can do as your surrogate father." Michael smiled. "Now off you go to your room. You must be exhausted and you'll need to settle in, so night-night."

"Good night and drive safely." Hannah smiled as she watched Michael leave through the hotel doors.

Once arriving at her room, Hannah slipped the pass card into the slot and was offered entry into a small but elegant room. She was welcomed by the room's television that's screen message offered her a personal welcome.

'This is incredible.' She whispered to herself and walked into the bathroom to draw herself a bath. 'I think I'll do as Michael suggested and treat myself to all the luxuries this room and London has to offer.'

She then remembered the message that had been handed to her

by the desk clerk upon her arrival. It was from Martha, asking that Hannah call her once she settled into her room. Slightly unsettled by the 'coolness' of the message, Hannah called the front desk to assist her in making the overseas call to her sister. Within a few minutes, Hannah was connected to her sister.

"Hannah, is that you?" Martha shouted into the phone.

"It's me Martha, but I don't think you have to shout. I can hear you clearly despite the fact there is a massive ocean separating us.' Hannah laughed.

"I'm sorry. I guess I thought that since you're so far away, I should raise my voice. How was your flight and how is London?"

"It was really good thanks, and I've only been in London for about two hours, but from what I've seen it's beautiful. I may not want to leave."

"Oh don't say that! I would miss you too much." Martha said with mocked horror.

"I'm only kidding. How is Paul? Did you drop in on Jane?"

"Yes, we stopped in at Jane's and she told us that Paul is improving slightly. He's still not out of the woods, but the doctors are pleased and have assured Jane that his prognosis is good."

"I feel so relieved. Thank you for doing that Martha."

"Well now you can relax and enjoy your visit to London. If anything changes, good or bad, I'll call you, but it seems he's going to be fine."

CHAPTER 56

Martha placed the phone back in its cradle after wishing her older sister a restful night. While it seemed strange not to have her in the house, Martha was grateful that Hannah had this opportunity to be free of any responsibilities and to enjoy a well deserved break. Given the pressures of Paul's accident and Kate's strangeness, Hannah needed to get out of the spotlight and being half way around the world seemed the perfect solution.

Martha's contemplations were interrupted as she jumped up from her seat remembering that she had forgotten a package in her car from Jane. Just after she rescued it from the back seat, her attention was drawn across the street to where she saw Kate just pulling into her driveway. Martha decided in that moment to seize an opportunity and approach Kate in the hopes of gaining some insight into the verbal attacks on her sister. Before she had the chance to back out from nerves she ran across the road stepping through the snow that lay heavily on the ground silencing her approach.

"Hi Kate!" Martha said brightly as she ran up behind her. Kate was visibly startled by Martha's voice and was momentarily speechless.

"Sorry I didn't mean to scare you, but I wanted to come over and see if we could talk?" Kate continued to stare at Martha without speaking, clearly confused by this request.

"I know this is short notice, but I would really like to talk to you." Martha pressed on realizing that she was probably sounding a bit desperate. "Maybe we could sit down in your kitchen and have a coffee? If you like I could run down to the coffee shop and…"

"Martha, under normal circumstances, that would be very nice." Kate interrupted unkindly. "But we both know that sitting down and having coffee together would be uncomfortable and really, I have nothing to say to you or your sister."

"I understand your resistance, but I think if you and I had a talk, then maybe I could help you." Martha explained cryptically.

"Help me what? I don't need help with anything. This is ridiculous Martha." Kate said as she slammed her car door shut and began to walk to her front door. Martha followed Kate and continued her appeal.

"Help you with Joe." Martha said simply.

"What do you mean help me with Joe? Are you trying to upset me Martha?" Kate spat angrily and then suddenly her face calmed. "Oh I get it. Hannah sent you over here because she doesn't have the nerve to face me herself."

"No, she has no idea. She's not even in the country. Believe me, this is spur of the moment. I saw you and I ran across the street to talk to you." Martha pleaded earnestly.

"Where is she?" Kate asked as she stared past Martha's face to focus on their home.

"She's in England on a business trip."

Kate considered this for awhile and then finally spoke. "Why are you so desperate to talk to me then? Why do you care?"

"Well believe it or not, I felt badly for you the other day."

"Yah, sure you did." Kate said unconvincingly.

"Look Kate, I think if we could sit down and talk out of the cold I could offer some insight into Hannah, insight that I know that you would benefit from. It would explain a lot of things and maybe you wouldn't feel so betrayed, particularly where Joe is concerned."

"I don't think so Martha. There's nothing you can say to me that will change my opinion of your sister and her sense of entitlement to what she wants." Kate said almost childishly.

"I'm not here to sell you on Hannah's behaviour. I'm here because I understand how you feel and I think you should just hear me out." Martha added with conviction.

"If you say the slightest thing that promotes your sister or her relationship with Joe, then you're out!" Kate threatened.

"You have my word. Let's go inside and while you put your groceries away, I'll make us coffees." Martha said conspiratorially.

CHAPTER 57

Kate remained silent as she turned and lead Martha up the driveway and opened her front door. The two women slipped off their coats and boots and made their way into the kitchen. After each of the delegated tasks was completed, Kate and Martha sat at the kitchen table uncomfortably stirring their coffees. Martha silently acknowledged that she was beginning to think that perhaps this wasn't a good idea after all.

Kate finally broke the silence. "Losing heart?"

Martha looked up at Kate and with a forced smile said, "Yes, I guess I am. I'm sorry Kate, I think I should go. I thought we could sit and have an honest talk, but I'm sensing your resistance and suddenly I'm lost for words." Martha pushed her chair back as she prepared to leave but before she could, Kate began speaking.

"Well let me do the talking first, so why don't you sit yourself back down." Kate instructed as Martha slipped back into her seat.

"Perhaps I should explain why I was so enraged the other day. You may already know this or maybe you don't, but I was involved in a serious relationship with Joe and since I was still struggling with my feelings for him, I decided to tell your sister about it. She betrayed me by seeing Joe behind my back. Not only do I feel foolish, but let's face it, a true friend would never have done that to me."

"I would understand that you would feel foolish, but she is not seeing Joe for the reasons you think." Martha had to admit that she felt if this conversation were to continue comfortably, her sincerity would have to be credible.

"What do you mean?" Kate demanded.

"You think they are together for romantic reasons, but that's not the connection at all." Martha stated strongly.

"Come on Martha! What other reason would there be for a man and a woman to be sneaking around together if it weren't for romantic reasons?"

"It's a ridiculous reason really but if you give me a chance, I'll explain it to you."

"This better be good, so talk." Kate ordered as she folded her arms across her chest.

"I have to give you a bit of history first about my family. I think you know that my parents died in a car accident about ten years ago. There was only one witness and they told the police that the accident seemed deliberate."

"Deliberate suggests another way of saying what exactly?"

"That someone or something forced their car off the road, but after a few years of thorough investigation, that theory was never proved and it became a cold case. I was never convinced that it was a deliberate accident. I mean honestly, why would anyone want to hurt my parents? They were just about the sweetest and kindest people you would ever want to meet. But no one ever asked me what I thought. That's the way it's always been with me and Hannah. I've always felt like a bit of a shadow, barely visible, which I attribute mostly to being so young when my parents died. In any case, I was merely an observer in the investigation because the police always dealt with Hannah."

"Look, I am really sorry about what happened to your parents Martha, and I know it must have been very hard for the two of you, but I still don't see the connection to Joe."

"I'm getting to that part. One day Hannah was out jogging and it started to pour down with rain and she met Joe who had been caught in the same storm. They got to talking and Joe told her that he often handled cold case files. Hannah explained that she knew first hand about cold cases and told him about my parents' deaths and so Joe offered to have a look at my parents' file."

"He's investigating your parent's accident?" Kate said incredulously.

"He is now and it's so senseless because all it does is dredge up a very tragic time. I am really upset that we have to go through all that again, particularly when I'm about to get married. But that's Hannah's decision, not mine."

"So why does Hannah want to reopen the case? Wouldn't it dredge up awful memories for her too?"

"Joe suggested improvements in the science of investigating these types of cases now that didn't exist then and that it might be worth having another look at my parents' case."

"I find it a bit odd that he would just reopen a case based on a casual conversation with someone he just met."

"Well, yes that's true, but then Hannah had some weird things happening to her like strange phone calls and someone sneaking around one night when she was home alone. Now those things don't necessarily point to my parents' accident I know, but then someone broke into the house and stole some things that had belonged to my parents."

"I wonder why someone would do that."

"I have to admit it was strange because the only value those things held was personal to Hannah. It looked as though whoever stole the box was looking for something specific because that's all they took." Martha offered robotically wondering why Kate didn't seem at all concerned that they had had a break in.

"Are you sure someone broke in? Maybe Hannah simply misplaced those things."

"Oh no, someone broke in for sure because Hannah was home."

"What? She was home! But then she must know who broke in!"

"No, when she realized someone was breaking in, she hid behind a chair so she didn't see the person clearly." Martha explained.

"Well, that doesn't mean that whoever took that stuff had anything to do with your parents' accident. Or am I missing something?"

"Joe had already begun questioning people about the accident, so he thinks it made someone a bit nervous. The only trouble is if they were looking for information that Hannah had that might implicate them, they didn't realize that she kept that information in a different box."

"...a different box?" Kate said almost silently.

"Hannah kept personal mementos in one box and in another box she kept all the information related to their deaths. I guess her thinking was to keep nice memories separated from bad memories. Anyway, usually both boxes are kept in her bedroom, but a couple of days before the break in, Hannah removed the one with all the information about the accident for Joe to look through."

"If they had done such a thorough job in the first place, why would Joe want Hannah's records?" Kate asked, clearly mystified.

"After the accident, literally, the next day, Hannah went to look at my parent's car after it had been towed so she could look at the damage and took all sorts of photographs. Then she went to the crash site she took even more."

"I'm sure the police would have taken the same photographs. That doesn't make sense."

"She actually went to the site of the accident just to see where they had died. That's when she saw the skid marks on the road and tire marks that were still imbedded in the snow bank. Since she had her camera in the car, she decided to take some more pictures. She told me then that she didn't know why she wanted those photographs but I think it was her way of trying to help herself deal with their deaths."

"So the police never asked for her photographs?"

"They looked through them, but, you're right, they had taken their own and felt they were all they needed. But Joe thinks he's on to something and wants to look at Hannah's photographs."

"And I suppose she was pretty happy about that." Kate offered.

"Happy? She was thrilled, ecstatic." Martha said shaking her head in disbelief.

"Are you supposed to be telling me all this Martha? It seems a bit strange that you're spilling the beans about the break-in and the investigation."

"I am telling you because you are under the wrong impression about Joe and Hannah being involved in a romantic way. I thought you would appreciate knowing the real reason. I know what it feels like to be disregarded and I just hoped it would make you feel better if you knew the truth. You and Hannah have been friends for a long time and I know she would never do anything to hurt you, just as you would never do anything to hurt her."

CHAPTER 58

The two woman sat is silence for a few minutes. Martha was not sure what to expect from Kate, whether she believed her or not, but she hoped her explanation was convincing.

"Why don't you put a stop to this Martha if you think its going to be so upsetting and pointless?" Kate suggested after some thought.

"You have to understand that Hannah has put most of her energy and heart into wanting this case to be properly solved. It's like she's stuck and can't get past my parents' deaths. Adam and I have given up trying to get her to date or even go out and enjoy herself. She just has to get the truth behind my parents' deaths out of her system before she can move on. Since I'm getting married soon, I don't want anything to spoil my plans or put a pall on the wedding day. So I keep my mouth shut because if I offer my opinion and tell her I don't agree with what she's doing, it will cause a lot of unnecessary tension between us."

"But Joe might find a link to something that was possibly missed. And the link just might be with Hannah's photographs."

"Yes there could possibly be a link. At least Joe thinks there is." Martha admitted, not sure where this was going to take her.

"Well think about it Martha. If Joe finds that link, it will certainly put a pall on the wedding as you say and all the days leading up to it because the case will certainly become the focus. Not you. Not your wedding." Kate offered gently.

Martha stared blankly at Kate and realized that she was right on target with her prediction. Martha also was struck by how these two women who were virtually forced into silence because of mistrust and uncertainty when they first sat down had now struck a level of trust and comfort with each other and any suspicion Kate possessed had now all but vanished.

"You're right Kate. I hadn't thought about that. I suppose I just expected that it would come up dry just like the last time."

"So, the threat to your piece of mind may be from photographs that Hannah took?" Kate prompted.

"It would seem that way."

"And Joe has the box now?"

"No, he hasn't picked it up yet. It's still in the kitchen."

"Well that's a good thing then." Kate said brightly.

"It is?" Martha said clearly confused.

"Yes because it will give you time to fix things..." Kate said leadingly.

"What do you mean fix things?" Martha asked innocently.

"If you think about it Martha, you don't want to have anything ruin your wedding day and if you think there's something in that box that could, well maybe..."

"Well maybe what Kate?" Martha said quietly hoping she would suggest a solution to her concerns.

"Well maybe you could look through the box and see what's in there. Find out what it is he might be looking for and get rid of it until after you get married."

"You mean temporarily dispose of it?"

"Temporarily or permanently, especially if you don't think the accident was deliberate. Probably it would be best if you destroyed it completely. Like you said, you will have to go through it all again. Let's face it, if Hannah took lots and lots of photographs, then one or two or more won't be noticed if they aren't in there."

"But how do I decide which ones to remove?"

"If the car that forced your parents off the road was never found, then the skid marks or the tire impressions in the snow could point to that car, so those would be the ones that I would remove." Kate suggested.

"Oh, of course." Martha said robotically, momentarily caught off guard by Kate unwittingly qualifying that she was aware that another car was involved. She was absolutely certain that she had not offered that piece of information to Kate. She wondered if at some point Hannah had.

"Look, I don't mean to offend you. I was just trying to help." Kate explained noticing that Martha appeared a bit uncomfortable with her suggestion. "It doesn't matter to me one way or another if you do what I suggest. It's your wedding."

"No, I'm not offended at all." Martha said recovering quickly. "I think it's a great idea. I won't be able to go through Hannah's things right away because Adam and I are away at our cottage for the next few nights, so I'll have to do it when I get back."

"I would be happy to go through them with you if you like." Kate offered kindly.

"That sounds like a great idea and I would love your help Kate. Two heads are better than one!" Martha said enthusiastically. "How about I call you when I get back from the cottage?"

Just then, Kate's phone rang and she ran to take the call. Martha turned to wave goodbye and began to leave the kitchen. Kate nodded and waved distractedly to Martha and then turned her attention back to her phone call. As Martha made her way down the hall, suddenly Kate was rushing past her.

"I'm sorry to be so rude Martha, but I have to run out quickly. Can you let yourself out?" Kate said impatiently as she pushed on her boots and grabbed her coat.

"What about locking your door?" Martha asked.

"There's a spare key hanging inside the garage door. If you could go get it and lock the door and put it back, that would be great." Kate instructed and without waiting for Martha's response, she ran out the front door and was gone.

Martha stood frozen in the hall and waited until she watched Kate pull out of the driveway and speed off down the street. As she slipped on her boots and coat, she began reconstructing her conversation with Kate. Did she make an assumption about her parents' car being forced off the road? Was she pretending not to know to spare her feelings? That seemed like too much of a coincidence.

Deciding to think about it later, she went out the front door and walked towards the side door to the garage. She turned the handle to the door and stepped inside to find it was shrouded in darkness. She groped around for a light and finally found a switch just to the left of the door. Once illuminated, Martha stood in her place as her eyes adjusted to the light. In front of her was a car covered completely in an old dusty tarp.

Not immediately curious, Martha focused on locating the key to Kate's front door. Just to her left, she spotted one dangling from a small rusty nail just slightly out of her reach. She was unaware there was a stair just below her feet and as she stepped towards the key, she lost her footing and fell directly towards the car. She grabbed onto the tarp hoping it would break her fall. Instead it slipped from its place and slumped like a blanket on top of her as she fell backwards onto the floor.

Momentarily dazed, she batted at the tarp to push it off and, using the bumper of the now exposed car, hoisted herself up off the damp floor.

'Well this is an old beauty.' Martha said to herself as she ran her hand along the passenger door. 'Well, maybe not so beautiful after all.' She mumbled as she examined a large dent and smashed headlight on the front passenger's side panel.

Her eye then caught a glint of what seemed to be a necklace dangling from the interior rearview mirror and peered in through the driver's window to get a closer look. It looked somewhat familiar but because the windows had been covered in a fine film of dirt, she could not see it clearly. Suddenly curious she tugged at the door's handle and the door pulled opened with a loud creaking noise. She slipped onto the seat and as her hand lifted to grasp the chain, she realized with horror that it was her mother's necklace.

On the passenger seat beside her lay the tin box that belonged to Hannah. And then with sickening clarity she realized why the car with a smashed headlight and crumpled fender was being hidden under a dusty old tarp in Kate's garage. This was the car that had been responsible for taking her parents' lives.

CHAPTER 59

Her first morning in London, Hannah woke to the sun spilling into her room. She checked the clock beside her bed and it read 9:00 a.m. She felt grateful for a full and uninterrupted night's sleep and, after showering and a quick breakfast, she went on a walking tour of the local area.

After about two hours, she felt the need to do some serious shopping and hailed a cab to take her to Harrods. If she thought the area around the hotel was remarkable, she was completely unprepared by the luxurious setting and the vastness of the store. As Hannah toured the premises, she noted the existence of an ancient Egyptian theme plainly to distinguish its most recent ownerships, remembering that the Al-Fayed family had in the previous year sold the landmark store for over $1.6 billion. It was patently clear that Harrods catered mostly to the wealthy and Hannah was surprised to learn enforced a dress code from its patrons as well as expecting all female staff to be wear makeup. Hannah recalled someone telling her Harrods had once hired a live Egyptian cobra to guard a pair of ruby sapphire and diamond sandals worth over $125,000.00.

The opulence of the store continued to greet her at every turn and on every level. She watched as a group of women, all of whom were in traditional Muslim dress, shopped for designer purses. Noticing her watchful gaze, one of the women finally turned to Hannah to question her right to be observing them.

"Are we taking too much time to choose?" The woman asked of Hannah.

"Oh no, not at all. Please just ignore me. I was just admiring your,

your, your..." Hannah blushed as she stammered hoping not to offend the woman.

"Chador?" The woman smiled as she held a portion of the luxuriant black robe that covered her body.

"Yes, chador..." Hannah repeated, hoping that her pronunciation was close to that of the woman's.

"Where are you from?" The woman asked kindly.

"Canada." Hannah answered simply.

"I'm very fond of Canadians, although I admit I've not visited Canada."

"You should one day. I should leave you to your shopping. I'm sorry to have bothered you." Hannah apologized.

"You have been no bother. Do you mind me asking your opinion?" The woman asked as she held up two purses - one a deep rich yellow and the other a soft grey. "Which purse do you like if you were to choose...I can't seem to decide?"

"The yellow is so unusual, but if I had to choose, it would be the grey one."

"I think the grey is nicer too. It's more expensive, but it's worth it to me. Can you guess what it is made of?" The woman asked in a soft lilting accent.

"I have no idea. It looks like leather, but what kind, I'm not sure." Hannah confessed.

"It's made of python skin." She answered with a smile while holding the bag out to Hannah.

"Did you say python?" Hannah responded by touching the bag instead of taking it from the woman. She was surprised by the softness of the rare skin.

"Yes, it is truly made of python skin."

"I had no idea that a purse could be made out of a snake." Hannah laughed.

"This purse is by a well known designer and she seems to prefer making her purses from exotic skins of snakes. Its value is £3,450.00." The woman stated calmly.

"What did you say?" Hannah almost shouted in disbelief. By this time the other women who were in this woman's company had gathered close by. Their robes were the same heavy black fabric, the quality unmistakable. Each woman's face was flawlessly and strikingly made up so that their eyes were thickly lined in black kohl and their lips each perfectly highlighted with scarlet lipstick. Hannah felt suddenly underdressed and plain in their presence.

"I said it is worth £3,450.00." She repeated as her friends exchanged quick smiles.

"But that's more than $7,000.00!" Hannah said with astonishment, suddenly forgetting her feelings of plainness.

"Do you think it's too much?"

"Oh no, not at all!" Hannah exclaimed with gentle sarcasm. "I think you should get two!"

"I think one is enough." She smiled as she extracted her wallet from her pocket.

"You're not kidding. Are you really going to buy that?"

"Yes, I am. I like you and trust your judgment. What's your name?"

"Hannah."

"That's a beautiful name Hannah. My name is Neema."

"Neema" Hannah repeated. "I've never heard that name before. Its very pretty."

"Thank you. It means 'born of wealthy parents'."

"Well that makes sense." Hannah laughed. "Where are you from Neema?"

"I was born in Egypt, but I live here now. What does your name mean Hannah?"

"My name means favour or grace."

"Well it suits you very much and it was so nice to meet you." Neema said.

"It's been nice meeting you as well and I really hope you enjoy your purse, and whatever you do, don't lose it!" Hannah laughed.

"I won't. I hope you enjoy your stay here." Neema offered as Hannah waved goodbye, with Neema's small entourage following closely behind her as they made their way to the cash counter.

CHAPTER 60

Feeling that she wouldn't be able to top the moment after Neema purchased her new and very expensive purse, Hannah decided it would be best to leave the store on a high note. Hannah realized she had been handed two opportunities to meet two extraordinary people in as many days. Her world was expanding and her life back home now seemed not only miles away but years away. Prior to leaving for London, Hannah believed she could never adapt to anything other than the comfort of what she knew and was even prepared to exist within that comfort. Since meeting Michael and now Neema, and because of all the changes that were unfolding back home, she felt she could now open her mind to new possibilities.

Hannah walked through Harrods to its front entrance and out onto Brompton Street to hail a cab. The ride back to the hotel offered welcomed relief to her tired feet and she looked forward to relaxing at the hotel. After paying the cabbie, she ran quickly into the lobby to make her way to her room when one of the front desk attendants called to her.

"Miss Hutton, you have a message in your mailbox." The desk clerk advised as Hannah made her way towards her.

"Thank you." Hannah responded and then took the note from the clerk's hand. She opened the pale blue sheet of paper that featured the name and crest of the hotel. It was a hand written note advising her that a taxi would be there to pick her up the following morning to take her to her meeting with Robert O'Shea in central London.

'I almost forgot about our appointment.' Hannah said quietly to herself.

"Is everything alright Miss Hutton?" The clerk asked.

"Yes, perfectly fine, thank you." Hannah smiled.

Hannah arrived at her room and after soaking in a hot bath, she decided to order room service. After finishing her meal and reviewing the documents for her meeting with Robert, she settled into a relaxed and peaceful sleep. It seemed that only minutes had passed before her phone was ringing for her wake up call the next morning.

'I don't know who invented room service, but I could get very used to this.' Hannah said again to herself after placing an order for morning coffee and a freshly baked scone with raspberry jam. 'And I have to stop talking to myself. That or get some new friends to talk to.'

Within the hour Hannah was being whisked by cab towards Robert's offices. She tried to picture what it would be like to meet someone she had only talked with over the phone. She imagined him to be tall with silvered hair and very slender, and since he and Paul had been friends for years, she knew he would likely be close to his age as well.

'I'll have to see if I'm right.' Hannah mumbled.

"Excuse me Miss? Did you say something?" The driver asked in a very broad northern English accent.

"No, I was just talking to myself. I seem to be doing a lot of that lately." She explained.

"Oh that's alright Luv, we all do. It's perfectly normal behaviour." The cabbie responded kindly.

After about a twenty minute ride, the cab driver safely dropped her outside the office tower of Robert O'Shea's offices. It was a stately white building featuring crimson double front doors. Hannah pushed through the heavy red doors and made her way down a long marbled hallway. A security guard directed her to the elevators that soon deposited her onto the sixth floor. Finally, she found her way down another hallway where she offered her name to Robert O'Shea's receptionist.

"Mr. O'Shea won't be a minute Miss Hutton." The receptionist informed Hannah after she had called through to his office. "Please feel free to have a seat."

As Hannah was about to seat herself she heard her name being called and turned to be greeted by Robert.

"Hannah, it's so good to meet you finally. I'm Robert." He said extending his hand to hers.

Hannah's idea of what she imagined Robert would look like was not far off but for the fact his hair was brown and he wasn't as slender as she expected. He led her down a long hall and after offering to take her coat, they settled into his office. They talked about her trip and he made certain that she was comfortable staying at her hotel.

"I'm glad you think it's so luxurious, its one of my favourites." He qualified. "Why don't we get all this business stuff out of the way first and then we can go out and have a relaxing lunch if you have time."

"I'd love to go for lunch afterwards. That sounds really nice." Hannah smiled.

After Robert had signed all the paperwork, they left his office and walked a short distance to a traditional English pub where they enjoyed a relaxing lunch. They discussed Paul at length and Hannah admitted her concerns over his health.

"I've known Paul a long time Hannah, and I'm sure he will be well enough and pull through. He's a fighter." Robert reassured.

"I know he is, but he's so concerned about his practice and I'm afraid he won't give himself the time to get properly rested." Hannah admitted.

"I have a very strong feeling that this accident will make him realize that life is too short to spend time worrying about his work. I reckon he will put things properly into perspective and assess what's really important and what's not. I won't be surprised if he decides to focus on his family and spend less time worrying about companies like mine."

Hannah looked intently at Robert and wondered if he knew more than he was admitting. It is quite likely that he knew that Paul was Sally's father. She was tempted to ask, but she didn't want to delve into the intricacies of this with a man she hardly knew. Hannah realized too that Robert was not aware of the close bond she had with Paul as he spoke honestly about the gravity of his accident little realizing the emotional impact it would have on her. She did not have the heart to tell him that his comments were distressing her. Her gaze changed to a smile that she hoped would not belie her concern.

"I guess all we can do is to wait and see. He's an intelligent man and he will know what's best." Hannah conceded.

"Have you had a chance to talk with him since you've arrived in England?"

"No, not yet. When I think about it, I realize its either too late or too early to call given the time difference." Hannah admitted.

"I'll tell you what, I'll go back to the office and give him a ring and I'll be able to get a sense of how he's doing. I reckon he should be awake by now. How about if I call you at the hotel later and let you know how he's doing?" Robert offered kindly as he waved off her offer to pay for her own lunch.

"I'd appreciate that Robert, thank you. Thank you for the lunch too. It was so nice to have finally met you."

"Shall I have my driver take you back to your hotel?" Robert asked after he had paid for their lunches.

"No thank you. I think I'm going to take advantage of some shopping and I'll make my way back on my own."

CHAPTER 61

Now midday, the streets of London were congested with taxis, buses, cars and throngs of people. Hannah pushed her way along Oxford Street ducking in and out of its many stores. With opportunities presented all around her to shop, Hannah bought only a few items. She felt unsettled by her conversation with Robert regarding Paul's health and decided that she would shop another day and hailed a cab to take her back to her hotel so she could await Robert's call. As she climbed into the taxi, she sensed the driver was not an affable man and so was grateful for the solitude since a protracted conversation would be out of the question.

The taxi pulled up alongside the curb to her hotel and she slid forward on the seat to hand the fare to the driver. Despite the lack of conversation between them, she decided to give him a generous tip not only for the quiet afforded her but also out of superstition in hopes that her kindness would generate a positive report from Robert.

Within minutes Hannah was walking through the lobby of the hotel when once again she heard her name being called. She realized that Robert must have already left a message for her and automatically she turned to approach the front desk where she was greeted by the desk clerk.

"Hello, do you have a message for me?" Hannah inquired expectantly.

"Let me check for you. Could I have your name please?" The attendant asked.

"Hannah Hutton, but I think someone just called my name. Perhaps it was the other attendant." Hannah offered.

"I'll check for you. I won't be a moment." The attendant smiled.

Hannah watched as the desk clerk checked her mail box and then spoke briefly to the other male attendant.

"I'm sorry Miss Hutton there are no messages for you."

"I don't understand. I heard my name called." Hannah said.

"I believe it may have been the gentleman standing behind you." The desk clerk offered.

"Behind me?" Hannah said not quite understanding but turned to look behind her.

She wondered if for just an instant her heart stopped beating. Her head seemed in conflict with what her eyes were telling her. It didn't make sense. She faltered briefly wondered if she was truly seeing Joe standing there before her.

"Is it really you?" She said only realizing when he answered that she had spoken out loud.

"It's really me." Joe replied as his face broke into a slight smile. Despite the confidence he felt in waiting for her, he now felt uncertain, even vulnerable, and had taken a liberty that he had no right to take. Despite his reservation, he held out his hand to her and to his complete relief she took it.

"I don't know what to say." Hannah admitted.

"That's so unlike you." Joe teased.

Hannah laughed that that was normally true, but this time she felt compelled to set her shyness aside.

"Clearly the last thing I expected is to see you standing in my hotel lobby and in England no less. But wait, is everything alright?" Hannah suddenly feared that he was there to deliver bad news from home.

"Everything is fine. Everyone is fine back home." Joe added. "I had some business to take care of here and I didn't want to pass up the opportunity to see you."

"Did you know before I left for England that you had business here?" Hannah asked sensing that it was too much of a coincidence.

"No I didn't. The opportunity surfaced after you arrived. I flew in early this morning, had a nap and then came here to find you. I called Martha and asked her where you were staying. I hope that was alright."

"No, I mean yes, of course that was alright. I…"

"I have waited in the lobby for awhile hoping that you wouldn't be upset that I was here." Joe interrupted. "I'm grateful that you didn't decide to go out dancing 'til the wee hours, but even if you had, I would have waited."

"I think the reason I am always so tongue tied is because you say and do things that I have no experience in knowing how to respond."

"I guess I haven't presented myself in the traditional way. Look, Hannah I was hoping that you might be free for dinner? Somewhere a little more relaxed?"

"I would love to go to dinner with you, but I have to admit I had lunch about two hours ago, and I'm expecting a call…"

"Oh of course, you have plans. I should have expected that." Joe confessed.

"No, no, it's not like that. I mean I don't have plans. I'm waiting for a call about my Uncle Paul. I feel so far away, and I was hoping he was improving."

"He is. I forgot to tell you. When I called Martha to ask where you were staying, she asked me to tell you that he was better and the doctors were hopeful that he would be home sooner than expected."

"Really? He really is?"

"Yes, really. But listen, if you would rather wait for your call to be sure, I understand and we can go to dinner another time."

"No, that's alright. If Martha told you specifically to tell me, then that makes me feel better."

"So, yes to dinner?"

"Yes, okay."

"How about going in about an hour? We don't have to eat right away, we could just talk." Joe suggested.

"Okay, but it should only take about half an hour for me to change. I think you've waited long enough." Hannah offered.

"Whatever works best for you. Take your time."

Within half an hour Hannah was back in the lobby where Joe was still waiting. He stood and watched as Hannah walked towards him.

"You look really nice Hannah."

"Thank you…for waiting."

Joe smiled and simply nodded. They looked at each other until it became uncomfortable. Joe broke the silence and as he spoke he slipped his hand on the small of her back to lead her towards the hotel's front door.

"I took the liberty of booking a reservation at a small Italian restaurant down the road. Shall we take a taxi or would you like to walk?"

"It's a nice evening, so let's walk. I think I've had my fill of taxi cabs." Hannah admitted.

As they made their way out of the hotel, they were greeted by a calm and warm night.

"You brought nice weather with you Hannah." Joe suggested.

"Really?"

"Yes, really. Normally we would be either wearing a coat or carrying an umbrella."

"I think you should take credit for bringing the nice weather since it was raining when I arrived." Hannah confessed.

"Okay, I'll take the credit but I have to admit, I really love the rain. In fact, I now prefer it over a sunny day."

"You do? That's unusual."

"Aren't you going to ask me why?"

"Okay, why?" Hannah laughed.

"Because I met you in the rain." Joe said simply.

"I remember. We did meet in the rain." Hannah said softly, but then suddenly lost for words.

Hannah and Joe walked in silence - Hannah quietly pleased because of his comment and Joe content simply to be in her presence. As if on cue, a gentle rain began to fall, so gentle that they both looked up to the sky to verify its existence. Within minutes the rain picked up its pace and began to fall in earnest. With no umbrella, Joe grabbed onto Hannah's hand and they ran laughing towards the restaurant. Minutes later they arrived at its doors, wetter but happier that their earlier conversation had been sealed by an offer of fate. The maitre d' welcomed them and noticing they had been caught in the rain, offered them a table for two near the fireplace.

CHAPTER 62

Hannah and Joe were offered menus and quickly decided on salads with pasta entrées and a bottle of Valpolicella. Their conversation remained light until after their server had poured their wine. Hannah sipped lightly as she listened to Joe recount his first visit to England years ago. After some time had passed, she felt the need to push Joe for the true reason behind his visit.

"Joe, why are you really here in England?"

Joe, clearly caught off guard by the question, hesitated, and then looked down at the table. He toyed with the knife that had been set before him, turning it this way and that, as though one direction would help him decide which way the conversation should go. He became mesmerized by it until Hannah believed he had forgotten that she was even there. She slid her hand gently across the table to interrupt his interest in the knife.

"Is it that bad?" She pressed.

"I hope you won't think so."

"Try me." Feeling a bit buoyed up by the courage her wine had given her.

"Okay. The real reason I came to England was to see you. I didn't want to wait any longer to tell you what I need to tell you."

"It sounds serious." Hannah laughed lightly and hoped that she appeared relaxed but silently felt a sense of dread.

"Let me start with this. I hope you remember my promise to you the night you called about Kate breaking into your home." As Joe spoke he gently released her hand and reached into his pocket.

"What promise?"

"Open your hand." Joe instructed and as she did so, he placed her mother's necklace into her palm. She looked down and looked back up to Joe's face with a look of disbelief on her face.

"You got it back from Kate! But how were you able to do that?" Hannah questioned quietly. Joe rose from his chair and without speaking took the necklace from her hand, placed it around her neck and secured the clasp. Hannah waited and once he returned to his seat, he began to explain.

"I think you will remember some of what I'm about say but, for the sake of it making sense I will have to repeat myself." Joe looked up for her understanding and Hannah simply nodded.

"You may remember that I explained to you awhile ago that Kate was a peripheral part of our group of friends. I admit I had had a relationship of, lets say, convenience with her during my first year of university. I tired of her and so she had made things uncomfortable for me for awhile when I made it clear that I didn't want a serious relationship with her, but for the most part, she kept her distance. During my second year of university I started dating a girl. It wasn't a serious relationship, but I liked her. She endured Kate's antics with a lot of patience. I admit, I didn't have the same amount of patience. Just as an example, there was an incident one evening during our final year where Kate had behaved so badly and was so embarrassing that I realized I needed to send her a very clear message. I was very angry with her and let her know."

"Was it at a small bar at the edge of town?" Hannah asked, trying to put the pieces together from the conversation she had with Kate at Martha's engagement party.

"Yes we were celebrating our graduation. Why?" Joe asked.

"The night of my sister's engagement party, Kate went into great detail about that incident. She told me that you were cheating on her and sneaking around behind her back and she caught you with another girl. I remember feeling so sorry for her."

"The event happened, but not at all the way she made it out to be. I realize now that her behaviour today might be considered stalking, and maybe it was even back then, but I was too young to realize it. I just remember that every time I turned around, or went somewhere, most of the time she was there too. She followed me everywhere. That night at the bar she witnessed my girlfriend with her arms around my neck and Kate lost it. She actually began hitting both of us while screaming disgusting remarks at us. She eventually had to be physically removed from the place."

"How horrible." Hannah mumbled realizing that Kate was quite capable of that kind of behaviour.

"Unfortunately, that night was the final straw and the relationship with my girlfriend ended. I had threatened Kate with a restraining order, but I couldn't be sure it would even matter to her. The best I could do was to get away and so the timing seemed right to go to England. I loved it here, every bit of it and I stayed a long time. But as much as I wanted to stay, I knew I had to go home to Canada.

About six weeks after I came home, I accidently ran into Kate. She behaved like we were dear old friends and insisted that we have a coffee together. I admitted to her that I felt it wasn't a good idea, but she assured me she had changed and she wanted a chance to explain herself. Stupidly, I thought that there would be no harm in having a coffee together. She reminisced about university and what wonderful times they were. Then she began talking about our relationship and admitted that she had gone to ridiculous extremes in order to have me. She was embarrassed and asked me if I could ever forgive her for the horribly insecure way she behaved.

When we parted company that day, I felt certain she no longer had any feelings for me. So when she invited me to a barbeque promising that a lot of my friends would be there, I accepted. I told her that I could only stay for an hour because I was meeting my parents for dinner later. When I arrived at the barbecue, I was the first one there. She assured me that the others would be there soon, but I have to admit I felt something was up. We chatted for an hour or so about nothing in particular and so I was completely unprepared for what was about to happen.

Another hour went by and still none of the guests had arrived. I needed to get home so I told her I was going to leave. She insisted that I stay longer. Then she came over and sat down beside me and took my hand in hers. She confessed that no one else was coming and that she had used the idea of a barbeque with all my old friends as a way to lure me there by myself. My heart sank. She said she still had strong feelings for me and was convinced now more than ever that we were meant to be together. I was so annoyed. I had let my guard down and she was back in my life again. I was angry at myself but I told her she was making a fool out of herself and I was not interested in her. Never was, never could be, and never would be. She got incredibly upset and pleaded with me to at least try.

I probably should have felt sorry for her, but I was so livid that she had wasted my time. I told her I was going home and started walking to the front door. She grabbed at my arm and said if I stayed she would make it worth my while. I pushed her hands away and made it perfectly clear that there was never going to be anything between us. She became almost childlike, crying and pleading with me over and over. I demanded that she grow up and stop begging. It was like a switch being turned off. She calmed down immediately, but the look that settled over her face was one of complete calm and resignation. Then she smiled, looked directly into my eyes, apologized, and said she hoped I had a nice time at the restaurant with my parents. She calmly opened the door and said goodbye. I was so relieved to be out of there.

When I arrived home about ten minutes later, I pulled into the driveway and noticed that my parents' car had a flat tire. I ran inside and said I would take care of it and suggested they drive my car to the restaurant and I would meet them there after I had fixed it. About an hour later after I had finished replacing the tire and cleaned up, my parents arrived back at the house. My father's face was absolutely white and my mother was sobbing. My dad said that on their way to the restaurant they had witnessed a terrible car accident. He said a car came out of nowhere, deliberately ran into the path of another car, hit it and forced it off the road. The driver sped off without stopping or even slowing down. My parents called the police and while they waited for the ambulance to arrive, my father ran over to the car to try and help but he couldn't get near it because it had gone down an embankment and had flipped on its side. He had no idea if the occupants were alive or dead. He could only wait. Finally the paramedics and fire trucks arrived. As the police questioned my parents, my father overhead the paramedics say the occupants of the car didn't survive the crash."

"My parents..." Hannah said numbly. The unlikely yet cruel coincidence of Joe's parents witnessing the final moments of Hannah's parents' lives had yet to strike Hannah. She focused instead on his words that confirmed those that she had heard years before where a deliberate act ended her parents' lives. All else at that moment, be it coincidence or fate, seemed irrelevant.

Joe gripped her fingers to confirm her discovery. "Are you alright Hannah?" Joe asked quietly. Hannah responded by simply nodding her head and asked Joe to continue.

"My parents felt compelled to go to the funeral to pay their respects and so I offered to take them. Sometimes small towns draw large interest to these types of tragedies, but this was like nothing I had ever witnessed. They were clearly respected and loved by many. The tributes were inspiring but the one that was most memorable was the victims' oldest daughter standing up before the congregation, so young and so vulnerable. Her grief was so raw and her words were so compelling."

Hannah's face fell as her eyes filled with tears. Memories of her parents' funeral were pulled cruelly into the present as she recalled that difficult day.

"I know this is painful Hannah, but I have to keep going because I want you to see the connection." Joe explained gently. Hannah simply nodded.

"We stayed for the reception afterward because my father wanted to offer his sympathies. I decided to wait out in the hallway for them. As I waited, I was surprised to see Kate walk through from the reception area. She looked lost and afraid."

"Kate was at my parents' funeral?" Hannah interrupted abruptly.

"Yes."

"What in the world was she doing at my parents' funeral?" She demanded.

"For a ridiculous moment I thought she had followed me, but then I realized that she hadn't even noticed I was there. I decided to forget my earlier determination to not have anything to do with her because I was curious as to why she was there too. But, when she saw me approaching her, she turned and ran back into the reception room. I assumed then that she wanted to avoid me because she was embarrassed by her behaviour when I had last seen her. Finally my parents came out of the reception and quite frankly I forgot all about Kate being there."

"I need to leave here." Hannah whispered. "Can we please leave?"

"What? Yes, oh of course, let's leave." Joe agreed. Joe threw more than an adequate amount of money on the table for the bill and ran to catch up to Hannah who had already made her way to the door. They made their way to the sidewalk before either spoke.

"I'm so sorry Hannah. In my attempt to explain everything I have been an insensitive idiot."

Hannah remained silent and continued to walk determinedly along the sidewalk to her hotel not even sure she was going in the right direction.

"Hannah. Please. I'm sorry." Joe insisted firmly as he ran up behind her. Hannah spun round and faced him. Her eyes were brimming with tears and the pain on her face was almost unbearable to him.

"I'm not doing this to hurt you Hannah. Honestly, I'm not."

"I want to hear this, but then I don't. It's so hard Joe. You came all the way here to tell me the truth about my parents' accident, and I want to know what you have to tell me, but I don't think I can bear it. Every day I think about that day when I lost them. Every day I wonder why they aren't here. My sister and I lost them at such a critical point in our lives, at such a critical point in their own lives, and I have done everything in my power to live as normally as possible beyond that injustice. I know that the police couldn't find the person who deliberately drove my parents off the road even though they tried so hard. But what I remember is the names of the witnesses were called Philpots, not Hastings. So why are you telling me that your parents were the only witnesses? It can't be possible."

Joe faltered momentarily as he realized with frustration that he had completely overlooked a simple but significant piece of information.

"My parents' surname is Philpot. My own father, Peter Hastings, died when I was only five. About a year after he died, my mother met and married a man named John Philpot and we moved to Stolpe, not far from where I now know you and your family had your family cottage. A few years after they married, John wanted to officially adopt me. My mother felt it would dishonour my father if I changed my name from Hastings to Philpot and while she agreed that John adopt me, she insisted I keep my biological father's name. I was so young when he died, I don't have many memories of him, except his name."

"So your parents witnessed the deaths of my parents. It seems like an incredible coincidence that years later I would meet you. And now you are here."

"Hannah, if you let me finish you will see the connection and understand everything. It doesn't have to be tonight. It doesn't even have to be here in England. I'll go home and I'll wait until you're ready after you get home."

Hannah looked beyond Joe's face and stared into the night. "Whether I'm here or back home, I don't have a choice but to hear it all do I?"

"You have to hear it. You should hear it. But I think you should be ready to hear it. I won't force it on you."

She looked back to his face and realized that he was struggling just as much as she was.

"I prefer to go back to the hotel and you can tell me there. That way, if I need to scream, no one will hear me but you." Hannah offered half jokingly. Joe nodded in agreement, and then in silence they walked the few blocks back to the hotel with Hannah leading the way.

CHAPTER 63

Once they had arrived at Hannah's hotel, she invited Joe to her room, sat down opposite him in the small sitting room in her suite and looked resolutely at Joe. "I'm ready now." She instructed, and, as if there had been no interruption, Joe continued.

"After the funeral, my parents tirelessly tried to help the police, and to their credit, they seemed determined to find the driver of that car. My father was consumed by it, losing sleep and even going back to the crash site time after time to see if he could remember something that he had missed. As the months wore on, he became a different man because it was all he could talk about or think about. About a year or so after the accident the police informed him that they had no choice but to close the case.

Whether related or unrelated, soon after that my dad had a heart attack and died. His death all but destroyed my mother and she asked me never to speak of the accident again. She needed to put it behind her because it became the focus of their lives and I think on some level she felt robbed of my father during the last two years of his life."

"I can understand that." Hannah offered solemnly.

"I could too and respected her request and never spoke of it again. Then, about a year ago, after I had joined the Special Units Department, I was visiting my mother and I was talking generally about some of the cold cases I was working on. Surprisingly, she mentioned the fatal accident that she and my dad had witnessed. She wondered if it was in my jurisdiction to reopen the case suggesting that it would be an appropriate tribute to my dad if I were to solve it. I reminded her of the promise not to speak of it again and asked why she had had a change of heart. She realized her grief initially compromised her thinking. My father's death was devastating to her but she realized that her anger wasn't productive. He always believed that those two young girls who lost their parents needed to know the truth. She pleaded with me to try and solve it."

"Have you?" Hannah asked without looking at him.

"I have."

"And that's why you're here."

"Yes." Joe confirmed quietly.

Hannah remained quiet but looked up at him, her eyes offering an invitation for him to go on.

"The investigation was slow at first but I knew if I stuck at it something would surface. Then one night I got lucky. Josh Hardcastle is a good friend of mine who I met in University and one night we were out having a beer together. He told me he had run into Kate who, by strange coincidence, had moved across the street from his brother's girlfriend. Kate asked Josh about me explaining that the last time she had seen me was at a funeral years before. Josh asked her whose funeral it had been and she said it was for a couple who had died in a car accident. She explained that she didn't know them but she had seen the accident and since they were local, she wanted to go to the funeral."

"When I got home later that night I kept thinking about Josh's conversation with Kate. There was something that was off about it, something that didn't make sense. And then it suddenly struck me what it was."

"What?" Hannah questioned innocently.

"Kate said she had attended the funeral because she had seen the accident. Since my father and my mother were the only ones to witness the accident, she couldn't possibly have seen it unless..."

"Unless she was making it up so she could justify following you to the funeral." Hannah guessed.

"Initially I thought that, but remember when you thought Kate's behaviour wasn't really about me, but about something else?"

"Yes, I remember."

"Well you were right." Joe confessed.

"Okay I was right, so why did she say she saw the accident when she didn't?"

"Because she did see the accident…"

"She did? But you said your parents were the only witnesses." Hannah interrupted clearly confused.

"She saw it because she caused it." Joe explained gently.

"What?" Hannah demanded.

"She was driving the car that forced your parents' car off the road."

"What?" Hannah said almost inaudibly, her face draining of all colour. "Why would Kate want to hurt my parents?"

"She didn't want to hurt your parents. She wanted to hurt me. She thought I was driving that car and so they were never her intended victims. I was."

"This isn't making any sense. What are you talking about?" Hannah shrieked.

"I discovered from the police report that the car your parents were driving was a 1997 red Honda Civic del Sol."

"Yes, it was a new car. They had only had for about a year." Hannah explained impatiently.

"When I saw the photograph of your parents' car, I realized it could easily have been my car. My car was a 1993 red Mazda RX7. Even though it wasn't new, I kept it in pristine condition so it looked almost new. From even a close distance both cars look similar. This is where Kate comes in. When I left her house that day to meet my parents for dinner, the calm she seemed to display was just an act. She was actually seething inside with anger. I believe that she wanted to avenge those feelings and knowing that there was only one route from my place to the restaurant, she drove to a certain point along the road and waited for me to drive by. When she saw what she thought was my car approaching, she quite literally and figuratively saw red and drove directly into its path, hitting it and forcing it off the road."

"You're telling me that Kate killed my parents?" Hannah demanded incredulously.

"Yes, unintentionally, but yes she did. I was her target, not your parents." Joe said as he leaned forward in his chair towards Hannah. "Her simple admission to Josh that she had seen the accident was indirectly a confession. It was innocent in its delivery, but guilty in its interpretation. I knew it wasn't enough to make a solid conclusion, so I had to be patient and wait until I had enough to go on to be sure that I was on the right track. I had to be careful that Kate was not aware of my suspicions. Josh knew I was investigating the case and I swore him to secrecy because if there was a slip up, then everything may have been compromised. The unfortunate events involving Sally and her ex-boyfriend offered me a way to protect you and insert a police presence on the pretense of a concern for retaliation from the ex."

"But it didn't offer me protection. Kate was in a rage and verbally attacked me since she was convinced that it was you who had put the police car outside my door." Hannah explained impatiently.

"I know, I know." Joe offered. "I understand that you had to endure her barrage of insults but I knew she hadn't discovered the real reason the car was there. Ironically, she was upset that the car was put there to watch you, but it actually was there to watch her so she wouldn't do anything to hurt you or your sister."

"Why in the world would she hurt me or Martha?"

"Once I was certain that Kate was involved and I began to investigate her whereabouts, and knowing that she had moved across the street from the victims' children, I just couldn't accept that it was pure coincidence.

"You think she deliberately moved across the street from us? Why would she do that?"

"There could be any number of reasons, and I won't pretend to know all the answers, but I'm convinced the main one is because of the crime she committed. There is a lot of power in what she did – ill-placed power, but power nonetheless. Two people had very different lives because of what she did. There is a psychology that some experts explain about people who commit murders. Some have an exaggerated attachment to the victim or victims, returning to the scene of the crime and will even attend the funeral to witness its impact like Kate did with your parents."

"That's sick." Hannah mumbled shaking her head.

"Initially, she may have had a strange curiosity about you. Maybe she felt a moral obligation to find out how you and Martha were doing since your parents had died. Maybe to ease what little conscience she had she hoped you both were alright."

"I suspect after all I know about her that we were the last things that mattered to her. I don't think she cares about anything but herself."

"I agree with that too. I also think she wanted to get close to you and gain your trust and loyalty. The better she knew you, the better she could influence you or intimidate you."

"So all along I have been manipulated by her?" Hannah asked simply.

"Yes she manipulated you as she had manipulated most things in her life I suspect. Not easy to hear Hannah, but she is the type of woman who is prepared to stop at nothing if she feels justified enough to have it."

"With no remorse or no concern except for herself." Hannah added.

"Hannah, the day I met you when we were out running, I had actually been following Kate who had been running behind you."

"She was following me?" Hannah said as a shiver spiked up her back.

"She was, but then it started to rain and she turned back. Just so she wouldn't see me, I ran for shelter and that's where you found me."

"But she wasn't a runner. I asked her so many times to try it and she just refused. So how does that make sense?"

"I suspect she was simply keeping watch over what you were doing, where you were going, who you were with... She must have always felt the pressure of discovery. Something must have triggered her concern and I think she found ways to follow you without you becoming suspicious. "

"And whenever she saw you, I was close by and it must have started to worry her that we might become close. She kept inferring that there was a romantic link between us, but she really wasn't concerned about that. She was really concerned that you would tie her to my parents' deaths."

"The only way I could keep an eye on her and make sure she didn't feel cornered was to follow her. I didn't intend to meet you that day in the rain, but I will always be grateful that I did. You possessed a vulnerability that I wasn't expecting and I became more concerned for you."

"What about Martha? Were you not worried about her?"

"Yes, of course, but not as much as for you. Martha spent most of her time with Adam. Whether by coincidence or design, Kate's interest focused on you because she saw you getting to know me. That was dangerous to her."

"Tell me about that day at the shopping centre. You and Kate were having a conversation and when you tried to end it, she made up a ridiculous excuse to chase after you to continue the conversation. She intimated to me that you were there to seek her out. Why didn't she become suspicious then as to why you knew me?"

"At that point she didn't put any importance on the fact that I knew you. She foolishly thought that I had come to town to seek her out. I actually still live in Stolpe, so I've been commuting back and forth for work. I told her that I was there working on a case and she became annoyed. Your presence was a welcomed relief to me because I could use it as an excuse to finish the conversation with her, but it was clearly an annoying interruption to her. Nevertheless, I was worried that she had seen me at all and it was a careless slip up on my part. I felt I put you in a vulnerable position and after that I had to be more careful and keep a distance."

"How long had you been watching her?" Hannah asked.

"About five months. We were hoping that she would do something significant that might incriminate her."

"Other than breaking into my house?"

"Yes, we had an unmarked car outside your house most nights. It wouldn't always park in the same place because we didn't want to raise suspicion. One night, the officer on duty radioed in to say that someone seemed to be sneaking around your house. Luckily, he just waited and watched and it ended up that it was Kate."

"Luckily...? Why didn't the police do something?"

"She could have easily explained that she was a neighbour and you and she were good friends. If we had questioned you, you would have agreed, and so it wasn't worth the risk to question her."

"That was the night someone was outside my house. I was terrified and then she called me and it was so late. I never did find out why she phoned me that night." Hannah thought back to that night when, ironically, she felt grateful to talk to Kate who calmed her down from her fears.

"I think she looked in the window and saw that you were home. I suppose she hoped you hadn't seen her, so she called to check. Even if you had thought to ask her why she called, she would have lied." Joe explained.

"Why was she there? Why didn't she just knock on the door?" Hannah asked fearfully.

"I think she wanted to make sure you weren't home so she could search your house to see if you had discovered anything about her. I think she stole that tin box because she thought it might contain information on the accident or about her. She must have wanted to assure herself that there was nothing in it to point to her involvement in your parents' deaths."

"None of this makes sense. Why would she take my mother's necklace and even be bothered to put it on. It was such a strange thing to do."

"It may have been relief or a way of rewarding herself for her deceit. I can only guess at how a mind like hers works."

CHAPTER 64

Hannah gently raised her hand to the necklace that was resting securely around her own neck. She couldn't quite put her emotions in order, feeling numb to all that she had been told. There was a bit of relief in knowing that her parents' deaths were solved but the bitterness she felt because of the senselessness was almost more than she could stomach and all at Kate's hand. The fact that she was beguiled by her manipulation and her friendship was humiliating.

"You still haven't explained how you got my mother's necklace back." Hannah stated.

"Martha got it back."

"But I don't think she even knew it was missing. In fact she didn't know that Kate had broken in and taken anything since you asked me not to say anything to anyone."

"Actually Martha did know. Right after you had left for England, I enlisted Josh's help to get together with Adam and Martha. He suggested that your Uncle Paul's place was not far from the airport. I felt it was best to let Martha know as soon as possible what I suspected about Kate, particularly since she was going to be on her own while you were in England. So, we met at Paul's home and I told Martha about the break in and that, among other things, she had stolen your mother's necklace and I wanted to get it back for you."

"She must have been so upset."

"Angry is more like it but upset for you. She confessed she didn't care much for Kate and always knew there was something not quite right about her."

"I always said she had an insight into people that I don't possess.

I think she was never comfortable about my friendship with Kate but had the grace never to interfere."

"Ironically in the end she did interfere and it forced Kate into a corner. You would have been proud by her determination to put an end to Kate's deception. It was really brave of her."

"What did she do?" Hannah asked innocently.

"I realized that we were always teetering on the edge with Kate. Even though I was convinced about her connection to your parents' deaths, most of it was circumstantial and of course we needed more than that. We were better off with a confession since hard evidence wasn't readily available."

"How would it be even remotely possible that she would confess? I would think that would be the last thing she would be tempted to do."

"Well I had a few ideas but most of them were shots in the dark. After I told Martha that Kate had broken into your house I explained to her that she was looking for possible evidence that could implicate her. I said to Martha that it was unfortunate in a way that we didn't catch Kate in the act. It wouldn't necessarily be a reason to implicate her but it would be a start. And then Martha suggested that we try to tempt her again."

"But she had already taken what she thought was the threat, so what was there left to threaten her?"

"Martha said that you had taken loads of photos and saved newspaper clippings as well as taking notes on all the conversations you had with the police about the accident. She said you even went as far to save part of a fender from the car that hit your parents' car."

"Yes, I did but I didn't keep them under the bed with all the other things because the box was too big, so I kept it in a blanket box at the end of Martha's bed."

"For some reason, Kate decided to only focus on the tin box under your bed and didn't bother checking anywhere for anything else. I suppose she didn't think there was anything else to look for. Anyway, Martha suggested that if Kate knew that there was something in the box that might point to her, it may prompt her into breaking in again."

"But how would she do that when we weren't on speaking terms with Kate?" Hannah asked logically.

"Martha offered to approach Kate and convince her that she was on her side and not yours and hoped that Kate would buy it. It was a stretch, but it was worth a shot. Luckily, that opportunity presented itself right after we all met at your Uncle's just as you were flying across the ocean. Martha had just arrived home when she saw Kate getting out of her car. So, not wasting any time and before she could lose her nerve, she ran across the road and pretended to offer an olive branch of sorts to Kate."

"And Kate bought it?" Hannah asked incredulously.

"Martha played her at her own game and Kate bought it hook, line and sinker."

"She never had any suspicions that it was all an act?"

"Martha almost lost heart in the beginning, and she was just about to get up and leave, when suddenly Kate asked her to stay. Martha confessed to me later that she felt horrible because she had to pretend that she resented you and your obsession about your parents' deaths. But her objective was to let Kate know indirectly that I had reopened your parents' case and that I was very close to solving it. We wired Martha so that if there was any trouble at all, we would know about it instantly. There was little risk to Martha, if at all. The main purpose here was the need to push Kate a bit and Martha felt she was the best person to do it, and it ended up she was."

"So you listened to everything that went on?"

"We did."

"I can't believe I'm hearing this. It couldn't have been easy to pull that off." Hannah suggested.

"Martha planted the seed that I was very close to solving the case, but wanted a bit more evidence. She suggested that I felt the key evidence might be in some of the photographs that you had taken of the crash."

"Didn't Kate think it was a bit strange that Martha was offering all this information?"

"A little bit, and actually Kate raised that concern too, but Martha convinced her that she resented the case being reopened because all the focus would be taken away from her wedding."

"So Martha was making it seem as though she was conspiring against me."

"That's right and by doing that she managed to earn Kate's trust. It was one of the hardest things she has ever had to do but she knew you would understand."

"I don't think I could have been convincing. I know it must have been hard."

"We practiced what she should and shouldn't say and to let Kate do most of the talking. She did a beautiful job. In fact, during one of the conversations where Kate suggested disposing of certain photographs, Martha pretended not to have any idea what Kate was talking about, just so Kate would keep talking. I thought for sure Kate would get frustrated with Martha and ask her to leave, but she didn't."

"You're not going to tell me that Kate trusted Martha enough that she gave back our mother's necklace?"

"No, Martha stumbled on the necklace quite by accident and the box she stole from you. But the best part, for implicating her anyway, she discovered the car that had been the missing link in your parents' car accident. Kate had kept it stored in her garage all these years."

Chills sparked up Hannah's spine as she realized that the evidence that led to her parents' deaths had been just across the road all this time. How many times had she walked past that garage never knowing what it contained?

"So you have all the evidence you need now to implicate her. This will be the end of it?"

"Yes, and just to seal the deal, we were waiting for her as she broke into your home again with the box of photographs that Martha had told her about."

"She must have tried to talk her way out of that."

"She tried, but she had a hard time explaining why she was ripping up the photographs."

"Don't tell me she destroyed all my photographs!" Hannah pleaded.

"No, we anticipated that she might try something like that, so we made sure we made copies of all your photographs. The ones in the box were duplicates."

"Her behaviour is like little stabs in my heart over and over again. One loss after another and there seems to be no end to her behaviour. I know losing those photographs might seem pointless but they really connect me to that day and make it real on some level. It helped me get through a lot of pain by focusing on the way they died. It must sound ridiculous to you." Hannah offered even letting a small smile cross her face.

Joe noticed a change or perhaps a resolve in Hannah, despite the smile. Even though the conversation was a difficult one for her, he hoped that in time she would come to terms with what had been done to her parents. Closure was not a word or an expression that he easily accepted since he had seen so much pain and raw emotion with his work. Was senseless and tragic loss ever afforded closure? He felt it a word that was thrown out too easily and felt that concession a more appropriate term based on the peace of mind that it offered to each individual victim. No one could determine when that point of concession would be. It could be separated by a word or a moment in time. Hannah had found that word or moment in time and Joe decided that was personal to her and it should stay that way.

"We did what we could to be as convincing as possible but also to protect you and everything that was important to you. There would have been no point in risking both and compromising what is sacred to you."

"I have to admit that I don't know quite how to feel about everything you've told me. It's a mixture of relief, anger, sadness..."

"Its okay, you don't have to explain. I can only imagine the impact this must have and it will take time for you to take it all in. The good thing is you don't have to go through it alone. You and Martha have a lot of support from not only me and Adam, but Sally and Josh."

"I know, I'm really lucky. Speaking of Josh, I don't think you ever told me how you two know each other."

"I thought I told you that we met in University."

"Oh, that's right, I forgot. And you've stayed friends all these years?"

"We have. In fact when I last travelled here to England after University, it was with Josh."

Hannah remembered the day that she and Josh had gone to Sally's neighbour's apartment and recalled the telephone call Josh had where it seemed he was talking about her. "Are you Jabber?"

"Am I what?" Joe asked appearing not to have heard her properly.

"Is your nickname Jabber?" Hannah clarified.

"It is. Where did that come from?" Joe laughed lightly.

"One evening Josh was helping me plan for my trip to England and he mentioned how he and his friend Jabber had travelled here together. He then explained that all his friends from University were given nicknames. The day we had been rescuing Sally, Josh got a call on his cell phone from Jabber. He acted so strangely towards me during and after that call. I must admit, I never put it together until now that it was you he was talking to. I guess I really have been foolish in not realizing so much of what has been right in front of me."

"I think you're being too hard on yourself. I found out that day that Josh was with you and I called him specifically to ask him not to mention that he knew me. I reminded him that I was still working on the case involving you and Kate. The strange reaction you were getting was likely concern for you. You couldn't have realized what was deliberately being kept from you. I had to be very careful because I couldn't risk it getting back to Kate in case it compromised the investigation. " Joe explained.

"Then why do I feel deceived by so many? It seems in the last few months, I've discovered so much of what I believed to be true has not been true at all. There have been too many lies and I have to admit that I was never sure what or who to believe."

"The only person who has betrayed you or wronged you in a deliberately cruel way is Kate. And while I know that's hard to understand and accept, it had nothing to do with you directly. You were never her target and neither were your parents."

"I don't know that I'll ever accept or forgive what she's done, but I do feel unsettled by all the deceit that has come from her actions and how it has involved so many people. It's causing me to be suspicious of everything. I don't want to live my life suspecting everyone's word and everyone's motives."

"I can only tell you that what Kate did was beyond understanding and no one expects you to accept it. She deceived you and manipulated you Hannah and that's never easy."

"I don't want to sound insensitive, but you lied to me too and so did Josh. I understand it was for good reason, but it's still unsettling to me."

"I wonder if I could offer you the idea of what I did was to borrow the truth rather than lying to you and I invited Josh to join me in that thinking. Believe me, he was hard to convince because he has so much respect for you."

"I don't think it makes a difference how you say it, lying or borrowing the truth. I would say it's the same thing." Hannah offered defensively.

"I know this may sound invented or convenient, but I believe that there are times when we all borrow the truth. We reinvent it or re-establish it during times when our intention is to protect rather than to deceive. I never liked keeping things from you, but my intention was always good. I was not only doing my job, but I was keeping a promise to my mum for my dad. If I let down my guard and confessed to you why I was watching you, you could have easily and understandably changed your behaviour towards Kate. It would only be human nature to expect that."

"I think this is going to take time for me Joe. I don't trust anything right now. I'm sorry to sound so ungrateful for all your hard work." Hannah confessed.

"I'm not expecting you to be grateful to me. I know this will take time and your trust being shattered may be the least of what you will have to endure in the next while."

"What do you mean?"

"I mean there will be a trial." Joe said simply.

"Of course, it's not over even when it's over." Hannah qualified.

"It won't be easy Hannah."

"Martha and I will have to go through it all again won't we?"